Natural PASSION

An Naturel Trilogy, Book One

ANNA DURAND

JACOBSVILLE BOOKS · MARIETTA, OHIO

NATURAL PASSION

Copyright © 2020 by Lisa A. Shiel
All rights reserved.

ISBN: 978-1-949406-17-7 (paperback)
ISBN: 978-1-949406-16-0 (ebook)
ISBN: 978-1-949406-18-4 (audiobook)

Manufactured in the United States.

Jacobsville Books
www.JacobsvilleBooks.com

Publisher's Cataloging-in-Publication Data
provided by Five Rainbows Cataloging Services

Names: Durand, Anna.
Title: Natural passion / Anna Durand.
Description: Marietta, Ohio : Jacobsville Books, 2020. | Series: Au naturel trilogy, bk. 1.
Identifiers: ISBN 978-1-949406-17-7 (paperback) | ISBN 978-1-949406-16-0 (ebook) | ISBN 978-1-949406-18-4 (audiobook)
Subjects: LCSH: Nudism--Fiction. | Nudist camps--Fiction. | Brazilians--Fiction. | Man-woman relationships--Fiction. | Oregon--Fiction. | Romance fiction. | BISAC: FICTION / Romance / Romantic Comedy. | FICTION / Romance / Contemporary. | FICTION / Romance / Multicultural & Interracial. | GSAFD: Love stories. | Humorous fiction.
Classification: LCC PS3604.U724 N38 2020 (print) | LCC PS3604.U724 (ebook) | DDC 813/.6--dc23.

Other Books by Anna Durand

Lachlan in a Kilt (The Ballachulish Trilogy, Book One)
Aidan in a Kilt (The Ballachulish Trilogy, Book Two)
Rory in a Kilt (The Ballachulish Trilogy, Book Three)
The American Wives Club (A Hot Brits/Hot Scots/Au Naturel Crossover Book)
Brit vs. Scot (A Hot Brits/Hot Scots/Au Naturel Crossover Book)
Dangerous in a Kilt (Hot Scots, Book One)
Wicked in a Kilt (Hot Scots, Book Two)
Scandalous in a Kilt (Hot Scots, Book Three)
The MacTaggart Brothers Trilogy (Hot Scots, Books 1-3)
Gift-Wrapped in a Kilt (Hot Scots, Book Four)
Notorious in a Kilt (Hot Scots, Book Five)
Insatiable in a Kilt (Hot Scots, Book Six)
Lethal in a Kilt (Hot Scots, Book Seven)
Irresistible in a Kilt (Hot Scots, Book Eight)
Devastating in a Kilt (Hot Scots, Book Nine)
Spellbound in a Kilt (Hot Scots, Book Ten)
Relentless in a Kilt (Hot Scots, Book Eleven)
One Hot Chance (Hot Brits, Book One)
One Hot Roomie (Hot Brits, Book Two)
One Hot Crush (Hot Brits, Book Three)
The Dixon Brothers Trilogy (Hot Brits, Books 1-3)
One Hot Escape (Hot Brits, Book Four)
One Hot Rumor (Hot Brits, Book Five)
One Hot Christmas (Hot Brits, Book Six)
Natural Impulse (Au Naturel Trilogy, Book Two)
Natural Satisfaction (Au Naturel Trilogy, Book Three)
Fired Up (a standalone romance)
Echo Power (Echo Power Trilogy, Book One)
The Mortal Falls (Undercover Elementals, Book One)
The Mortal Fires (Undercover Elementals, Book Two)
The Mortal Tempest (Undercover Elementals, Book Three)
The Janusite Trilogy (Undercover Elementals, Books 1-3)
Obsidian Hunger (Undercover Elementals, Book Four)
Unbidden Hunger (Undercover Elementals, Book Five)
Willpower (Psychic Crossroads, Book One)
Intuition (Psychic Crossroads, Book Two)
Kinetic (Psychic Crossroads, Book Three)
Passion Never Dies: The Complete Reborn Series

Chapter One

Eve

On the well-mowed lawn in front of me, four nude people batted a tennis ball back and forth over a net by striking it with the wedge-shaped wooden boxes fitted over their hands. Each player had one thug, the official name for the box-shaped thingy. They were playing miniten, a version of tennis unique to the nudist community, and having a ball doing it. They laughed whenever someone missed the ball and cheered whenever they hit it and the ball went sailing over the net. Miniten was more relaxed than tennis, making it the perfect sport for people who preferred to stay au naturel. No sports bras or jockstraps required.

Ah yes, this was my life. I entertained naked people for a living. Running a nudist resort involved a lot more than keeping my guests entertained, though. It also brought a slew of boring, unpleasant tasks like bookkeeping, meal catering, laundry service, and anything else my guests required. This was Au Naturel Naturist Resort LLC, but I was the only member of the company. That meant my guests were solely my responsibility, whether they wanted to be called nudists or naturists.

I leaned back against a tree, my hands in the pockets of my shorts. My tank top and short-shorts seemed downright tame compared to the unabashed nudity of the folks enjoying a friendly game of miniten and the spectators observing from the lawn's periphery. Four of them were over sixty, one was over eighty, and three were younger. Only one belonged to the millennial generation, but Ollie Jackson wasn't exactly a buff specimen.

Not that I cared what they looked like. Not that they cared either. I admired my guests' attitude toward the human body and their carefree outlook on life in general. Besides, Ollie had the cuteness factor, both in his looks and his personality.

"Hey, Eve!" Sylvester Norris shouted to me, waving. The breeze ruffled his shoulder-length gray hair. Other parts of him flapped too, but the seventy-two-year-old didn't seem to notice or care. He grinned at me. "When are you going to join the party?"

Every summer Sylvester and his wife, Ruth, visited my establishment, and every year he asked me when I might "join the party," meaning when would I get naked along with my guests. Though I admired their unashamed attitude toward nudity, I had no desire to shed my clothes.

"Maybe another time," I called to him.

That was my standard answer to the obvious question: Why did a woman who refused to strip down own a naturist resort?

I supposed it was kind of like owning a tattoo shop but having no tats of my own. Still, being the proprietor of a nudist resort did not mean I had to strip along with my guests. I took care of them like any good innkeeper would, but I kept my clothes on at all times—in public, and in private while in the company of other people who were not my lovers.

Ruth slapped her husband's arm. "Leave the girl alone, Sylvester. We're not evangelists for nudism."

"Naturism," said Ollie, my youngest guest at twenty-four. The only item he wore on his body was a pair of eyeglasses. "Get with the twenty-first century, guys. The word nudist is totally an old fart thing."

Sylvester winked at Ollie. "We are old farts, pipsqueak."

I smiled. Couldn't help it. My regular guests who came back year after year were like family to me. Even Ollie had been visiting my establishment for four years, at least three times a year. Two of those stays consisted of weekend-only trips, but every summer he enjoyed a two-week holiday here.

Except this year he was staying for six weeks. I wondered why, but it wasn't my business.

"Catch you guys later," I said, pushing away from the tree. "Gotta fix lunch and get ready for the new guest."

Everyone waved and shouted goodbye to me.

I ambled back to my house. It sat fifty feet away from the two-story building that served as the guest quarters. My little ranch-style house didn't look like much on the outside, but inside it had a spacious kitchen and a photo studio. As I walked through the main door, straight into the kitchen, my gaze flitted to the framed photos on the walls. Every wall in my house featured samples of my photography. The older images were of normal stuff like animals and scenery.

Everything from the past five years was…less normal.

In the photos, nude people of every age, size, and color frolicked. Nudists playing miniten. Nudists playing chess. Nudists having a picnic. Nudists gathered around a bonfire toasting marshmallows. Nudists… Well, let's just say I had photographed human beings in the buff doing more activities than anyone who wasn't a nudist would've realized people of that ilk engaged in. None of the images were lewd or sexual in any way. Whether they called it nudism or naturism, these folks weren't in it for erotic reasons. They simply preferred to go clothes free.

Nope, no porn here. I took tasteful pictures of my guests, but only of the ones who signed a release form. I posted the images on the resort website and also on some stock photo sites to earn a few royalties, but I had no illusions I'd become a famous documentarian of the naturist lifestyle.

Photographing nudists. Who knew this was where I'd end up? Not me, for sure. This resort in the boonies of Oregon was a long ways from New York City.

I threw open the refrigerator, grabbing ingredients and tossing them onto the large butcher-block island. My guests would be hungry after their morning exercise. The ones who hadn't participated in miniten had chosen other forms of physical fitness, everything from weight lifting to jogging. After lunch, they'd want to relax in the hot spring. Oregon in the summer was usually pleasant, making the hot spring a year-round attraction.

We hadn't reached prime bug season yet. I checked my supply of insect repellent, then got to work on lunch.

Twenty minutes later, I'd whipped up the appetizers and salads and was about to start in on the main course when the house phone rang. I had a cell, but the landline offered more convenience when my guests needed something. All anyone needed to do was punch the green button on any phone in the guest house to ring the one in my house. The digital display on the base unit told me which room was calling, whether it was a guest's room or the dining hall. This one originated from the supply closet that doubled as my handyman's office.

I nabbed the handset off the wall, cradling it with my neck while chopping lettuce. "What's up, Quentin?"

"Got a problem," Quentin Smith said in his gruff voice. My sole employee wasn't known for his cheerfulness, but he performed magic on the plumbing and anything else that needed fixing. "The room for the new guest is toast."

"What?" I dropped the lettuce and my knife, gripping the phone in my hand. "There was a fire? I didn't smell any smoke."

"There's no fire," he grumbled. "A pipe burst in the wall, but nobody knew about it until I came in here to make sure everything was good for the new guest. The place is wetter than a moose after a dip in the hot spring. Don't think anybody wants to sleep in that bed. Might as well paint yourself green since you'd be covered in mold by morning."

"Shit. What are we going to do?" I glanced at the clock and cursed again, too softly for Quentin to hear. "The new guest will be here any minute."

"You'll have to use your spare room, at least until I can get the pipe fixed and clean this place up."

We were booked up in the summer with a waiting list to boot. I'd hosted the occasional guest in my house when there was a problem with their room, but the spare room was mostly for my friends and relatives. Maybe I should've felt weird about letting strangers into my home, but it wasn't any different than if I'd owned a bed and breakfast.

"It's your choice, boss," Quentin said. "I can put a canoe in here and tell 'em to get paddling."

"Hilarious." I rubbed my forehead and sighed. "Okay, I'll put him up in the spare room. But please, Quentin, get that room cleaned up as fast as possible. My house doesn't have all the amenities for guests and the decor is girlie. I don't think a man is going to appreciate the pastel bathroom or the pink sheets on the bed."

"The new guest is a man?" Quentin made a noise that reminded me of a growl. "Maybe you should send him to a motel in town until the room here is fixed."

"Everything's booked up. The Pioneer Days festival is this week."

"Yeah, forgot." He growled again. "I'll get to work right away and see how fast I can fix this puppy."

"Thanks, Quentin."

I hung up the phone.

A guest in my house. The new guy would be nice like all my guests, I was sure. I knew his name and where he'd come from—Valentim Silva from Los Angeles—but nothing else.

Outside, the crunching of tires on gravel alerted me to Mr. Silva's arrival.

I snagged a little remote from the counter and sprinted out of the house toward the driveway.

A black pickup truck was stopped at the gate.

Breathing hard from my sprint, I stopped fifteen feet from the gate and punched a button on the remote in my hand. The gate rolled open. The truck had dark windows on the sides, and the glare of sunlight obscured my view through the windshield as the vehicle passed me. I trotted after it, gesturing for my newest guest to park near my house instead of in the gravel area set aside for guests. He seemed to get the idea, pulling up behind my pickup.

His made mine look like something I'd gotten from a junkyard. My Dodge Ram was six years old and lacked the ooh-la-la factor of this guy's Ford F-250 Limited Super Duty. I recognized the model. I'd seen one at the car dealership in town, though I'd gone there strictly to window shop. No way could I afford a new truck, especially not an F-250 Limited. It cost at least eighty thousand dollars.

Great. A rich guest. My little place was not a luxury resort, and the last time I'd hosted a wealthy guest, the woman had bitched about everything.

The driver's door swung open just when I reached the truck.

Panting, I rushed up to meet my guest. "Hi, welcome to Au Naturel Naturist Resort. I'm—"

My voice ceased working the instant the man jumped out of the car and turned toward me.

A god had stepped out of the luxury pickup. My gaze insisted on taking in the full picture of my newest guest, wandering over his entire body. Tall and muscular in an athletic way, he boasted skin lightly bronzed by the sun. His dark hair curled around his ears to kiss the lower edge of the lobes. His cocoa slacks clung to his thighs, accentuating the powerful muscles underneath. The top two buttons of his white dress shirt hung open.

My attention stalled on his chest and the elaborate tattoos that covered the swath of skin I could see.

He ran a hand through his artfully mussed locks, and his full lips curved into a relaxed smile.

All of my guests arrived wearing clothes since airports frowned on nude travel, but this guy's clothes struck me as designer quality. Most people showed up wearing shorts and T-shirts.

The god offered me his hand. "Valentim Silva. But you can call me Val."

He spoke with a light accent I couldn't quite place. In fact, it was so light I wouldn't have picked up on it if not for the lilting way he said his full name.

I settled my palm in his, my gaze drawn to his warm brown eyes. "Eve Holt. I own the resort."

"Yes, I know." He held on to my hand for a second or two longer than necessary for politeness. "I have seen your website. Your photographs are wonderful, very artistic."

"Thank you."

None of my previous guests had ever looked like him. I'd hosted attractive men before, but they were dim stars in the far reaches of the hotness galaxy. This guy was a supernova standing two feet away from me.

He peered over his shoulder at the guest house. "Is my room ready? I'm a little early."

I fanned myself with one hand, suddenly hot despite the temperate weather.

"Ms. Holt?" he said. "Are you all right?"

Shit. What was wrong with me? I cleared my throat and stuffed my hands in the pockets of my shorts. "I'm fine."

He raised his brows. "My room?"

My mouth opened, a response on my tongue, but I froze before uttering a syllable. His room. The one that had been flooded. Double shit. This man, this human supernova in designer slacks, was going to be sleeping in my spare room. Oh no, this wasn't a disaster at all.

It wasn't like I had to sleep with him.

No, I didn't have to…

"Come with me," I said, waving for him to follow as I headed for the house. "Your room was flooded, so you'll be staying in my house until the cleanup is done."

He grabbed his bag from inside the truck and came up beside me, smiling in a way that made my heart skip. "In your house? That's very generous of you, Ms. Holt."

"Call me Eve."

"Thank you, Eve. I don't want to put you out, though. Maybe I should stay in town."

"All the motels are booked up."

"I could sleep in my truck."

"You are my guest," I said, flashing him my professional smile, "which means it's my responsibility to take care of you."

My body had some very, very wrong ideas about how to take care of Val Silva. I ignored those thoughts. I didn't sleep with guests anymore. Besides, I was way too busy to waste time on a roll in the hay with a hot newcomer.

I glanced back at his vehicle, the spiffiest rental any guest had arrived in. "That's one fine truck you've got there. Somebody who can afford a luxury pickup could afford to stay at a luxury naturist resort too, I'm guessing. I hope you won't be disappointed by the accommodations here."

"Not at all." He stopped to gaze out at the large lawn where the miniten net was still set up and where guests lounged in Adirondack chairs or on chaises. "It's beautiful here, very quiet too. I'm used to the noise and crowds in LA."

I stopped too. We were halfway to my house, but I had to let my newest guest enjoy the scenery a bit. He was paying for the scenery. A forest of conifers covered the property, though the two acres around the guest house and my home were open. Puffy little clouds dotted the blue sky. With a temperature in the seventies, we were enjoying perfect weather for nudists.

"Since we're out here," I said, "let me point out the main features of the resort."

He threw me a sideways glance. "Well, I can see there's badminton or tennis. Or could it be miniten? Nudists love that game."

"All of the above. But we have a lot more to offer." I pointed in the appropriate direction for each feature as I listed them. "The lawn also hosts flag football and other sports. That little brown building over there is the sauna, but that's mostly used in the winter. The big building is the guest house, and inside it you'll find rooms with private en suite bathrooms, an exercise room, a dining hall, a game room, and a self-serve pantry filled with snacks. There's a pop machine in the downstairs hallway, along with a coffeemaker and water cooler in the dining hall. Those are available twenty-four seven, along with the pantry."

"Sounds like you have everything."

"There's more." I pointed at the dirt trail that disappeared into the woods. "We have nature trails too, and a natural hot spring as well as a small private lake."

"Impressive. A resort with all these amenities should be more expensive."

"There are plenty of luxury resorts in the world. I want to offer an affordable, family-friendly place where naturists and nudists can experience the wilderness without sacrificing the creature comforts."

"And that's why I decided to come here." He turned toward me. "For the friendly atmosphere. Your website says I'll find that here."

"You will. My guests are good people." I eyed his truck again and couldn't hold back my curiosity any longer. "Where did you find a fancy truck to rent? I would've picked you up at the airport if you'd told me when your flight was arriving. You left that question blank in the online registration form."

"That's because I didn't fly. I drove here in my own truck, not a rental."

"You drove from LA? That's a twelve-hour trip."

He shrugged one shoulder. "I wanted the privacy and quiet."

Deciding I'd been nosy enough, I started for the house and waved for him to follow. "Come on. I'll show you the spare room."

Val smiled again, this time with a warmth that exceeded friendliness. Not that he was leering at me. Flirtatious seemed like a more accurate description of his expression.

No more sleeping with guests, Evie.

Val caught up to me, that smile deepening. "I appreciate your hospitality and plan on taking advantage of it often while I'm staying here. If you don't mind."

"That's what I'm here for."

"Are you a nudist, Eve?"

"No. I run the place, that's all."

"Too bad." He skimmed his gaze up and down my body. "I've never seen a woman more worthy of the nudist lifestyle."

This guy was trouble. Sexy, flirty, down-and-dirty trouble.

And I hadn't slept with a man in almost a year.

Val winked at me, still smiling.

Oh yeah. Big, big trouble.

Chapter Two

Val

I trailed Eve into the house, letting myself enjoy the view of her luscious ass cupped by the shorts that barely covered her bottom. The woman had a body any man would worship, even the ones who preferred other men. Her curves were a work of art, and the freckles on her lightly tanned skin hinted at creamy coloring under the surface. I wanted to lay her down in the grass and crawl up her body, exploring every inch of her with my tongue and lips.

We would be naked, of course. I was a nudist after all.

But she wasn't. Eve owned a nudist resort but kept her clothes on. Somehow, that made me want her even more. Fantasizing about what treasures she hid under those shorts and that tank top could keep me entertained for days.

Eve led me through a large kitchen, waving an arm to indicate it. "This is where I make the food for all my guests, but meals are served in the guest house. While you're staying here with me, you can grab a snack or a pop from the fridge anytime you like."

"Will I take my meals in the guest house or here with you?" *Please say with you.*

Eve paused on the threshold of a hallway, whipping her head around to look at me. The long locks of her strawberry-blonde hair bounced around her shoulders. Her bright-blue eyes widened briefly, and she caught one side of her bottom lip with her teeth. "I guess that's up to you. I eat here."

"I'll have my meals with you, then." I couldn't stop staring at her lips, full and pouty, and the way she was biting down on her lower lip. What would she taste like? The flavor of her mouth would be different from the flavor of her cream, and I wanted to sample all of it. All of her.

She sucked in a deep breath, her breasts lifting, and exhaled it in a rush. "Moving on..."

Already, I was deeply in lust with those breasts. Not too small, not too large, just right for holding in my palms while I suckled the tips.

My fantasies about her breasts ended when she spun away from me and started down the hallway. I counted four closed doors.

Eve pointed at the first door on the left. "That's the bathroom. We'll have to share." She twisted her head around to give me a sheepish smile. "Hope you don't mind girlie things. The bathroom is pastel-colored and full of my stuff."

"Doesn't bother me." My mind went straight to a fantasy of me shaving her legs in the shower. "I have two sisters, and they left their things everywhere in our house when we were children. I know more about feminine hygiene than most men would want to."

"I bet. Over there is my photo studio," she said, pointing to the door opposite the bathroom. "My bedroom is at the end of the hall on the right. You might have noticed the other doorway leading out of the kitchen. That's the living room, where you can relax and watch TV if you want." She walked up to the next closed door on the left, turned toward me, and pushed the door open. "Here's where you'll be staying."

"Directly across from your bedroom."

"Both bedrooms have locks on the doors, if you want to ensure privacy."

"Hardly seems necessary." I set down my bag and leaned against the jamb of the open door, probably standing closer to her than was necessary or appropriate. Fuck appropriate. The sweet, fresh scent of her enveloped me, and I wouldn't give that up one second sooner than I had to. "Thank you for sharing your home with me, Eve."

"No problem."

I tipped my head to the side, studying her. "May I ask a personal question?"

"Sure."

"Why does a woman who's not a nudist own a nudist retreat?"

"For the money." She hunched her shoulders. "I know that sounds crass, but it's true. I make a decent living catering to the clothing-optional set."

"That's not crass. It's smart." My attention stalled on her breasts and the faint lines of the bra that held them up in perfect position. I would get her naked as soon as possible. I had to. My cock insisted on it, and I'd never had much luck fighting my carnal urges.

Eve glanced into the bedroom. "Oh, I forgot your welcome packet."

While she sprinted down the hallway to the kitchen, I carried my bag into the little room and set it on the floor beside the bed. The mattress was a decent size, large enough for me—and for Eve too, if she should join me. A dresser with a large attached mirror was pushed up against the wall, and a pair of accordion doors probably concealed a small closet. A telephone, cordless and seated in its charging base, sat on a little round table tucked into one corner while an old-fashioned clock with large hands counted the hours, minutes, and seconds.

A window overlooked the lawn where the miniten net was still set up.

The distinctive clapping of sneaker-clad feet on the wood floors drew my attention to the doorway.

Eve, breathless and smiling, clutched a large basket in her arms. It was full of items I couldn't quite make out, thanks to the large, blue-satin bow tied to the handle with its long ribbons hanging over the entire basket.

She marched to the little table, set down the basket, and plucked a manila envelope from inside it. She waved the envelope at me. "Here's your welcome packet."

I strode up to her and accepted the envelope.

"You've got a map of the property," she said, "with all the attractions noted, along with brochures for things you can do away from the resort in the local area. You'll need to wear clothes if you go off site." She pried open the metal tabs that held the envelope shut. "There are also coupons for local restaurants. The national forest borders my property on three sides, but there's no fee to hike on that land."

She pulled the envelope's flap out, seemingly to encourage me to examine its contents. Her expectant look confirmed my assumption.

I slid the contents out and flipped through them. "You are thorough, aren't you?"

"Yep." She stepped back and gestured toward the basket. "This is your welcome kit with samples of everything you might need."

I leaned in to examine the items. "Sunscreen. Lip balm. Foot moisturizer. Body lotion. Aloe. Insect repellent. Calamine lotion." I glanced at her, my brows raised. "Are you expecting insects to be a problem?"

"Not usually, but twice we've had an invasion of no-see-ums." She feigned disgust. "It's not pretty. Then there was the year we had an outbreak of poison ivy." She tapped the pink bottle of calamine lotion. "You may never need this, but trust me, if you do, you'll be glad you have it."

"You take good care of your guests." I considered what she'd said a moment ago. "No-see-ums?"

"Teeny-tiny bugs that will eat you alive and you may never even see them. They're also called midges." She faked an exaggerated shiver. "The no-see-um attacks were like something out of a horror movie. You need super-strong insect repellent for that. It might melt your tattoos, but at least you won't get bitten up."

One corner of her mouth twitched upward, and I knew she was teasing me. I liked that. "My tattoos are made from molten steel. I think they'll survive your insects."

She waggled her eyebrows. "You haven't seen the mosquitoes yet."

I grinned. She was the most adorable, sexiest woman I'd ever met.

Eve leaned her bottom against the table. "Here are the rules. No staring at women's breasts or anyone's private parts. Maintain eye contact. You're welcome to wear clothes anytime you want since this is a clothes-optional resort rather than a clothes-free one. Footwear is fine, but do not walk around in your underwear."

"I never bother with underwear."

"Okay." Her brows crinkled, but if I'd shocked her, she shook it off quickly. Clearing her throat, she continued. "Always shower before using the sauna or the hot spring. Always put a towel on a chair or other surface before sitting down on it. No PDAs—public displays of affection—other than a quick hug to say hello or a quick peck on the cheek. Hand holding is acceptable. Oh, no barn doors open when you're sitting or lying down in the presence of other guests."

"Barn doors?"

"It means don't have your legs spread so everyone can see your privates."

"Ah, I see. You don't need to go through all of this. It's not my first time at a nudist resort."

She folded her arms over her chest. "Everyone hears the rules the first time they come here. It's protocol."

"All right. I'm listening."

"No reaching during meals. If you need something, ask someone to pass it to you." She waved a finger toward my groin. "Make sure none of your bits intrude on anyone else's space. And if you absolutely must relieve yourself outdoors, whether it's number one or number two, please find a secluded spot where you can take care of things. No photography without express permission from the people involved. Do you have a cell phone?"

"Yes."

She dug a small, folded sheet of paper out of the basket, handing it to me. "Put a red dot over the camera lens, please. If your phone has more than one camera, please put stickers over all of them."

I obeyed, applying red stickers to the tiny lenses on the front and back of my phone.

Eve nodded her approval. She started to push away from the table but stopped. "One more thing. Men tend to get embarrassed when I bring this up, but it's necessary. If you get an erection when you're outside of this house, please put a towel over your lap or roll over onto your side. If you're in the hot spring or the lake, you can just stay put until the problem subsides."

She watched me like she expected me to blush or get upset.

Most men probably would have, but no one who knew me, or knew of me, would think I'd ever get embarrassed about something like developing a hard-on in public.

I chuckled. "Don't worry. I'm shameless."

"No need to pretend you're cool with it. I'm used to my male guests getting flustered when that happens."

I studied her expression for some sign she was teasing me again but found none. "You really don't recognize me, do you?"

She raked her gaze over my body. "If we'd met before, I'd remember."

Eve Holt had no idea who I was. Her attentiveness and attraction to me had nothing to do with my reputation or my past behavior. It was…refreshing.

"You're good to go," she said. Her gaze flicked to the clock on the wall. "I need to finish getting lunch ready. Once you're settled in, come find me in the kitchen."

"Thank you, Eve."

"I'm just doing my job." She moved toward the door, hesitating on the threshold. "If there's anything else you need, just ask."

"Don't trouble yourself on my account."

"It's no trouble. I'll let you get settled."

She disappeared down the hallway.

I shed my clothes and shoes, then headed into the kitchen.

Eve stood at the island placing food items into plastic trays and closing up each tray with a red plastic lid. She glanced up when I walked into the room.

Her eyes flared wide. She stared at me for a moment before blinking furiously like she was waking from a strange dream. Her cheeks pinkened. She bowed her head to focus on her task. "I see you've made yourself comfortable."

"Are you carrying all that food to the guest house by yourself?"

"My handyman, Quentin, will be here any minute to help."

I approached the island across from her. "I would be happy to help too."

"That's not necessary. You're a guest." She kept her head down but lifted her gaze to me. "Besides, handling food in the nude is a health code violation."

"How many guests do you have?"

"The number varies." She slapped the lid onto a tray and laid her hands on top of it, swiveling her gaze up to me. "The guest house has ten rooms with two queen beds in each. Some people bring tents to sleep out, and others come in RVs and sleep in those. Currently, I have seventeen guests, including you."

"And you manage all of this on your own. Just you and a handyman."

"Well, I do outsource dinner. Tonight, it's pizza delivered from a restaurant in town, with salad for the vegans."

I arched a brow. "Town is eighteen miles away. I didn't realize anyone delivered that far out."

"Normally, they don't. I have special arrangements."

She stacked four trays and lifted them in her arms.

I rushed around the island, intending to take them from her. "Let me help."

"You're a guest, and you're naked."

"I'm also not the sort of man who lets a woman do all the work alone. My sisters would whip me for not lending a hand." I turned halfway toward the hall. "Let me put some clothes on, and I'll help you. Please, I insist."

She set down the trays and raised her hands. "I surrender. Knock yourself out."

I sprinted back to my room and yanked on an outfit that seemed more appropriate for serving lunch than my designer clothes—a T-shirt, jeans, and sneakers. When I got back to the kitchen, Eve was waiting with her elbows braced on the island. She moved to pick up those four trays again, but I hurried over to take them from her.

A knock vibrated the door as a male voice hollered, "It's me, Eve."

"Come on in," she said.

The door swung open. A well-tanned man in jeans and a T-shirt, with clunky boots on his feet, pushed a metal cart into the kitchen. He dragged another metal cart behind him, and I could see a third parked a few feet outside the door.

"Sorry I took so long," the man said. Deep wrinkles carved lines into his face when he squinted at my hostess in what seemed like a strained attempt at a smile. "We better hurry, Eve. The natives are getting restless and might start gnawing on each other if we don't get them their food pronto."

The man looked at me, his squint deepening. "Guess you've got help already."

Eve cleared her throat. "Quentin, this is our newest guest, Val Silva. Val, this is my handyman extraordinaire, Quentin Smith."

Quentin offered me his hand, realized I couldn't take it with the trays in my arms, and pushed his cart toward me. "You can set those down here."

I deposited the trays on the cart and offered him my hand. "A pleasure to meet you, Mr. Smith."

"Just Quentin." He shook my hand, eying me up and down. One corner of his mouth twisted downward, then smoothed out. "Welcome to Au Naturel Naturist Resort."

"Hungry people are waiting," Eve said, stacking four more trays on the counter.

When she tried to pick them up, Quentin and I reached for them at the same time.

I yanked them out of Eve's hands and slid them onto the cart's lower shelf.

Quentin's mouth tightened.

"No fighting, boys," Eve said. "There's plenty of work to go around."

Her handyman pursed his lips, his gaze narrowing on me.

Did he have a special fondness for my hostess? If he did, he'd have to take a step back. For the next two weeks, I planned to be the one monopolizing her attention and seducing her into sharing my bed.

Chapter Three

Eve

For the next fifteen minutes, Quentin and Val competed in a bizarre race to ferry their carts across the fifty-foot gap between my home and the guest house and get their trays into the dining hall and unloaded. I pushed the third cart but gave up on keeping up with the men. Val seemed to think their little race was funny, but Quentin was not amused. I supposed he'd gotten used to being my one and only assistant. It probably didn't help that we'd slept together last summer.

Oh yeah, *that* had been a mistake. Ever since, Quentin had developed an odd possessiveness toward me. The sex had been decent, but not worth this aggravation.

When we'd gotten all the food offloaded in the dining hall and placed on the buffet tables, I encouraged Quentin to stay there and get himself some food before the teeming horde of hungry nudists descended on the buffet. He got the hint and took it.

Back in my kitchen, Val helped me put the last of the trays onto a cart.

"Let me take the last cart," I said. "You'll want to get out of your clothes, I'm sure."

He opened his mouth, and by the look on his face, I knew he wanted to protest.

"Go on," I said. "I insist. This is a nudist resort, after all. You came here to enjoy yourself sans clothing. And I can manage to push one cart."

Val stared at me for a few seconds, then he whipped off his clothes. Stretching his entire body, he let out a long, satisfied sigh. "Much better."

I leaned against the island admiring the view. Damn, that man had a killer body—decorated with just enough tattoos to give him that bad boy look. I'd hosted plenty of athletic male guests, but Val made them all seem like couch potatoes with beer bellies. He was lean but well-muscled, with washboard abs and strong thighs. I let my gaze travel down his body, starting with his face, moving down to the corded muscles of his shoulders and arms and along the center line of his torso. His skin was smooth with only the barest hint of dark hairs. Near his hips, those hairs grew thicker and longer, tapering down to the most beautiful set of manly parts I'd ever seen.

Oh yeah, he was well-muscled and well-endowed. Spectacularly well-endowed.

His penis hung slack and soft but proved no less impressive for its lack of arousal. Veins rippled along its length, though the skin looked smooth otherwise. I imagined taking his thick girth in my hand, exploring his flesh, fondling his sac.

No more sex with guests, remember?

Val cleared his throat deliberately.

I tore my gaze away from his dick and intended to look him in the eye, but his impressive pecs and biceps distracted me. "Are you ready to go?"

"Yes, I'm ready."

He infused those words with enough innuendo that even a nun who lived in a remote Himalayan convent would've understood his meaning.

I couldn't resist glancing at his cock one last time.

"Let's go, then," I said, rolling the cart toward the door. "Can't let all those naked people starve."

He pulled the door open for me and smirked. "I'll be hungry even after lunch is served."

Once I'd wheeled the cart across the threshold, Val nudged me out of the way. "I don't think my nudity will contaminate the food when it's inside covered trays. Let me at least push the cart to the guest house door for you."

"I guess that would be okay."

While he steered the cart down the dirt path to the guest house, I granted myself permission to ogle him a bit more. His tattoos fascinated me. The black designs adorned the upper part of his chest as well as his right arm. The ones on his chest were abstract patterns, but the one on his arm represented a stylized dragon that curled around his biceps and spit black flames from its open mouth.

I let my attention wander to his ass and the way it flexed with his every step. With all those taut muscles, along with his easy sensuality and complete lack of shame, he definitely had the raw material to be a fantastic lover.

Not that I would sleep with him. Way too complicated.

We finished stocking up the buffet table while Quentin chomped on his food, watching us from a table in the back of the dining hall. He kept squinting at Val but avoided looking at me.

Just what I needed. A jealous ex-lover on the premises.

I hurried outside to ring the lunch bell. Literally. I had a big brass bell attached to the side of the guest house and rang it to alert my guests it was mealtime. A few straggled in from the direction of the hot spring, but most emerged from their rooms. I returned to the dining hall only to be waylaid by Ruth Norris.

"What a hunk," she said, nodding toward Val. "About time we got some real eye candy for the ladies."

Should a gray-haired woman with seven grandchildren be talking about eye candy? It seemed weird, but I'd gotten used to Ruth's un-grandma-like comments over the past few years.

I slipped my arm around her shoulders. "Don't tell Ollie that. He thinks he's our man candy of the month."

"That dear, sweet boy is fine looking. But he"—she rolled her eyes toward Val—"is prime, grade-A beefcake."

"Cool down, Ruth. Sylvester might hear you."

"Oh, he doesn't mind. My hubby knows I'm window shopping." She cast me an impish sideways glance. "I heard a rumor the new guest is staying in your house."

"His room got flooded by a burst pipe. He's in the spare room until Quentin gets the cleanup done."

"I see," she said with a bit too much emphasis. "At least you'll be close by to keep an eye on Mr. Tall, Dark, and Beautiful when the Kitten Brigade shows up. They'll eat that poor boy alive."

Val, done introducing himself to other guests, sauntered up to me and Ruth. "Shall we go, Eve? I'm looking forward to a private meal with my hostess."

Ruth's lips tightened in a knowing smile. "Private meal? My, Evie, I didn't realize you were expanding your services."

I stuffed my hands in my shorts pockets. "It's a special case. Val is staying in my house—by necessity, of course—and I invited him to have his meals with me."

Ruth winked at me. "I'm sure the Kitten Brigade has nothing to do with it." She caught sight of her husband, flapped her fingers at him in a mini wave, and said, "I'll leave you to your private meal. Nice to meet you, Val."

She patted Val's arm, then toddled off to join her husband.

I waved for Val to follow me out of the dining hall. We'd made our way down the long hallway and out the side door, heading toward my house, before he spoke.

"Kitten Brigade?" he asked.

"That's what the older ladies have named them. They're a group of twenty-something girls who started coming here on their spring breaks from college." I pushed open the outside door to my kitchen. "They've come here every summer for the past four years. They are, shall we say, very enthusiastic in their admiration for attractive men. The term Kitten Brigade came about because Ruth said those girls would be called cougars if they were older. Since they're young, they must be kittens. I pointed out baby cougars are called cubs, but Ruth insisted kitten was a better term."

"A cougar, meaning a woman who pursues younger men."

"Yes. But the Kitten Brigade does not discriminate based on age. They'll pounce on any man, old or young, as long as he's of legal age."

"They sound awful."

"Oh, they're not so bad. When they come here, they want to have fun. I know they all have steady jobs, though, and not as strippers. Some are in grad school studying law, anthropology, or psychology. Others are accountants, advertising copywriters, and other serious stuff."

"When will these kittens arrive?"

"Later this week."

The door clicked shut behind us, and I went to the fridge, pulling it open. "Want a sandwich?"

He moved up behind me, leaning around me to peer inside the fridge. "Let me make lunch for you. After making a meal for all those guests, you must be tired."

No, not really. Staring at his gorgeous bod kept me awake and energized.

The heat of him, so close against my backside, sent a tingly shiver through me. And God, the way he smelled. Spicy, woodsy, tempting as hell. My lids fluttered half shut as I drew in another lungful of his scent.

"Are you all right?" he asked in a sexy rumble, his lips grazing my ear.

"Mm, fine." I forced my lids to open all the way and wriggled away from him. "If you want to make lunch, be my guest."

"I am your guest." He bent to study the contents of the refrigerator. "But I'd love to feed you."

Conversation seemed like the best way to tame the desire simmering inside me or to at least distract myself from it. I perched on one of the stools on the other side of the island, my hands clasped on the wood surface. I wiggled my butt until I found a comfortable position. "May I ask you a personal question?"

"Go ahead." He smiled at me over his shoulder. "I'm not shy."

No kidding. I'd spent five years catering to the needs of people who preferred to go sans clothing, but none of them had the audacity of Val Silva.

"You live in Los Angeles, right?" I said. "But your accent, I can't quite place it."

"I've lived in Los Angeles for five years, but I'm originally from Porto Alegre, a city in southern Brazil." He grabbed packages of cheese and deli meat, tossing them onto the island. "I've spent a lot of time in America. When I was fifteen, my father was appointed the Brazilian ambassador to the US. We lived in Washington, DC, for three years. After that, I went to Harvard."

"The university?"

"Yes." He tossed a package of bacon onto the island, peeking at me over his shoulder. "Is there another kind of Harvard?"

"No, I guess not." Why had I asked such a dumb question? *Jeez, Evie, get a grip.* "What do you do for a living? Are you a lawyer? I only ask because you seem smart and well-off."

He turned toward me and set down the condiments he held in both hands. Head tipped to the side, he observed me like I was a confusing creature. "You honestly have no idea who I am, do you?"

"You're Val Silva." I folded my arms on the island. "Are you from a super-rich family or something?"

"No," he said slowly. "I was a football player—soccer to Americans—for years until an injury forced me to retire. Now, I take modeling jobs when I feel like it."

"When you feel like it? Guess you made a good living at soccer." I ran my gaze over his muscular, tattooed chest. "You probably get paid a lot for modeling, with a body like yours."

He chuckled. "Thank you for the compliment, but that's not why I get high-paying modeling jobs."

"Why, then?" Realizing I was being kind of rude, I held up a hand. "Sorry, never mind. It's not my business, unless you want to tell me. I swear I'm not normally this nosy."

"I don't mind your questions." He bowed his head, focused on sorting the items he'd procured from the fridge. "Most people don't need to ask questions. They know all about me before they ever lay eyes on me."

"Are you famous?"

He set his hands on the island, leaning into them, and lifted his head to look at me. "Infamous is more accurate."

The house phone rang.

Damn, I wanted to know why Val was infamous, but I couldn't ignore the phone. My guests only called when there was an urgent issue.

"Hold that thought," I said and rushed to grab the phone off the wall. "Hello."

"You forgot dessert," Quentin said. "The guests are not happy."

"Oh. Sorry. I'll bring it over right away."

"Not like you to forget anything."

"I'll bring the desserts," I snapped. "Get back to work on the burst pipe."

"Plumber can't get here until tomorrow."

"Fine, whatever. Goodbye."

I hung up, oddly flustered by my phone call with Quentin. He had interrupted my conversation with Val, and I was annoyed. Why? Val was just another guest, one I would not sleep with ever, under any circumstances. Been there, done that, had the mental bruises to prove it. My mistake with Quentin last year had done damage I hadn't realized until today.

Until Val Silva showed up.

My gaze flicked to him. "I forgot to take the desserts over to the guest house. Gotta do that now, sorry."

"I'll help."

"That's okay, I can manage. The desserts are in the guest house fridge, which is always locked. I have the only key."

And I needed a little break from being alone with a nude, intensely hot man.

I left Val alone in my kitchen and jogged over to the guest house.

Chapter Four

Val

Eve came back a little while later but insisted she had work to do in her office, which was in the guest house. She grabbed the lunch I'd made for her and took off again, though not before encouraging me to go out and mingle with the other guests.

I wanted to mingle with her. Alone. All day and all night.

She really had no idea who I was or what I'd done. I had no shame about any of it, but I always ran the risk new people wouldn't appreciate my infamous past. Maybe my football career alone wouldn't have made me a celebrity, but my affair with a movie star certainly had. Our scandalous public behavior had made us a favorite of the tabloids. I'd assumed Eve was flustered around me because she knew about my indiscretions. Everyone with an internet connection seemed to know.

Eve didn't.

I ate my lunch alone before wandering over to the guest house.

A cheerful older woman with gray hair rushed up to me the instant I walked into the dining hall. The other guests seemed to be finishing up their dessert.

The woman, whom I'd seen with Eve earlier, seized my hand with both of hers. "We weren't properly introduced before. I'm Ruth Norris. It's so nice to meet you, Val. Eve told me absolutely nothing about you except your name."

Because Eve knew next to nothing about me.

I smiled. "It's a pleasure to meet you, Ruth. Thank you for the warm welcome."

"Let me introduce you to everybody."

"No need. I met them earlier."

"But you didn't get the Ruth Norris special introduction." She leaned in and whispered, "I saved you dessert, but Sylvester had to stash it in our room so these chow hounds wouldn't gobble it up. I'll get it for you after the introductions."

"Thank you, but there's no need to go to any trouble."

"It's no trouble, dear." She patted my cheek.

Ruth shepherded me around the room, presenting me to every one of Eve's guests. They all had nothing but praise for their hostess, though some of them commented that she needed a "good man" in her life. Ruth stated outright she thought I was that man.

I wanted to fuck Eve, but a relationship could never work. She didn't belong in my world any more than I belonged in hers. For a week or two, yes. For life? No. Besides, according to all my new friends, Eve did not date.

Ollie Jackson, the youngest guest in residence here, kept staring at me, though not with jealousy. He seemed confused. When Ruth introduced us, Ollie pushed up his glasses and said, "Have we met before? You seem familiar."

"I don't think we've met, but I do run into a lot of people when I'm working."

"What do you do?"

Ruth gave Ollie's arm a casual slap. "Don't interrogate the boy. Let's not scare him off on his first day."

I thanked heaven for Ruth's interruption. Ollie's question didn't upset me, but I preferred to avoid answering. This vacation was supposed to be an escape from my life and sharing too much would ruin that. But if I were completely honest with myself, I didn't want to talk about my life because I didn't want Eve to know about my escapades.

What did it matter? I planned to have sex with her, as many times as possible, but I did not want a relationship.

Ollie scratched his head, ruffling his curly blond hair. "I'm sure I've seen you somewhere."

I cleared my throat and changed the subject, not so deftly. "Eve has had no boyfriends since you've known her?"

Ruth chortled and squeezed my shoulder. "Don't worry, sweetie, she's free."

Ollie contorted his lips. "Well, it's not entirely accurate to say Eve's had no boyfriends. There was that thing with Cody and Aaron two summers ago."

A threesome? Eve? She didn't seem like the type, so that must not have been what Ollie meant.

Luckily, he explained. "See, Eve had a thing with Cody in the spring, but that ended. Then, when Cody and Aaron were both here for the summer, she had a thing with Aaron. Cody got righteously ticked about that." Ollie gestured with his hands to emphasize his words. "He kind of assumed Eve was, like, his girl and nobody else's. She'd told him it was totally and forever done with, but the guy did not want to give up."

"Cut to the chase, dear," Ruth said. "You're boring Val."

"Not at all," I said. "What happened, Ollie?"

"Well…" Ollie leaned closer, his voice dropping to a whisper. "Cody started pushing Aaron around. You know, physically pushing him. They yelled and stuff. But finally, Aaron had enough, and he slugged Cody." Ollie held up two fingers. "Twice. That dude had a black eye and could hardly chew for a week."

Ruth tsked. "Ollie is exaggerating. The black eye is true, but Cody had no trouble chewing."

"Tell me, Ollie," I said, "what did Eve think of all that?"

He scrunched his face and puckered his lips in a silent *oooh*. "She was royally pissed. Told both of them to take a hike. She even banned them from the resort for life."

A man with salt-and-pepper hair, whom I'd met but whose name I'd forgotten, jumped up and waved his arms. "It's nature hike time!"

He spun toward the dining hall doorway. Everyone else looked in that direction too.

Eve stood there with an enormous backpack slung over one shoulder. She'd switched her sneakers for hiking boots. "That's right. I've got the bug spray and sunscreen, plus bottled water. Are you guys ready to go?"

Her guests nodded. Some shouted, "Yes!"

"We're heading to the lake, so grab a quick shower first. Don't want to spread any germs, do we?"

"Evie's a germophobe," Ollie quipped, grinning at our hostess.

"Ha-ha. It's resort policy, as everyone knows, and good hygiene. Let's meet up outside."

Guests started to move toward the door.

"Remember the shoes, people!" Ollie shouted. "You want blisters? I sure don't. And does anybody remember the Great Barefoot Disaster of last summer?"

The entire group hurried past Eve, headed for their rooms to retrieve their shoes, leaving me alone with our hostess.

"Do you want shoes?" she asked.

"It's probably a wise choice. Mine are in your house."

She turned and waved for me to follow. "Let's go get them. We'll meet the gang outside."

While we walked back to Eve's house, I asked, "What was the Great Barefoot Disaster?"

"Last summer, the Kitten Brigade decided to go barefoot on a nature hike." Eve winced. "They didn't see the ant colony until it was too late. Velvety tree ants were nesting under a rock. One of the girls tripped over it. Those ants bite if you disturb their nest."

I grimaced. "That must have been unpleasant."

"Since then, nobody goes into the woods without shoes."

Once I'd rinsed off in the shower and put my shoes on, Eve and I met up with the others in the area between the guest house and Eve's home.

"Everyone all sprayed up and sunscreened?" Eve asked.

The group nodded.

"I've got extra if you need it," she said. "Aloe and antihistamine spray too, just in case."

"You're a worrier," I said.

"I've been hosting nudists for five years. It's experience, not worrying."

Eve led us past the miniten net and down a trail into the woods. I took the backpack from her, despite her eye roll when I did it. We ambled down the trail with Eve pointing out various flowers and bushes, explaining what they were and how they fit into the ecosystem. She pointed out birds too, as well as smaller creatures on the ground. I couldn't focus on anything she said. The sight of her round ass moving, stretching her shorts with every sway of her hips, distracted me.

I had to keep imagining ants attacking my dick to prevent a hard-on.

Fifteen minutes later, we reached a small lake. Eve instructed me and Ollie to set out the picnic blankets she'd somehow stuffed into her backpack along with everything else. She unpacked bottles of water and a plastic box filled with single-serve bags of potato chips and tiny pink cakes nestled in a smaller plastic box with wax paper separating them.

She'd brought a snack for us. The woman thought of everything.

After lunch, the group took a swim. Well, everyone except Eve. She waded into the cool water up to her knees but stepped no farther.

"What's the matter, Evie?" Ollie asked. "Did you see *Jaws* one too many times?"

She smiled and shook her head. "There are no great white sharks in this lake."

Ollie splashed her, making Eve laugh. The water soaked her shirt, and her taut nipples became visible through her bra.

I had to stay in the water several minutes after everyone else retreated onto the shore. Eve's wet T-shirt had left me in a state that wasn't suitable for mixed company.

While we ate dessert, Ollie told me his version of why Eve didn't date. "I think she got sick of guys fighting over her. I mean, every hetero dude who comes here wants to crawl inside Evie's pants and make a home there."

"Every man?" I tipped my head to indicate Ruth's husband, Sylvester.

Ollie snickered. "Every dude who's not married or on social security. Then again, maybe Sly does secretly want to get up in Evie's shorts."

"Does everyone call her Evie?"

"No, man, only special peeps." He hooked a thumb toward Ruth and Sylvester. "Me and the old farts have been coming here for years."

I didn't normally ask strangers personal questions, but Ollie seemed comfortable with me, and my curiosity prodded me to ask. "Have you and Eve…"

"Done the deed? No, dude, we're just friends."

"Are you gay? It doesn't matter to me, but I wondered, since you said every straight man who comes here wants her."

"Not me. I like girls, but not older women."

"How old are you?"

Ollie shoved half of a little cake into his mouth and chewed it up before answering. "I'm twenty-four. Been coming here since I was twenty." He gave me a knowing smile. "Eve's thirty, since you're dying to know."

Maybe I was dying to know everything about her, and maybe that contradicted the idea of a fling. My curiosity didn't care about that. It pushed me to find out more but asking Ollie to tell me those things was not the way to go. I wanted in her shorts as much as anyone, but I didn't need to know all about her unless she chose to tell me.

After the nature hike, the group split up and spread out. Some went inside to play board games while others opted for sunbathing. Ollie offered to help Quentin with the repairs to the water-damaged room. Despite his every attempt to talk the boy out of it, Quentin wound up letting Ollie be his assistant. I didn't want to think about what disasters might befall a nudist who engaged in home repairs.

I participated in one game of hearts before I abandoned the card table to find Eve.

The door to her office on the second floor hung open. She was concentrating on her computer screen, one hand poised over the mouse.

Pausing in the doorway, I drank in the sight of her shapely legs and those lush breasts I longed to taste.

She noticed me and smiled. "Come on in."

I sat down in the chair beside her desk, resting an arm on the desktop.

"Bored with hearts?" she asked, her gaze returning to the screen.

"Card games have never appealed to me."

"Mm-hmm," she said absently as she moved her mouse around and clicked it twice.

"Take a break, Eve. Come to the hot spring with me."

"I don't swim with guests." She moved and clicked the mouse, moved and clicked, moved and clicked. Her eyes darted but stayed focused on the screen. "Maybe Ollie will go with you."

"He's entertaining, but I'd rather spend time with you."

"Too busy." She typed on her keyboard, her fingers clacking the keys in rapid motions. "Maybe later."

She was paying minimal attention to me, and that had to change.

I propped my ankle on my knee. "May I call you Evie?"

"Uh-huh."

"All right, Evie. I wanted to fuck you in the hot spring, but since you won't stop working, this desk will do."

She froze. Though her head did not move, her eyes swiveled toward me. "What did you say?"

"I want to fuck you, *linda*. Right now."

Chapter Five

Eve

That's what I thought you said." I slumped back in my chair, considering the man who'd announced in a matter-of-fact tone that he wanted to fuck me on my desk. "You weren't kidding about being shameless. And you seem to have confused me with someone else because my name is Eve, not Linda."

"*Linda* means beautiful in Portuguese. You are beautiful, Eve, and we need to fuck."

"Sorry, but I don't sleep with guests anymore. It's way too complicated."

"Because two men once fought over you."

"Who told you about that? It must've been Ollie or Ruth." I shook my head, trying to frown but not pulling it off. I couldn't really be mad at them. They meddled out of love. "I knew I should've had them sign a nondisclosure agreement."

"Ruth thinks we're a cute couple." He held up a hand the second I opened my mouth to speak. "Not that I agree with her. I'm not interested in a relationship, and if we have sex, I won't get into a fist fight over you."

"That incident was the last straw, yes, but I'd already started to think getting involved with guests was a bad idea, business-wise."

He rested his arm on the corner of my desk. "I've been told you don't date either."

"Who said that?"

"Your guests."

Ruth and Ollie, no doubt, blabbing again about my personal life. I appreciated their concern for my happiness, but it was misplaced.

"Were they mistaken?" Val asked.

"No, but not dating isn't a conscious choice. I live way out here and always have guests to take care of, even in the winter. Hunting for men isn't a priority." I picked up a pen and braced it between the index fingers of both hands, my elbows on my chair's arms. "I tried online dating, but men are such cowards these days. They only wanted to talk to me through what they saw as anonymous messages on the dating sites."

"What about the town near here?"

"I go into town to buy supplies, not troll for dates." I toyed with the pen, lifting one end and then the other repeatedly. "Besides, guys who aren't perverts or losers are like Bigfoot. Even if they exist, you're never going to catch one."

Val drummed his fingers on the desk, studying me with a curious expression. "Relax, Eve. I don't want to date you."

"You want sex. Yeah, I caught your drift earlier." I tossed the pen onto the desk. "Why did you say you're infamous?"

"Because it's true. Haven't you looked me up online yet?"

"I don't invade the privacy of my guests."

"Anything that's online isn't private."

"Most of it should be. The world really doesn't need to know what everyone ate for lunch today, with close-up pictures of the food."

"True." He studied me again, studied my face. "A young, beautiful woman like you should have a lover."

"And you're volunteering for that job? Thanks, but I'm good the way I am." I rocked my chair, clasping my hands over my belly. "I'm not that young anymore."

"You're thirty. Ollie told me. That is young."

"So you've been quizzing my guests about me, eh?" I smirked. "In that case, how old are you?"

"Thirty-seven." He leaned forward. "I know you want me, I can see it when you look at me. I want you too, and there's no reason why we shouldn't act on our mutual desire."

"I've known you for a few hours."

He shrugged one shoulder. "You know what I look like naked. What more information do you need?"

"Maybe we won't even like having sex with each other."

Val chuckled. "I've never had a complaint."

Yeah, I had no trouble believing that. His body seemed to have been designed by Aphrodite herself to be the perfect sex machine.

Still, I shook my head. "I don't sleep with guests."

"But you do sleep with your employees."

"What? Why would you think that?"

"It's obvious from Quentin's jealousy and the way he glares at me."

I was pretty sure my entire face scrunched up for half a second. "Okay, yeah, I did sleep with him last year. It was a mistake."

"Do you mind if I ask why you did it? Was it one time or an ongoing affair?"

"Nosy, aren't you?" I grabbed the polished rock that served as a paperweight on my desk and rolled it in my hand. What the hell. I might as well tell him. "It was once. I'd had one too many margaritas on Mexican Monday."

"Was he drunk too?"

"I wasn't drunk. A little tipsy, that's all." I wrapped my fist around the paperweight. "But no, he didn't drink that night."

A muscle ticked in Val's jaw. He hissed a breath out his nostrils. "He took advantage of you."

"No, I make my own decisions."

"You'd been drinking. He hadn't. The bastard should never have seduced you." Val's lips compressed into a line. "I hate men who take advantage of women."

"Chill out. It wasn't like that." When his lips flattened again, I added, "I take responsibility for all my decisions, good and bad. If it doesn't bother me, it shouldn't bother you either. And for all you know, I'm a slut who throws herself at every man she meets."

His mouth relaxed, and his jaw stopped ticking. "All right, it's none of my business. I'm sorry for getting upset about it. Growing up with sisters has made me overly protective of women in general."

"That's not a bad thing. It's sweet."

He ran a hand through his hair, leaning back in his chair. "Let's talk about something fun, like when you're going to strip for me."

A poorly stifled laugh snorted out of me. "Whoa there, cowboy. I don't sleep with guests, remember?"

"I'll be the exception."

He rose from the chair with panther-like grace, unfurling his nude body with a languor that I felt sure was purposeful. He wanted me to get a spectacular view of every inch of his skin, from those tattoos all the way down to his impressive dick, and farther down to his powerful thighs. The man had a mouthwatering body, for sure. And no shortage of confidence either.

Everything about him was sexy as hell.

Maybe I should break my rule this one time. With him. In my bed. For hours and hours and hours.

Slickness blossomed between my thighs.

He moved closer, placed one hand on the arm of my chair, and bent to aim those heated brown eyes straight into mine. His breaths tickled my skin. "I don't want to date you. I won't be jealous when we say goodbye and you find someone else to warm your bed. Relationships aren't in my wheelhouse. But I'm staying for two weeks, and I'd love to enjoy you while I'm here."

"Sounds like you don't care if I enjoy you."

"That's a given." He licked his lips. "You want to touch me, don't you?" With his free hand, he picked up one of mine and guided it to within inches of his cock. "I want you to do it."

He let go of my hand, leaving the decision up to me.

I closed my fingers around his cock. It was hot and firm, thickening in my hand.

Val took a slow, deep breath, his eyes going hooded. "*Te quero*, Eve, and when I'm inside you, I guarantee you won't be thinking about anyone or anything else. You won't be thinking at all." He covered my hand with his, pressing my skin more firmly to his erection. "In case you had any doubts, *te quero* means I want you."

He let go of my hand.

I held his cock for a moment longer, reluctant to give up the feel of his inflamed flesh. We stared into each other's eyes, my breaths growing heavier while desire tingled through my sex and tightened my breasts. When I finally withdrew my hand, I couldn't help myself. I thrust that hand into his hair and tugged him in for a kiss.

Our lips touched, gently at first, then with more and more pressure until our mouths were fused. I opened for him, and he plunged his tongue inside my mouth, sliding it over mine, teasing the roof of my mouth, consuming me while I consumed him, the flavor of his mouth electrifying me while the warmth of his lips seemed to blossom outward into my whole body. He tasted so good, like exotic things I couldn't describe but that I longed to savor for the rest of eternity. The delicious warmth engendered by our lip-lock suffused every part of me and penetrated deep into the core of my sex.

God, the man could kiss. I clenched my fingers in his hair, loving the silky texture of those wavy locks. He plowed deeper, coiling his tongue around mine, and groaned with intense pleasure.

Despite the fact I was sitting down, my knees got weak. My ears rang, and I realized I'd stopped breathing.

Someone knocked on the door.

Val jerked away from me, still bent over my chair, and glanced over his shoulder at the open doorway.

Quentin, his fist on the jamb, scowled at Val before looking at me. "Need to talk to you about the repairs in the damaged room."

He spoke through clenched teeth.

I wondered how long Quentin had been standing there, how long he'd watched me and Val together. The door had been open, but both Val and I had our eyes closed until Quentin knocked. Would he have spied on us? Yesterday, I would've said no without hesitation. Today, after witnessing Quentin's jealousy, I wasn't so sure. I didn't want to believe it.

No, he wouldn't do that.

Val straightened but did not turn toward my handyman, probably because his dick was at half-staff.

Pushing my chair back, I got up. To Quentin, I said, "I'll meet you in the room in a minute."

Quentin's lips twisted into an annoyed slant, but he stalked off down the hall.

I smoothed my shirt, like it mattered if my tank top got wrinkled. "I don't sleep with guests, Val. That's my final word on the matter."

I moved to the door but paused on the threshold when he spoke.

"You say that now," he said, "but a second ago you would've let me do anything to you. If your handyman hadn't interrupted us, I'd be fucking you on your desk."

He was right, but I wouldn't tell him that.

Instead, I walked out of the room.

My phone chimed, indicating a new text message, while I was trudging down the stairs to the first floor. Sheesh, I needed to install an elevator. Going up and down the stairs multiple times per day got exhausting. I stopped halfway down the stairs and dug my phone out of my pocket to check the new text. It was from my mother.

You OK? she asked.

I typed my response: *Yes. Why?*

No call last week.

Busy, not dead.

Not like you to stop calling.

I really had been busy, even before the pipe burst in the guest house. Doing everything myself, except for the handyman work, required a lot of time. I typed on my phone's screen. *I'm fine, gotta go, will call later.*

Maybe we need to come for a visit, Mom replied, *to check on you.*

Oh no, absolutely nooooooo way. Sure, my family knew I owned a nudist resort and had no problem with that. But the last thing I needed was my parents meeting Val and seeing how much I lusted after him. I was sure I failed miserably at hiding it. I cherished my privacy, and unlike Val, I wasn't shameless.

Part of me envied his total disregard for what others thought of him.

No visit necessary, I typed to my mom. *All fine, talk to you soon.*

Mom at last said goodbye, and I stuffed the phone in my pocket.

I glanced up the stairs, but I couldn't see Val or the door to my office.

That kiss. His lips on mine had sparked something deep inside me, a kind of hunger I'd never known with any other man. I craved him. When he'd announced he wanted to fuck me, I'd gone instantly wet.

My original assessment had been right. That man was sexy, flirty, down-and-dirty trouble.

Stay away, Eve, keep your hands and mouth off him. I could do that. No problem.

As I trudged down the stairs, my mind replayed the sensations of our kiss.

Not sleeping with him. No way.

Who was I trying to convince?

Chapter Six

Eve had disappeared by the time I walked out of her office. I'd needed a few minutes to recover from our kiss, from the lust that had gripped me when our lips met and I tasted her mouth for the first time. Her lips were soft and flavored with a hint of peppermint, but her lip balm hadn't been the taste that left me halfway to hard and craving more of her. Eve's natural flavor intoxicated me.

When I was finally suitable for public viewing, I ambled outside and glanced at the lawn. The miniten net had been removed. Several guests were laying out yoga mats on the mowed grass while Ollie took up a position in front of the group as if he planned to lead the session.

He spotted me and waved. "Come join us, Val. You do yoga, don't you?"

"Yes, and I'd love to join in."

Maybe a good session of downward dogs would distract me from thoughts of Eve's lips and her luscious body. I loved fantasizing about her, but getting a hard-on wasn't conducive to socializing with the other guests.

"I don't have a mat," I shouted to Ollie.

"No problem. You can get one in the exercise room. We'll wait for you."

Nodding, I trotted back into the guest house and down the hall to the exercise room I'd spotted earlier. Yoga mats, rolled up and sealed with shrink wrap, were stacked inside a large wooden box. A sign on the box said, "New yoga mats. Write your name on the sheet and $10 will be added to your bill. The mat is yours to keep." Eve took every precaution to keep things sanitary and convenient for her guests. I admired that about her. Eve was beautiful, yes, but also smart and capable.

The sheet in question was hooked onto a clipboard that dangled from a chain attached to the wall. I scrawled my name on the sheet and took a mat, peeling the wrapping off and dropping the plastic into a trash can on my way out. Ollie and the rest of the yoga fans had already laid out their mats by the time I got back to the lawn. I spread mine out.

"We'll start with a warm-up," Ollie said.

"No glasses?" I said. "Don't trip over your mat, Ollie."

He rolled his eyes. "I'm not that nearsighted. Now, everybody assume mountain pose. Feet spread to hip width. Let your mind go and really feel your feet. Stretch your toes up and then relax them down again."

I followed Ollie's instructions without thinking about it, my mind wandering to other thoughts. Eve. Her lips. Her scent. Her flavor. The faint pinkness of her cheeks after our kiss. I wanted to do more than feel her soft lips on mine. I wanted all of her, naked and wet and—

Fuck. I had to stop imagining all the things I wanted to do to her, or this would turn into porn yoga.

With a great effort of will, I concentrated on Ollie's instructions and on attaining a relaxed and thought-free state of mind. Ollie might've been young, but he led our yoga session with all the composure and patience of someone much older. By the time we got to the headstand pose, I'd stopped thinking at all. Serenity took over, and I let myself enjoy the sounds of nature around us—the singing of birds, the whisper of the breeze fluttering through the trees, the gentle intonations of our teacher.

I was vertical and upside down when I noticed Eve hovering at the lawn's edge.

She watched me, her head tilted to the side, her lips curved in a slight smile.

Only a few of us had attempted the headstand pose since it was an advanced move. Maybe I wanted to show off for Eve, because I found myself lifting one hand to wave at her. Held up by one arm, I began to teeter just a little.

Eve's eyes widened. Her mouth fell open.

I dropped my hand back onto the mat before I tumbled over, an outcome that wouldn't impress Eve and certainly wouldn't make her want to crawl into bed with me. Still, I was never above showing off to impress a woman.

"Okay," Ollie said, his voice a bit strained from holding his headstand, "time to ease out of it."

Moving slowly, I bent my knees and pulled them down toward my chest, then lowered my toes to the mat and rolled into a kneeling position.

Eve clapped and grinned.

She definitely looked impressed.

I waved to her again and probably smirked, though I resisted the urge to run over there, throw her over my shoulder, and cart her off to the nearest private spot, indoors or out.

The second Ollie announced the session was over and thanked us for attending, I sauntered across the grass to Eve.

"Wow," she said, "you've got the strength of a superhero."

Her compliment made me smirk again. "I appreciate the comparison, but I can't lift a building with my bare hands."

"I'm thinking you could if you really wanted to." She stretched out a hand to fondle my biceps. "You've got some powerful muscles."

Her voice had turned huskier, infused with sensuality.

Mission accomplished. I'd impressed Eve.

"Hey, Val!" Ollie called out.

Eve's hand lingered on my arm, but I tore my gaze away from her to glance back at Ollie.

"Forgot your mat," he shouted, pointing at the one I'd abandoned.

"Sorry, I'll get it." I asked Eve, "When will I see you again?"

"Dinner, probably. I've got work to do, and I need to get back to the drowned guest room. Had to get a tape measure from the house for Quentin."

That's when I noticed the tape measure she held cupped in one hand, almost hidden inside her curled fingers.

"Do you practice yoga?" I asked.

"Yes, but not in public." She gave my biceps a squeeze, her gaze trained on my arm. Her tongue slipped out to moisten her lips. "And not in the nude."

"We should have a private session, just the two of us. I can help you master the one-handed headstand."

She pulled her hand away from my arm and met my gaze. "I'll see you later, Val. Have fun with the other guests."

I enjoyed the view from behind as she sashayed toward the guest house door.

After rolling up my yoga mat, I headed into Eve's house and down the hall to my room. I checked my phone for messages, discovering I had one voicemail from Wendy Yu. I groaned. The last thing I wanted to do on my vacation was talk to my agent, but I never ignored phone calls, emails, or texts.

I dialed Wendy's number.

"Val," she said in her usual cheerful tone, "so glad you called me back. We've got an offer for a magazine spread."

"Not interested."

"The shoot isn't for six weeks. Plenty of time for you to finish your secret sabbatical and come home."

Was LA home? It had been for years, but lately, I'd started to wonder.

"Still not interested," I said. "Turn down all offers until I tell you otherwise."

"At least tell me where you are."

If I did that, Wendy would make sure a gang of paparazzi descended on the resort within twenty-four hours. My agent had done wonders for my career when I'd switched from football to modeling, but I wasn't sure I wanted that life anymore. When I'd mentioned my doubts to Wendy, she had told me to "have a vacay, bang someone, and get over it."

"Please respect my privacy," I told her. "And give me time."

"Just tell me it's not someplace trendy like Ibiza. You have an image to uphold."

"No jobs, Wendy. Understand?"

She sighed loudly. "Fine. But if your sabbatical takes too long, your career might dry up."

I wasn't sure I cared if it did. "Goodbye, Wendy."

Before she could complain, I disconnected the call.

How had I gone from Olympic glory to preening for the camera? I used to enjoy modeling, but these days, I wanted…something else. Something more. What that meant, I still hadn't figured out.

For now, I'd settle for getting Eve Holt in my bed. Or in the grass. Or in the hot spring. Anywhere and everywhere I could have her, I would have her.

The rest I'd think about later.

Chapter Seven

Eve

After discussing the necessary repairs with Quentin and authorizing him to proceed, I returned to my office to finish my boring business tasks. That's what I intended to do. But my mind kept flashing back to that kiss, to the feel of Val's lips on mine and his tongue tormenting me. I couldn't deny he'd been right when he said I would've let him do anything to me if Quentin hadn't interrupted us. I thanked heaven he had, but I also cursed the fates for getting in the way.

It was for the best. I should not sleep with Val. He'd admitted he was infamous, though I had no idea why. He had all but told me to look him up online.

No, I would not do that. His past didn't matter since he was nothing more than a guest.

I returned my attention to the computer screen. The numbers in my accounting software blurred. My mind reeled me back to the moment when Val's lips had touched mine. He smelled so good. He looked so good. Damn, he was sex on a stick slathered with warm caramel sauce and whipped cream. Watching him do yoga in the nude, that had transformed my desire into a living, breathing creature scrabbling to get out and have its way. I would never forget the sight of Val in a headstand pose with one hand raised to wave at me, a sexy smirk on his lips.

How could he hold that pose? The man must have supernatural powers.

My mind conjured images of all the positions he might pull off in bed and how deliciously naughty it would feel to let him fuck me. *Get a grip, Evie.*

For ten more minutes, I tried to do that. Really, I tried. My fingernails tapped on the desk instead of the keyboard, and I couldn't focus on the screen for more than two seconds.

Oh, screw it. I could check him out. He'd clearly wanted me to, and Googling him did not mean I would crawl into his bed in the middle of the night.

I opened my web browser and searched for Val Silva. A bunch of results popped up, including several women with the same name, but the top five results were all about my Val Silva.

Not mine. My guest.

The titles of the web pages listed in the results solved the mystery of his infamy. "International soccer star shucks his clothes to celebrate winning game," said an American newspaper. A sports website stated, "Former Olympic football champ Val Silva bares all on the field to celebrate World Cup win." Browsing the articles, I learned Val hadn't received any severe punishment for his antics, since both times he'd stripped after the final whistle and not during the game. The first time, he'd received a warning. The second time, he'd been fined and suspended for one game as well getting arrested, though his influential father got him out of jail with no charges filed.

It was the fifth search result that stopped me.

The article came from a gossip website. The headline read, "Silva-Taylor sex tape: Football champion Val Silva and Hollywood star Marina Taylor caught with their pants down, again."

My mouse pointer hovered over the link to the full story. I shouldn't click the link. No, I really, really, really shouldn't.

I clicked the link, wincing at my inappropriate curiosity. Was it inappropriate? He'd sort of suggested I look up his infamous behavior. He must want me to see the tape.

The article talked about Val's history of stripping down during football matches, usually after he'd scored the winning goal. I skimmed through the description of his athletic achievements, including the fact he'd led the Brazilian Olympic team to a gold medal and had been the star player of his professional football club. Later, he'd been instrumental in his national team claiming three World Cup wins. Every time, Val had scored the pivotal goals.

Then I got to the part about the video.

All I saw was a still image from the video with all the sensitive bits blurred out. Val sat in a chair with a woman straddling him. Her head was thrown back, and his eyes were closed. According to the text, the sex tape went on for fifteen minutes, with Val enjoying his lady friend in various positions and giving her several "happy endings." His video sex partner was the movie star Marina Taylor, according to the article, though I'd never heard of her, since I paid little attention to celebrities. The story went on to explain Marina had become as infamous as Val was for her scandalously risqué behavior in public, and the two of them had even received their own celebrity couple nickname, Valarina. The couple had also sprinted across the stage—naked, of course—at the Oscars, but nobody bothered to press charges for the incident. It was Hollywood, after all, the land of outrageous behavior. Marina was quoted as saying, of their sex tape, "Val and I have nothing to be ashamed of. He's a god in bed, and I'm blessed to have enjoyed the pleasure of his company."

His company? She'd been lost in ecstasy in the image from the video.

Val had given no comment on the tape.

The fact I'd never heard of any of their escapades was hardly surprising. I avoided social media, tabloids, and gossip shows.

I browsed a bit more of the search results and glanced at magazine spreads he'd posed for since retiring from football. Damn, but he was photogenic. Not that the fact surprised me. In person, he was drop-dead hot and sex incarnate. In photos, he made every other male model look like an amateur. I searched for his sex tape too but couldn't find it.

Okay, enough snooping. I closed my web browser. Now I knew why Val had said he was infamous. He had flaunted his nudism in public and starred in a sex tape with a famous actress. Mystery solved.

Again, I tried to get back to work.

My mind wouldn't let me. I fantasized about being the woman in that video, about all the things he might do to give me multiple happy endings.

I gave up and went outside to check on my guests.

Ollie and Sylvester were playing checkers, their board lying on the grass though they sat on towels, while behind them, other guests played volleyball. Ruth sat beside Sylvester, observing the checkers game.

When Ollie spotted me, he patted the grass beside him. "Sit down, Evie. Take a load off."

I accepted his invitation. For the better part of an hour, I watched Ollie and Sly shifting the red and black disks around the playing board, each of them winning several games. We all joked and laughed and talked about what to do tomorrow. The Pioneer Days festival was up and running, so we decided that might be a nice change of pace. Yes, the nudists would need to wear clothes, but they were cool with that. The rest of the gang agreed it sounded like a fun outing.

Eventually, Val came up the path from the woods, alone. He smiled at me, then joined the volleyball game.

I tried soooo hard not to stare at his penis, the way it bounced whenever he jumped up to hit the ball. Really, I tried. But every girl has her limits, and eventually, I allowed myself to grab the occasional glance. That man had the best ass I'd ever seen, not to mention the best dick.

After the checkers marathon ended, Ruth and Sylvester retreated into the guest house, taking the checkers board with them. Val had disappeared into the guest house with his fellow nudists.

I got up and stretched.

Ollie stood too. He twisted his lips this way and that, scratching his nose. "Do you know where Val's from?"

"He lives in Los Angeles, but he's originally from Brazil. Didn't he tell you?"

"I didn't think to ask." Ollie folded his arms over his chest. "I know I've seen him somewhere before."

"Well, he used to play professional football. His teams won the Olympics and the World Cup."

Ollie's brows cinched together, wrinkling the skin above his nose. "Football. Val Silva." His eyes widened, and he snapped his fingers. "That's it. He's the soccer player who kept ditching his clothes during games."

"That's right. I'm not sure if he wants to talk about it, though."

Ollie gave me an *oh please* look. "I'm a naturist. I know how to be discreet. But nobody should ever be ashamed of taking their clothes off."

"I think it's a crime to do it in public, at least in the US."

He flapped a hand in a dismissive gesture. "Only because the authorities have sticks up their butts."

A crunching sound drew our attention to the gravel driveway. A car emblazoned with the logo of the pizza restaurant parked alongside the guest house.

"Dinner's here," I said, and Ollie and I headed for the guest house.

I tried to grab a few slices of pizza and duck out to go eat in my own home, but Val insisted I sit beside him throughout dinner. He didn't touch me and never reached for anything. That a shameless exhibitionist like him followed the house rules surprised me, but the way he included me in every conversation made me feel oddly happy. One discussion involved everyone gushing about how amazing I was for running the resort all by myself. I smiled tightly and thanked them for their kind words. I wanted to bow my head and pull my hair over my face to hide. Their effusive praise made me uncomfortable.

During the entire meal, I resisted the frequent urge to slide my hand up Val's muscular thigh under the table. It would've been a violation of the rules, but I had a feeling he wouldn't have minded. Still, I stuck to my decorum.

By the time the pizza party ended, it was nearly ten o'clock.

When I told Val I planned to get some work done in the living room before going to bed, he shook his head and retreated into his room.

Half an hour later, I'd had enough work. My eyes were tired and gritty, so I shambled barefoot through the living room doorway into the kitchen. There, I paused to shut off the light and then made my way down the darkened hallway toward my room.

A wedge of light shined through the partly opened door to Val's room, spraying its glow across the wood floor in the hall. I did not peek through the opening when I walked past his room.

Hooray for my self-control. I almost pumped my fists in the air.

I had just pushed the door to my room open and was reaching for the light switch inside when a noise from across the hall caught my attention. A thump, that's what it had sounded like.

A long, low groan originated from Val's room.

Staring across the hall, I considered what to do. Should I go check on him? What if he'd fallen and hit his head? I couldn't have a guest dying of a cracked skull. I needed to check.

Decision made, I approached the door.

It hung open about six inches, enough to let the wedge of illumination spill out—and enough to grant me a view of him. My belly quivered, and my skin came alive with a tingling excitement that raised every hair on my arms and my nape.

Val reclined in the wooden chair by the desk completely naked, as usual, his feet on the floor and his big body slouched. He had his head thrown back, resting on the chair. His full lips were parted, his eyes closed. With one hand, he gripped the chair's arm. With his other hand...

Heat ripped through me.

With his other hand, he pumped his rigid cock in a leisurely, decadent rhythm. His chest rose and fell with his heavy breaths. Little grunts and groans escaped his lips. Every so often, he would lift his hips into the thrusts of his hand, and the chair would tip back a smidgen only to smack down again when his ass slapped onto the chair.

That explained the thump I'd heard. And the groan.

He raised his head, eyes still closed, his face tight with need.

I sidled up to the wall, hidden in the shadows but with a clear view of him. I should've walked away. Should've gone to my room and...masturbated while imagining what he was doing in his room. Shit. A good host would leave right now. Then again, he had left the door open. He must've known I would hear him. Maybe he wanted me to watch.

Or march in there and mount him.

God, I wanted to climb astride him and drive us both to screaming orgasms.

My sex had grown so wet I felt the slickness every time my legs shifted the tiniest bit. I could smell the scent of my arousal, and my clit throbbed. Oh, did it throb. I couldn't remember the last time I'd been this turned on. Maybe I never had been before.

He threw his head back once more, his mouth wide open, and hissed in a breath. He groaned it out, the sound resonating deep in his throat and chest. That hand stroked his length faster while the fingers of his other hand clenched the chair's arm harder.

I unhooked the button of my jeans and slid the zipper down inch by inch, so the sound was almost inaudible. Powerless to resist the urge, I slipped my hand inside my damp panties and stroked my mound.

His hand pumping, pumping. His rock-hard cock glistening. His palm and fingers encircling his shaft. The tip so red, begging to be sucked.

My mouth watered. I plunged a finger between my folds, rubbing my nub.

His back arched. He rocked his hips up, thrusting into his own hand, his breaths harsh and fast. The need to come wrenched his features, and as he pumped wildly, he sucked in a breath and held it.

Hunger pulsated through my clit, and holy fuck, I was on the verge of coming already. I rubbed faster, rougher, desperate to hit my release with him, but I couldn't stop it. The orgasm seized my body. I mashed my face into the wall to muffle my strangled whimpers. I squeezed my eyes shut, rubbing until I'd milked every last spasm of pleasure from my body.

I opened my eyes, still stroking myself lightly, and looked at Val.

A milky jet erupted from his cock.

He let out a hoarse cry, pumped twice more, and slumped in the chair. Sweat sheathed his tattooed arm and chest and dampened his hair. He grabbed a towel from the desk and began to wipe down his shaft.

Watching Val clean himself up after beating off, it got me all hot again. I couldn't stop myself. I ground my finger into my clit until another orgasm barreled through me, hard and fast. Flattening my back against the wall, I gritted my teeth and swallowed my own cries. Once the climax subsided, I could breathe again.

My cheeks flamed, not only from my climax. What had I done?

I tiptoed back to my bedroom and shut the door behind me. When I flopped backward onto the bed, the springs squeaked. What on earth had I been thinking? Spying on Val while he masturbated was bad enough, but I'd gotten myself off while watching him. Twice.

Damn if those hadn't been the best orgasms of my life.

I changed into my nightie and crawled under the covers. For a long time, I lay awake reliving those moments in the hallway and remembering the look on his face when he'd come. We couldn't work as a couple, I knew that much. Val and I had nothing in common. He was a celebrity with a checkered past, the kind of man who relished the spotlight and loved the big city. I liked my quiet life in rural Oregon, running my family-friendly naturist resort. Of course, he'd made it clear he didn't want a relationship with me and that he wouldn't start a brawl if another man expressed interest in me. He wanted sex, pure and simple.

Even that seemed like a bad idea. He was so…naughty. And I had a feeling if I got it on with him, one taste would never satisfy me.

No sex with Val. Decision made. He never needed to know I'd spied on him.

If I could just get my body to go along with that resolution…

Chapter Eight

Val

E ve was cooking breakfast when I walked into the kitch-
en the next morning. Instead of those very-short shorts and
that tank top, the outfit I'd loved yesterday, she wore tight
pink jeans and a loose-fitting white blouse. Her curves looked no
less enticing in this outfit. She couldn't be frumpy even if she'd
tried, not with that body.

"Good morning," I said, taking a seat on a stool at the island. Eve
had already laid out place settings on the island, one on either side.

Across the island from me, she paused in frying up something
in a skillet and glanced my way. "Good morning. Breakfast is almost ready."

"What about your guests? Don't they eat breakfast?"

"Their food is hot and waiting for them in the dining hall of the
guest house."

I raised my brows. "It's seven o'clock. When did you get up?"

"Five thirty." She turned back to her cooking, stirring whatever
it was with a wooden spoon. "I hope you like scrambled eggs, bacon, and pancakes."

"You didn't need to cook all of that for me. Especially not after
making breakfast for sixteen other people."

"Oh, it's no trouble. I made the same thing for the other guests, so
all I had to do was save a few pancakes for us. The bacon was pre-
cooked and warmed up in the microwave, so that was no trouble. I

made fresh eggs, though." She smiled at me over her shoulder. "I hope you're hungry."

"*Estou verde de fome.* It smells delicious."

"Thanks, but I have no idea what that first thing meant."

"I said I'm starving." I winked. "In Portuguese."

"Wish I knew another language, but I barely passed high school Spanish."

"Maybe I'll teach you Portuguese—or Spanish, if you like. I'm fluent in both."

"Wow. I'm impressed." She shut off the stovetop burner and carried the frying pan to the island, then portioned out the eggs onto our plates. "Eat up. Can't have a guest starving on my watch."

I pointed at my plate. "You gave me more than you gave yourself."

"You're a big, strong man who can do a one-handed headstand. I assumed you'd need more protein than I do."

"That sounds rather sexist," I teased.

"I'm committing sexism against myself? Not sure how that works. If you don't want the eggs, I'll dump them down the garbage disposal."

"No, I'll eat them."

She set the frying pan in the sink.

I watched her reheat the pancakes and bacon in the microwave, though my attention frequently wandered to her ass. Her loose-fitting shirt seemed to make those perfect cheeks even more enticing.

Once she'd portioned out the rest of our meal, she perched on her own stool and picked up her fork, spearing a chunk of eggs.

"Did you sleep well last night?" I asked.

She froze with the forkful of egg poised between her open lips. Her eyes rolled up to stare at me. "Huh?"

"I asked if you slept well."

"Oh. Yes, fine." She shoved the food into her mouth and chewed it. "How about you?"

"Very well." I ate some of my food while keeping an eye on her, trying to gauge when would be the right time to bring up the subject of last night. After eating half of a pancake, I couldn't wait any longer. "Did you enjoy the show last night?"

Eve dropped her fork. It clattered onto her plate, and the chunk of pancake impaled on the tines broke in half. "Excuse me?"

"Last night. When you watched me. Did you enjoy it?"

Her eyes flew wide, and her cheeks turned slightly pink. "I—well—"

I picked up a slice of bacon and bit off a piece.

She sat up straighter, staring down at her lap, and took a deep breath that she exhaled little by little. At last, she raised her face to me. "How did you know I was there?"

"I saw you in the mirror."

"Mirror?" She winced as realization hit her. "The one on the dresser. I didn't think about that."

"That mirror was angled just right to let me see you." I bit off another piece of bacon and chewed it so I could take a moment to savor the pinkness of her cheeks and the way her breasts rose and fell. "You came, didn't you? I heard the little noises you tried to muffle by pressing your face to the wall."

To her credit, she didn't look away or try to deny it. Despite the faint blush coloring her cheeks, she stayed calm and resolute.

"Why deny it?" she said. "Yes, I came. Twice."

I couldn't help smirking. "Eve Holt won't go nude in front of her guests, but she is a voyeur."

"How is it voyeurism when you left your door open? I bet you did that on purpose, hoping I'd see you."

"Do you?" I chuckled. "All right. Yes, I did. I wanted you to see what you're missing."

She shook her head, her lips stretching into a closed-mouth smile. "I'd already seen that. I Googled you yesterday. Unfortunately, I couldn't watch your sex tape since I found only a still photo from it."

"The leaked video was taken down by the site where the thief uploaded it. At least half the world had already seen it by then." I dipped my finger into the syrup on my plate and thrust it into my mouth, drawing my finger out slowly, loving the way Eve's breath caught when I licked it and sucked the tip. Maybe she guessed that I was imagining doing the same thing to her. "I have the original on my phone if you'd like to see it. Marina and I recorded it on my phone, and I didn't bother to delete it. I never imagined my assistant would leak the tape. After that, everybody had seen it anyway."

"Did you watch your own video last night? Is that why you were jerking off?"

"No, I was fantasizing about you." I reached across the island to rub my thumb over her lips. "You can kiss me again anytime you want, anywhere you want. And I don't mean you can do it in the kitchen or in the bathroom. I mean anywhere on my body."

As her gaze traveled over me, the parts she could see above the island, the stiff peaks of her nipples jutted against her shirt. When her eyes met mine again, her pupils had enlarged.

I swirled my fingertip in the syrup on my plate, keeping my gaze nailed to hers. "How hard did you come for me last night?"

She touched the fingers of one hand to her throat, grazing them down to her collarbone. When she spoke, her voice had gone sultry. "Those were the best orgasms I've ever had."

"It'll be better when I'm inside you."

We studied each other for a moment, her lips parted and her cheeks rosy, while my cock stiffened. I had to have her soon or I'd go insane. Never in my life had I hungered for a woman the way I hungered for Eve Holt. Our kiss yesterday had only heightened my lust for her.

She cleared her throat, wriggled on her seat, and set her hands on her lap. "No, Val, I will not be kissing you again. I won't sleep with you either."

"Don't want to sleep, Eve."

"I'm not getting involved with you in any way." She shoved a piece of pancake into her mouth and devoured it, her throat muscles working as she swallowed. "I like my simple life out here in the woods. Nothing and no one is going to derail that." She stabbed her fork into her pancake. "You are trouble, Mr. Silva. You strip naked in public and save your sex tapes on your phone. I wouldn't be surprised if you leaked that tape yourself."

I licked the syrup off my finger and leaned into the back of my stool. "My personal assistant leaked the sex tape. The second I found out, I fired him. I'm not ashamed of what the world saw, but I can't have an assistant who betrays me for money. As for stripping in public, those were publicity stunts. I knew my football career wouldn't last much longer, and I wanted to see what kind of offers I'd get if I did something outrageous to make myself more of a celebrity."

"What offers did you get? Starring roles in porn movies?"

"Some of those, yes, but I turned them down. The offers I liked the best were for modeling work, so I accepted a lot of those."

She leaned back too, eying me with a renewed interest. "I saw a few of the spreads you did for magazines. You look good in print."

I raised a brow. "But not in person?"

"You know the answer to that."

"Mm, yes." I couldn't help smiling. "I gave you the best orgasm of your life without laying a finger, or a tongue, on you. Imagine what I can do when I'm touching your body."

"As intriguing as that sounds, the answer is still no. We are not getting involved."

"I don't want to date you, *linda*. I want to have sex with you."

She hopped off her stool. "And I told you no. You are the hottest mess I've ever seen, and I don't need the complications. A notorious athlete turned model who likes to strip in public and who starred in a sex tape. No thank you, Val."

"Not interested in complications. Just sex, nothing else."

"Uh-huh." She carried her plate to the sink. "I've heard that before. Quentin swore sex wouldn't change anything and we could go back to being just friends after. Instead, he's jealous of you even though I haven't slept with you yet. The last thing I need is you getting jealous of every man who speaks to me."

"I'm not the jealous type."

"Heard that before too." She turned around and braced her bottom against the counter. "No sex, Val."

I got up and strode around the island to stand in front of her. Inches separated our bodies. I placed my palms on the sink counter at either side of her hips, bending my head to meet her eyes. "You say that this morning, but last night you came twice from watching me get off. You want me. I want you. There's no reason to make this more complicated."

She wrinkled her nose. "Yeah, right. Guys always think they mean that, but they don't."

"I do. Sex only, *bebê*."

"Yeah, I can guess what that one means. You called me baby, didn't you?"

"That's right." I brushed my lips over hers, and she sucked in a breath. The feel of her mouth on mine brought my cock to attention, but she didn't seem to mind the hard length rubbing against her belly. I nipped her lower lip, then brushed my tongue across it. "Let's do it right now, right here in the kitchen."

"What if paparazzi show up and snap lurid pictures of us through the window? You are a notorious celebrity, after all."

"My life won't touch yours. No one knows I'm here, I made sure of that." I slipped my hand under her shirt, finding the waistband of her jeans and hooking a finger inside it. "I told only my parents and my sisters where I would be, and they're in Brazil. No one will find me. I drove instead of flying partly to keep anyone from tracking me. Mostly, I wanted to escape from my life for a while."

"What, did you release another sex tape?"

"No." I skimmed my finger along the inside of her waistband until I found the button on her jeans. Unhooking it slowly, I licked at the seam of her lips. "Let's enjoy each other, Evie. That's all I want and all you want too."

I tugged her zipper down and pushed my hand inside her jeans, inside her panties, to palm her mound. Her desire had drenched the soft, curly hairs that tickled my skin.

She sucked in another breath. "I don't have time for this. Gotta clean up the breakfast dishes from the guest house and—" She exhaled a breathy moan when I dived a finger between her slick folds. "We're all going to the Pioneer Days festival after lunch, so there really isn't...oh...time."

I thrust my whole hand between her folds, rocking it to rub her flesh. The scent of her desire wafted around us. She smelled incredible.

"Val, we can't," she said, though her voice was a throaty whisper and her head had tipped back, exposing the delicate column of her throat. Her fingers gripped the counter's edge harder, making tendons rise on the back of her hand. "I have to get to work. This place doesn't run itself."

"No, you're not leaving yet." I dropped to my knees in front of her, then dragged her jeans and panties down to her ankles. "Not until I've tasted you."

I grasped the backs of her thighs and lifted, hoisting her ass onto the counter.

Movement outside the window pulled my attention to the view, and for a second, I swore I noticed a shadow out there. It disappeared so fast I decided it must've been a cloud passing over the sun.

And I had more important concerns at the moment.

Eve glanced around as if expecting to see paparazzi outside one of the windows. "We can't. I can't. What if—"

"No one will know what we're doing. Unless you scream."

I shoved my head between her thighs, burying my face against her mound and thrusting my tongue between her folds. Her cream tasted sweet and tangy, and the musky scent of her drowned my senses. I draped my arms around her hips while I lapped at her flesh, circled my tongue around her taut nub, and raked my tongue down her cleft and back up to suck her clit into my mouth.

Her fingers plunged into my hair. "Oh, Val, yes."

A knock rattled the door.

I kept licking and suckling her nub, too inflamed by the flavor and heat of her to give up her body or to care who the fuck was knocking.

She whimpered, her nails scraping my scalp.

A more forceful knock rattled the door.

"Eve?" Quentin called. "You in there? I need your input with the repairs."

"Stop," she hissed to me.

I pulled back enough to look up at her. The blouse she wore had gotten bunched around her hips. "Tell him to go away."

"Can't do that." She planted her feet on my chest and pushed me away. "This is my job, Val."

While I sat back on my haunches, she shimmied her hips as she pulled her jeans and panties up, then zipped up and hurried to the door.

Her hand on the knob, she glanced back at me. "Better, um, go into another room or something."

She nodded toward my groin and the erection waving at her.

I leaned against the island. "Afraid your handyman will be jealous?"

"Unlike some people, I don't flaunt my sexcapades for the world to see." She flapped her hands, shooing me away. "Go."

I moved behind the island where Quentin wouldn't see the state Eve had gotten me into here in the kitchen.

She slipped her feet into the flip-flops she kept beside the door, pulled the door open partway, and sneaked outside. She yanked the door shut after her.

I shook my head, smiling. Stubborn as she was, Eve wanted me as much as I wanted her, and we would be fucking soon.

Very soon.

Chapter Nine

Eve

I ordered him not to do it, but Val insisted on helping me clean up the dining hall, take the dishes back to my house, and wash them. He even rushed back to the house to put on skintight jeans and a T-shirt, in accordance with the health code. Quentin tried to help too, but Val kept swooping in first to do everything. He seemed impervious to Quentin's hot glare and his snide comments. My handyman called my newest guest "a human bulldozer" and "an exhibitionist with a one-track mind" as well as "a mosquito buffet waiting to happen." The last one didn't make sense since Val was currently wearing clothes, but Quentin chortled at his own joke anyway.

The three of us carried the dishes back to my house. When Quentin tried to squeeze in to claim the sink first, Val casually asked whether my handyman had finished the repairs "you keep needing your employer's input on."

Quentin's face turned beet red at that comment. His nostrils flared—something I thought human beings couldn't do, but Quentin sure could. He fisted his hands, seeming about to erupt.

A fist fight was the last thing I needed, so I shooed Quentin out of the house, telling him to get back to work on the repairs.

I tried to shoo Val away, but the man was so large and strong I couldn't budge him. Even kicking his feet didn't make an impression. He flashed me a smile and went back to washing the dishes. That meant I stood beside him drying those dishes and trying not to stare at his ass. Those tight jeans didn't conceal much, though I couldn't see the bulge of his dick since he was leaning into the counter.

My mind kept flashing me back to earlier today when he'd shoved his face between my thighs. God, that had felt incredible. His hot, slick tongue working my flesh. His lips sucking. His fingers pressing into the backs of my thighs. I'd been so close to climax. If Quentin hadn't knocked on the door, I might have enjoyed a rockin' orgasm. Instead, I had to take care of the breakfast mess while my body throbbed from thwarted bliss.

Oh, and I remembered the glimpse I'd gotten of his aroused cock. When I'd pushed Val away from me, I'd seen it. Damn, the man was beyond well-hung. His erect penis was bigger, thicker, and even more impressive than when it hung slack. I wanted that inside me. I wanted him. More than anything, I'd wanted to tell Quentin to go to hell so I could mount Val right here in the kitchen.

Too complicated, I reminded myself. He was a notorious celebrity.

Well, I didn't have to get attached to him or get enmeshed in any kind of relationship. We could have sex, period. I could satisfy this outrageous craving for him that had me acting like a horny teenager and then move on.

Letting him go down on me in the kitchen? For pity's sake, I was thirty, not sixteen.

Once we'd finished with the dishes, Val turned to face me and leaned his hip against the counter. "Why don't you have a dishwashing machine?"

"Those things are expensive, and you have to practically wash the stuff before you put it in the dishwasher anyway." I replaced the dish towel on the little hanger attached to the counter, only in part as an excuse to look away from him and his hot bod, not at all disguised by his clothing. "I'm not above manual labor."

"You need more than a handyman. You need a team of employees."

"I've done fine so far."

He touched my arm. "When was the last time you took a day off?"

The warmth of his hand on my bare skin set off a flurry of goose bumps. My nipples went hard. I struggled to keep from sounding breathless when I told him, "My work habits are none of your concern."

He moved closer.

Too close. I could smell him, that indefinable essence of man that made everything inside me perk up and take notice. No, it wasn't the essence of man as in any old man. It was the essence of him.

His fingers curled around my arm. "Why haven't you hired anyone else? Why only Quentin?"

I noted the way his voice took on a faint sharp edge when he spoke my handyman's name. "It's complicated."

"You can tell me. I won't post it on Twitter." He winked. "I save that for sex tapes."

"Uh-huh." I considered walking away but decided I had no reason not to tell him the truth. I faced him and said, "When I started this business five years ago, I didn't have much money. My dad inherited this place from his great uncle, but he and my mom wanted to retire to the Florida Keys, not to the Oregon wilderness. They gave me this property. My parents also gave me ten thousand dollars to get started with, and I took out a loan for the rest, mainly to pay for building the guest house. I paid off the loan six months ago, which means I don't have enough left over to afford more employees or the other improvements I'd like to make."

"I would be happy to invest."

Folding my arms over my chest, I squinted at him. "Invest? That would mean you get your money back eventually, but I don't think that's what you really mean."

"Call it a gift, then."

"Oh-ho, no." I shook my head, wagging a finger at him. "I don't accept payment for sex."

A smirk stretched his lips. Amusement sparkled in his eyes and crinkled the skin around them. "That almost sounds like an invitation to fuck you."

"You think everything I say is an invitation."

"Because it is." He wrapped an arm around my waist, tugging me into his big, firm body. "We both want the same thing, sex with no strings. Stop fighting it. At the end of two weeks, I'll go home and we will never see each other again. What have you got to lose?"

My sanity. My self-respect. My heart.

I wouldn't fall for him. I barely knew Val, and I had no intention of getting to know him better. Sure, that's why I'd explained my financial situation to him. Ugh. As much as I would've loved to take a wild roll in the hay with him, I needed to shut this down ASAP.

"Sorry," I said, wriggling out of his hold, "I don't sleep with guests. Right now, I have to do some stuff in my office and then I need to make lunch. After that, we're all off to the Pioneer Days festival." I scrunched my lips, trying not to smile. "You'll need to keep your clothes on for that."

He tapped a finger on my lips. "I know that, Eve. I'll help you with lunch."

"No way. You are a guest, so go mingle with the rest of the gang."

Val stared at me for a moment, his full lips twisting into a half frown. He gusted out a sigh and nodded. "All right. I will mingle."

"Good."

He sauntered to the door, pausing there to glance back at me. "But I won't give up on seducing you."

Val walked out the door.

Once it clicked shut after him, I almost sagged into the counter. Whew. One calamity averted. For now.

He wouldn't give up. I believed that. For some bizarre reason, an infamous football star and unabashed nudist who liked to tape himself having sex had set his sights on me, the non-nudist proprietor of a low-rent resort who refused to sleep with guests.

Maybe a roll in the hay with him would be worth the risk of repercussions. He kept telling me he wasn't the jealous type and he didn't want a relationship. So maybe, just maybe, I could take the roll with him. Oh yeah, my body loved that idea.

Chapter Ten

When Eve strolled out of her house at one fifteen, her guests were waiting for her in the grassy area between her home and the guest house. I'd made sure to be in the front line. Eve stopped a short ways from us, gripping the strap of the huge purse she'd slung over one shoulder.

Her brows lifted a touch when she saw me.

I'd changed clothes for the occasion, though I doubted Eve would appreciate my ensemble. She had, I was sure, hoped I'd keep my entire body covered so she might feel less inclined to ravish me. Though I hated disappointing her in any way, this one time I had to do it.

Her gaze traveled the length of my body. Her raised brows lowered and cinched together over her nose.

Maybe my clothing surprised her. I was, after all, wearing swim shorts with a brightly colored zigzag print, a sleeveless T-shirt, and the latest, impossible-to-get style of Nikes that featured a bright pattern not unlike my shorts. I'd taken off my bucket hat and my Ray-Bans so I could see Eve clearly, though I held them in my hands.

She looked incredible in her pink jeans and white blouse. Here in the sunshine, the blouse became semi-transparent, revealing the outline of her bra that barely covered her gorgeous tits. She wore white sandals that exposed her toes and the shiny pink polish on them that matched the polish on her fingernails. She'd painted her nails since I had left her in the kitchen.

Just looking at her pink nails made me want to fall down at her feet and suck her perfect little toes one by one.

A straw hat with a wide brim perched on her head at a slight angle, shading her face. She adjusted the strap that held the hat in place and smiled at me. "Nice outfit, Val. I suppose that's the latest fashion in summer menswear."

"It is, but I augmented it with my own style."

"Naturally." She eyed my clothing again. One side of her mouth kinked upward. "Your style is definitely unique."

Every other man in our group wore subdued clothing—khakis, denim, shirts in earth tones. Ollie had opted for a bright-blue T-shirt, but even that was subdued next to my clothes.

"Why blend in?" I said to Eve. "I enjoy standing out from the crowd."

"No kidding." She feigned a surprised face. "I never would've guessed."

Ruth patted my arm. "This is a good sign, sweetie. Eve is flirting with you. I've never seen her do that with anyone else, not even the gentlemen she had flings with."

"I am not flirting," Eve said. She darted her gaze around the crowd, gripping her purse strap in both hands, and cleared her throat. "Not that it would be anyone's business if I were."

Her cheeks had turned a lovely shade of mottled pink. It almost matched her jeans.

Ruth hurried over to Eve and hooked an arm around her shoulders. "It's okay, Evie. We're all glad you found a man who excites you. Maybe you'll even let him take you on a date."

The idea of exciting Eve excited me, but Ruth would be disappointed about the dating suggestion. Neither I nor Eve wanted that.

"Thanks," Eve muttered. She stepped away from Ruth, lifted her chin, and called out, "Everybody in the bus. It's field trip time."

We all piled into a decommissioned school bus, once a yellow monstrosity but now painted sky blue. I hadn't noticed the bus on the property yesterday, but Ollie had explained that Eve kept it on the far side of the guest house, hidden in the shadows of tall trees. She didn't want a bus to be the first thing her guests saw when they arrived at the resort.

The afternoon had turned warm but not so hot we would be uncomfortable in the bus during the drive into town. Besides, someone—Eve, I suspected—had opened all the windows some-time earlier to let in fresh air. The vinyl bench seats had been re-upholstered with soft beige fabric and seemed to have acquired more cushioning than any school bus I'd seen before. The benches featured seat belts too. Eve did everything she could to make her guests feel comfortable and safe. It was no wonder they kept coming back to this place.

Every bench seat had at least one person occupying it by the time I stepped onto the bus. I scanned the interior, looking for a good place to sit.

Ollie waved at me. He had taken the front seat on the left side.

I nodded to him.

He scooted closer to the window and patted the seat beside him. "Take a load off, Val. This bus isn't exactly a Ferrari, or even a Chevy Volt, so it's a longer ride to town than if you were in a car. That's why Eve made the seats cushier and had better shock absorbers installed." He patted the spot beside him again. "Take a load off."

"Thank you." I settled onto the seat. "Does Eve organize a lot of field trips?"

"At least one a week. She likes to give us something to do other than sit around naked and contemplate our navels."

"Can't say I've spent much time doing that. My navel isn't that interesting."

"Belly buttons are weird, aren't they?"

I hadn't seen Eve's belly button yet, but I had a feeling her navel would be as sexy and fascinating as the rest of her body. The thought made my cock stir.

Quentin stomped onto the bus and dropped into the driver's seat. He flashed me a tight frown.

Eve bounded up the steps and faced her guests. "Everybody ready to go?"

Heads nodded. Voices murmured.

"Good," she said. "Buckle up, guys."

While everyone else secured their seat belts, she glanced around as if looking for something.

"Forget something?" I asked.

"I'm looking for a place to sit."

I patted my thigh. "My lap is available."

She clamped her lips between her teeth, clearly struggling not to smile.

Ollie hopped up. "Take my seat, Eve. I'll hang with Fred."

Before Eve could respond, Ollie squeezed past me and trotted toward the rear of the bus.

"Well," I said, "looks like you're sitting with me. Do you prefer the window or the aisle?"

"I'll take the window."

She sidled past me, and I got a close-up view of her bottom sheathed in those skintight pink jeans. Resisting the urge to palm her cheeks tested my willpower, but I managed to restrain myself.

Quentin started up the bus. It lurched forward.

Eve grasped the metal bar that separated our seat from the steps.

I placed a hand on her hip to offer support.

She raised her brows at me but settled onto the seat, sticking close to the window, careful to keep a gap between us.

"I'm not contagious," I said. "And I'm not even naked. Should I be offended that you're hugging the wall?"

"Sorry." She relaxed, moving a little closer. Her blue eyes studied me. "You must be rich, right? I mean, your truck is ultra-expensive and you're a famous athlete slash model."

"I have more than enough money, yes."

"Why did you come to my little bargain-basement resort? You would've been more comfortable at a luxury club."

"I like your resort. Besides, I value privacy and friendliness more than luxury."

Her lips curved into a sweet smile. "Well, you definitely came to the right place if you're looking for privacy. We're in the boonies."

"That's part of why I chose your place for my vacation."

"What's the rest of the reason?" She winced. "Sorry, I'm being way too nosy."

"Not at all." I draped my arm across the seat back, angling a few degrees toward her. "I told you I've seen your photographs. Your talent impressed me, Eve. I've done a fair bit of modeling, and you are better than the fashion photographers I've worked with. Do you sell your pictures?"

"Yeah, on stock photo sites."

A gray head popped up behind our seat. Ruth peered over the seat back at us and winked at me. To Eve, she said, "Don't forget to tell Val about the sessions tomorrow. I bet he'd love to pose for you."

Ruth's gray head retreated.

I looked at Eve. "Sessions?"

She focused on the floor, scratching the back of her neck. "Uh, yeah, I do private portrait sessions for my guests. Nude portraits. It's an add-on. The guests who want it pay an extra fee."

"How much?"

"A hundred dollars."

"Sign me up."

Her fingers froze mid-scratch. She rotated her unblinking eyes toward me. "You've posed for famous photographers. Why would you want me to take your portrait? All those other pictures of you ought to be enough."

"Those photos weren't for me, they were for magazines and billboards." I leaned closer, lowering my voice to a whisper. "I'd like to have an intimate portrait, and I would love for you to take it."

"Billboards? Jeez, you really must be famous."

"I was, briefly. It's not important." I leaned in more until my lips hovered an inch from her ear. "Will you photograph me?"

She stared straight ahead for a minute or more until, at last, she rolled her shoulders back and announced, "Yes, I'll photograph you."

"Thank you. I'm looking forward to it."

She swiveled her head toward me, those lustrous eyes zeroing in on mine. "Me too."

For the rest of the trip, we talked about nothing of importance. She told me funny stories about her past guests, and Ruth joined in to share her own stories. Soon, everyone on the bus was chiming in with tales of the shenanigans at the resort. None of it was salacious, though the antics of the Kitten Brigade skirted the line. I was both looking forward to and dreading the day when those young women arrived.

The Pioneer Days festival was fun, but I would've preferred to have Eve all to myself. Our group stayed within sight of each other the whole time. Ruth, Sylvester, and Ollie stuck close to Eve and me. Quentin had opted to stay in the bus at Eve's suggestion. I got the impression she was growing tired of her handyman's jealousy. About damn time, I thought.

When we got back to the retreat, a delivery car from a local bistro was waiting in the driveway. Somehow, Eve had arranged to have our dinner hot and waiting for us. When I asked how she pulled that off, she shrugged and said, "The restaurant has an app. I placed an order while everybody was getting back on the bus."

She thought of everything for her guests. I wondered when she'd last done something for herself.

Naturally, I asked her that question.

"I keep telling you, it's my job to take care of my guests," she said. "My needs are last on the list."

"What needs of yours aren't being met? Maybe I can help."

"I don't need any help."

Eve joined the group for dinner in the guest house. She enlisted Ollie to assist with the cleanup, waving me away when I tried to join in. Was she avoiding me? That wouldn't work for long. Tomorrow, I'd be posing for her. A private session with Eve Holt was worth a lot more than a hundred dollars.

Eve retreated to her office after cleaning up the dinner mess.

I waited in my room, lying on the bed, with the door halfway open.

At eleven o'clock, Eve sashayed down the hallway. When she spotted my open door, she leaned in to peek at me. "Thought you'd be asleep."

"I'm a night owl." I stretched and sighed. "Why don't you lie down with me?"

She shook her head, her lips twitching up at the corners. "Thanks for the offer, but I'm used to sleeping alone."

"Who said anything about sleeping?"

"Good night, Val."

She moved away from the door.

I sighed again, this time with disappointment. "Good night, Eve."

After a few minutes of trying to read a book on my phone, I gave up. Eve's curves kept invading my thoughts, driving me crazy with visions of what I could do to that body. I set my phone down and took my rock-hard cock in my hand. If she wouldn't join me, I'd take care of things on my own. Maybe she'd overhear and decide to join me.

By the time I'd come, I realized Eve wasn't going to walk through the door and beg to take my dick in her mouth. Just the thought of her doing that made me hard again. I tried to sleep, but the sensual woman slumbering across the hall from me tormented my dreams.

Tomorrow. We would fuck tomorrow.

If we didn't, I'd need tranquilizers to get through another night.

Chapter Eleven

Eve

O h, Val, yes." I slipped my hand between my drenched folds, stroking myself while remembering the dreams I'd had last night. Dreams about him. About us together. Naked and writhing and devouring each other in every way imaginable. I whisked my fingers up and down my cleft, and my breaths grew shorter and sharper.

A fist rapped on my door.

I froze, halfway to my happy ending, panting and burning for release. "Who is it?"

"Val. I've made you breakfast."

"What time is it?" I could've glanced at the clock on my bedside table, but I'd lost the ability to move even a single muscle. My hand was still between my legs.

"It's five thirty," he said. "This is when you normally get up, so I made sure to be up first. It's the only way I'll get the chance to do something for you."

Oh, he'd done something for me all right. He'd turned me into a sex-obsessed idiot who spied on him while he masturbated and got myself off repeatedly while thinking of him. I hadn't watched him last night, though I had my suspicions he'd done himself a favor at least twice. His bed had been thumping, and I'd heard his grunts.

Big mystery why I'd endured intensely erotic dreams last night that forced me to do myself a favor…or two, or three. Maybe this was the fourth time. I'd lost count.

"May I come in?" Val asked.

"Uh…just a minute." I snatched a tissue off the box on the table and wiped my fingers with it. Jumping up, I straightened my nightie. "Come in."

The door opened. Val sauntered inside.

He swept his gaze over my rumpled sheets and then up to my face. "Your cheeks are pink. Aren't you feeling well?"

Alive, that's how I felt. Aching and tingling in all the right places. The sight of his nude body did not help matters.

"I'm fine," I said. "Thank you for making me breakfast. I'll be there in a minute, after I get dressed."

"Don't dress on my account." He raked his hot gaze over my body. "You can wear nothing at all. I'm a nudist, remember?"

Right. Hard to forget that fact. Even if I'd been tempted to go naked this morning, with him, it was a bad idea.

Tempted? I wanted to tear my nightie off right this instant.

"I'll, ah, see you in a few minutes," I said. "In the kitchen."

"Whatever you want." He sauntered out of my bedroom.

How would I survive two weeks with him? Quentin had better finish repairing Val's room in the guest house fast.

I dressed in my favorite shorts and a mint-green crop top, then joined Val in the kitchen.

He'd cooked me a huge breakfast—an omelet stuffed chock-full of veggies, sausage, and three kinds of cheese. A plate of buttered toast waited beside my breakfast platter, with jars of every kind of jam and jelly I owned lined up next to it. He'd made hash browns too, plus adorable silver dollar pancakes.

I didn't even mind that he'd made breakfast while naked. Since this was a private meal, rather than one for the other guests, I decided he hadn't violated the health code.

After gobbling up my breakfast, I insisted on washing the dishes.

"I'll allow it," Val said, "only if you let me help you get breakfast ready for the guests."

"For the millionth time, you *are* a guest."

"No, I'm your slave."

The tone of his voice, deep and rumbly, told me he meant "slave" in a different way from what most people would've meant. Later today, I'd photograph his gorgeous, nude body—just the two of us in my little studio, inside this house, away from the other guests. Having him as my slave? That made my tummy flutter.

"Fine," I said. "You can be my breakfast assistant if you get dressed first. Straight after that, though, I have to prepare my studio for the portrait sessions."

"I can help—"

"You're sweet to offer, but I prefer to get things set up on my own." I hopped off my stool. "You came here to be nude and free, but you've spent half the time in clothes because you insist on helping out. I feel like I've cramped your style."

"There's no cramping. I like assisting you."

"As a favor to me, why don't you hang out with the other guests until it's your turn in the studio?"

He bowed from the waist. "If that's what you want, *linda*, your slave will obey."

Since he'd been the last to sign up for a session, he'd gotten the last time slot. I would photograph him after everyone else, meaning I would have no easy excuse to cut the session short. Did I want to cut it short? Why was I trying so hard to avoid having sex with him? We were both adults. No one but his family knew he'd come here. His wild life would not tarnish mine, which meant I had no excuses left.

Right, because that had worked out so well before.

The last time I'd engaged in casual sex, it had triggered a hairy situation. Quentin still seemed to think he owned me. And the more I thought about what Val had said, about Quentin taking advantage of me in my tipsy state, the more I wondered if he was right.

Val wouldn't be like Quentin. He would stay for two weeks and go home. We would never see each other again.

Quentin I had to look at every day.

Maybe I should've fired Quentin, but firing an employee I'd slept with might trigger legal ramifications I couldn't afford. Besides, Quentin did his job very well and was the only handyman I'd found who didn't mind working at a nudist resort.

Five hours later, Val and I had taken care of breakfast for the guests and I had photographed a dozen of them. The portraits weren't sexual, but rather just like regular portraits somebody might get at a regular photo studio. The only difference was my subjects were naked.

My little studio occupied a space that had originally served as a bedroom. The room featured one curtained window, various lights plus an umbrella, several backgrounds I could set up and swap out quickly, a fan to offset the heat from the lights, and extra power outlets

I'd had installed to accommodate my equipment. If my guests needed a drink during our shoots, I went to the kitchen to get it for them. A stereo tucked into the corner provided mood music. I preferred something relaxing to keep my guests in a good mood.

The centerpiece of my whole setup was my camera, of course. A couple years ago, I'd upgraded to a Canon EOS 5D Mark IV DSLR that cost over three thousand dollars. It had seemed like an extravagance at the time, but I'd earned back the cost and then some thanks to these photo sessions. My guests loved getting tasteful images of themselves to take home.

Right on time, Val strode into my studio.

He turned his head left and right, admiring the room like it was the inside of the Sistine Chapel. "Very nice. This is a professional studio."

"Mm-hmm." I gestured toward the chair set up in the center of the room. "Have a seat."

"In the chair?" He walked a circle around it, scrutinizing the piece of furniture, then stopped and shook his head at me. "I won't be posing in a chair."

"Well, I guess you can stand for the whole session."

"No, Eve." He moved the chair out of the way and sat down on the floor. "This will do."

"Okay, if you really want to sit on the floor the whole time, I guess—"

He stretched out on his side, his head propped up with one hand. "I'm ready."

"Uh, people generally sit or stand for portraits."

"No boudoir photos? I'd think at least a few people would want that."

I couldn't resist skimming my gaze over his body and licking my lips when I reached his groin. "Only a couple of people wanted sexy photos. My guests like that my pictures are tasteful and respectful. The ones who wanted boudoir stuff were older couples looking to spice up their love lives." Somehow, I managed to tear my attention away from his manly bits to meet his gaze. "Are you sure you wouldn't rather sit on the chair like everybody else?"

"Would you want me to be like other people?"

No, absolutely not. "The floor is awfully hard to lie on for very long. I've got an idea."

Racing into the corner of the room where I'd stashed various props and background screens, I retrieved a padded mat, more like a cushion really. Val got up when I started dragging the bed-size cushion toward him. He grabbed one end and took the thing away from me, laid it down where he'd been a moment ago, and stretched out on his side again—this time on the crimson cushion.

"Comfy?" I asked.

He patted the cushion. "Yes, very."

"Normally, I use the padded mat for photographing babies and toddlers." I drank in the sight of Val the human supernova laid out across the crimson mat, and my mouth watered. Seriously, it did. "The color suits you."

"How would you like me?"

The erotic rumble of his voice, molten and decadent, rippled heat through me. I gripped my camera against my belly, and though I tried not to ogle him anymore, I failed. His nude body standing up or sitting down was breathtaking. Lying there stretched out like a Roman emperor awaiting his concubine… God, he was beyond hot. Especially the way he kept looking at me. Brown eyes warm as melted caramel. Tongue flicking out to moisten his lips. And that penis, so thick and long. Holy hotness. I'd never seen anything as gorgeous and tempting as Val Silva.

Why was I resisting the urge to get horizontal with him? I knew there'd been a reason, but suddenly, I couldn't remember what it was.

His lips slid into a sensual smile. "Are you going to photograph me? Or would you rather join me here on the floor?"

My mouth opened, but I couldn't summon any words. Join him? Yeah, oh hell yeah, I wanted to do that.

Why shouldn't I? Maybe he was the kind of bad boy I tried to avoid, but it wasn't like we had paparazzi way out here in the boonies of Oregon.

Screw it. I wanted him, he wanted me, and we were both consenting adults.

"Let me take a few shots first," I said. "You are paying for this session, after all."

He tipped his head to the side, not blinking when he asked, "And then you'll join me?"

I wandered over to the stereo and the iPod docked to it. Yeah, I was old school. I didn't like listening to music on my phone the way a lot of people did these days. Flipping through my playlists, I found an album that fit the mood, a collection of songs by Delerium. An ethereal feminine voice crooned to a sensual, exotic rhythm.

"Yes," I said, returning to Val and raising the camera, "after I take some shots, I will join you."

He skated his palm over the velvety cushion beneath him. "Naked?"

I regarded him through the LCD screen on the back of my camera, framing up a good shot. "Since we'll be having sex, yes, I'll take my clothes off."

A grin spread across his face, lighting up his entire expression.

I pressed the shutter button, capturing a shot of him in that moment when he'd realized I wanted to fuck right here, right now. My heartbeat sped up, and my nipples pearled. He had a killer grin, for sure.

"You should be a model," I said, taking another picture. I peeked at him over the top of my camera, though he couldn't see it. "Oh wait, you already are."

As I moved around him, snapping shot after shot, I got more and more aroused by the sight of him. He didn't preen or do any of the silly poses hotshot models might do. He followed my directions, lifting an arm or sliding a hand into his hair. Honestly, the man looked incredible doing nothing at all. He didn't need to pose, he simply needed to be.

"On your back," I said.

He rolled onto his back and linked his hands under his head.

After one more shot, I set my camera on the chair he'd moved out of the way.

"Is the session over?" he asked.

"Yes, the photography session is." I took hold of my shirt's hem and flipped it up and over my head, letting it sail down to the floor. "But we're just getting started."

He stared at my flimsy bra, and his dick began to swell.

The thin lace of my bra left most of my breasts exposed and revealed the dusky pink of my nipples. They pushed against the fabric, aching for his touch. I shimmied my hips more than necessary as I eased my shorts down over my hips. They fell to the floor, and I stepped out of them.

Val groaned.

My panties were as flimsy as my bra.

I reached behind my back to undo my bra one hook at a time. Once I'd freed them all, I shrugged the bra off my shoulders. It fluttered to the floor, joining my shirt and shorts.

His dick rose up like a flagpole.

Licking my lips, unable to tear my gaze away from his cock, I wriggled out of my panties.

A groan resonated in his chest.

I dropped to all fours and crawled toward him until I straddled his body. My face hovered over his groin and the beautiful, rosy-tipped erection I craved.

"Eve," he said, turning my name into the most erotic thing I'd ever heard, "you surprise me at every turn. I'd expected I would have to seduce you. Instead, here you are climbing up my body with a ravenous look on your face."

"Mmm, I am ravenous." I licked the head of his cock. "For this."

No more excuses. No more waiting.

I gave his erection another long, slow lick. "I want you in my mouth, Val."

Chapter Twelve

Val

I must've been gaping at the woman crouched over the lower half of my body. I couldn't help it. Eve Holt, the woman who'd sworn she wouldn't get naked with me, wanted to take my cock in her mouth. She had already surprised me with her sudden announcement she wanted to have sex. Her little striptease had made me hard, but her desire to give me a blow job stunned me. Wasn't this the same woman who'd said she didn't sleep with guests anymore?

Not that I was complaining. The most enticing woman I'd ever laid eyes on wanted to suck me like a lollipop. What man in his right mind would say no?

I slid a hand into her hair. "You're incredible, Eve. You can be sure I'll go down on you next."

She laved my crown with her tongue, making me suck in a breath. "I look forward to that. But first, I've got to eat you up."

"Don't make me come. I want to save that for when I'm inside you."

"Whatever you want."

"Already have everything I wanted—you, naked, about to let me fuck you."

She puckered her lips and blew a stream of air across my crown. I groaned.

Eve opened her mouth wide, lowering it to within millimeters of my cock, and exhaled a long, hot breath onto the tip. She raised her head to look at me. "You've got the most beautiful dick I've ever seen."

What else could I do? I grinned like a fool. This woman drove me wild and turned my brain to mush. I combed my fingers through her hair, amazed by her unabashed enthusiasm and by the sheer beauty of her body and her spirit. Other women had gone down on me, but none did it with the tenderness and enjoyment Eve displayed.

"So big too," she said in a husky tone, her breath teasing me with each syllable. "Can't wait to have this inside me."

"Neither can I. Let's skip the foreplay and—"

She ducked her head, pressing her mouth to my inner thigh, and dragged her lips up my flesh. Her silken hair had fallen over my cock to tickle my skin as she moved.

"Fuck, Eve," I growled, my fingers clenching in her hair.

The vixen lifted her head to switch to my other thigh, this time licking and nibbling her way toward my groin. When she'd almost reached it, she raised her head to hit me with a wicked little smile. "I love an ice cream cone before the main course."

"Ice cream?" I said, sounding as baffled as I felt. Baffled and intrigued, not to mention so hot for this woman I was fighting the impulse to flip her over and bury my face between her thighs.

She dragged her tongue up my dick, from the base to near the tip. Humming with pleasure, she did it again. Her eyes drifted partway closed. "Better than ice cream. Better than dark chocolate cake with cream cheese frosting, which I thought I loved more than sex." She took another long, sensuous lick. "May have to re-evaluate that. You are the most delicious thing I've ever tasted."

No woman had ever talked to me the way she did while doing what she was doing to me. Maybe I'd died and this was the afterlife, with Eve as my angel guide. She certainly seemed determined to kill me with pleasure.

Her lips sealed around my cock and sank down, down, down until she'd taken as much of me as she could into her mouth. She moaned, the sound vibrating my flesh.

A choked sound spluttered out of me.

She grasped the base with her fist and began to move her mouth up and down, sucking gently, moaning like I was her first meal in weeks. I thrust both hands into her hair, shut my eyes, and let the sensations flood over me. Her soft, warm tongue. The heat of her breaths. The way her hair teased my skin. Every time she pulled her mouth nearly free of my flesh, the dampness left behind by her lips and tongue sent a rush of coolness over my skin. I levered into a sitting position, keeping one hand in her hair, and spread my other palm on her back to caress her in long, slow strokes. The pressure escalated, little by little, with every swipe of her tongue and brush of her hair.

Every muscle inside me went taut. I teetered on the edge, and if she kept going...

She sat up and swept her tongue across her lips.

I almost came just watching her do that.

"Mmm," she said, "I enjoyed that way more than I usually do. Loved it, actually."

She'd loved it. I couldn't comprehend the full meaning of those words, not in my current condition.

"On your knees," I said. "It's your turn."

"My knees?"

"Yes." I lay back on the velvet cushion. "Move this way."

I curled my finger repeatedly, gesturing her to move closer. She rose to her knees and crawled toward me. Her brows crinkled in the sweetest way when I kept crooking my finger, but still she inched ever closer.

"Stop," I said. "That's perfect."

Her glistening pink cleft was positioned above my head. I stretched my hand up, sliding my fingers into the soft, curly hairs on her mound. She bit her lip. I caressed her with my finger-tips. She released her lip gradually, her gaze hooded, and my cock throbbed. Eve Holt was beautiful, yes, but she was also the most sensual woman I'd ever known. Whether she realized how her every movement and expression fired up my libido, I didn't know. Her sensuality seemed innate, a part of her she couldn't have hidden if she'd tried.

I skated my other hand up her thigh to curve it around her hip. "You're incredible, Eve. Your body is stunning, but it's what I see inside you that makes me want you so badly."

She smirked. "You're only saying that because you're staring at my vagina."

"No, I'm staring at you." I palmed her mound, my gaze exclusively on her face. "I've never met a woman like you before. I doubt I ever will again."

She stopped blinking. Stopped breathing too, I suspected. Her gaze locked onto mine, the color of her irises seeming deeper and bluer.

"What is it?" I asked.

"That sounded almost…romantic."

"Almost? I must not have said it right."

"This is casual sex, remember?"

"I know, but I can still pay you a compliment. Can't I?"

What I'd said did sound a lot more romantic than the things I usually told women. I would compliment their bodies, not—what had I called it?—the things I saw inside them. This woman made me lose my mind. Anything I'd said to her was instigated by lust, nothing more. I'd met her the day before yesterday, for fuck's sake.

"Sure," she said carefully, "compliments are fine. But don't go getting the idea we might be dating or whatever."

"No worries." I grinned, hoping she would believe what I was about to say. "Relax, Eve. I want your body, that's all. I'm even less interested in dating than you are."

To prove my point, I shoved my hand between her legs, nestling it between her slick folds. The heel of my hand covered her clit. I ground my hand against that erect little nub until her eyes fluttered shut and her mouth fell open on a throaty moan. The hunger evident in that sound sent any blood that was left in my brain rushing south. I kept rubbing her clit while I stretched my fingers out to stroke her flesh, my longest finger nudging her opening.

She slapped a hand over mine on her hip. "Oh Val, I want you. Now. Please."

"You've got me." My voice had gone as husky as hers, strained by the need we both endured. I'd never been so aroused by a woman, so desperate to thrust into her moist heat and lose myself inside her. "In a minute, I promise."

I gazed up at her belly, the way it quivered the slightest bit, and higher still to those perfect breasts rising and falling with every breath she sucked into her lungs.

She gazed down at me, her lips parted. They'd turned a deeper shade of rose. She rocked her hips, pushing the heel of my hand harder into the rigid tip of her clit. "Don't stop. Please don't stop."

I would in a moment, but not yet. The longer I watched her, the more turned on she got, the harder I fought to hold back my raging need for her. I wanted to fuck Eve like I'd never wanted to fuck any woman. And I didn't want her to come until I was deep inside that lush body.

Her head fell back. A long, luxurious moan resonated through her.

I shifted my hand lower and plunged two fingers inside her. With my thumb, I worked her nub.

"More," she begged, "more, please, more."

Her plea shattered my willpower. I lunged my head up and gripped her ass with both hands, latching my mouth on to her nub, suckling and nipping, scraping my tongue over the rigid tip while my fingers dug into her cheeks, relishing the sound of her panting breaths. She clutched my head, her nails raking my scalp, and bucked her hips every time I sucked on her nub. I gazed up at her face while I worked her body, my breaths shortening and blustering through the hairs on her mound. Urgency gripped her features. She stopped breathing, and her body went stiff.

"Oh no," I said, pulling my mouth away from her flesh, "I'm not letting you come yet."

Her head snapped up, and she gaped at me. A delicate flush colored her cheeks.

I skimmed my hands up and down her thighs.

She kneed me in the side. "That was a dirty trick."

"Maybe, but I think you like it dirty. Besides, you didn't make me come."

"You told me not to." She bent her knees to sit on my lap, her wet and swollen flesh inches from my cock. "Do you have a condom?"

I patted my chest and hips like I was searching for one. "Sorry, I don't have any pockets to keep anything in."

"Right. You're always naked." Her gaze flicked down to my erection. She licked her lips. "Do you have any condoms anywhere? I don't. I'm on the pill, but…"

"Have some in my room." I ran my hands up her thighs again. "You'll need to move off me so I can go get one."

She glanced at my erection again and sighed, then slid off my lap.

I sprinted out of the studio.

Chapter Thirteen

Eve

I lay on my back on the velvet cushion, waiting for Val to come back with a condom. If I'd planned for this to happen, I would've stashed an entire box of Trojans in this room. Despite my reckless craving for him, I'd vowed I would not sleep with Val. So much for that resolution. Lying here, burning with desire, I couldn't remember any of the reasons why I'd sworn to avoid sex with this man.

Minutes elapsed. A few turned into several. Several became an uncomfortably long time.

"Val?" I called out.

When he didn't respond, I shook my head. Of course he wouldn't hear me. He was probably still in his room down the hall rummaging around for his box of rubbers. I got up and moseyed out of the studio, intending to swerve right toward Val's room. A noise from the direction of the kitchen made me pause. I leaned to the side so I could get a peek into Val's room. Since I couldn't see him, I figured he'd gone into the kitchen, maybe to get some chocolate syrup we could drizzle over each other's bodies.

I walked into the kitchen—and gasped.

The door to the outside hung wide open, and Quentin had his fist clenched, ready to lash out.

Val slumped against the wall massaging his jaw.

No, this couldn't be what it seemed to be. Quentin couldn't have punched Val.

"Get the hell out of here," Quentin snarled. He shook his fist in the air between them. "Or I'll lay another one on you. And this time, I'll draw blood."

I gaped at my handyman. "What do you think you're doing?"

Quentin's gaze veered to me. First, his eyes bulged. Next, his jaw dropped. His shock morphed into something else, something darker. One side of his mouth slanted upward while his tongue traced the inside of his lower lip. His wide eyes narrowed as he took in the full view of me.

Totally naked.

Maybe I should have run out of the room or at least snatched up a dish towel to cover part of myself, but I was too pissed.

I focused on Val when I asked, "What happened here?"

"He hit me," Val said, his voice surprisingly calm under the circumstances. He straightened and narrowed his gaze on Quentin. "I was coming back from my room when I heard the knob on the kitchen door jiggle. Came in here to check it out. That's when this bastard crashed through the door and attacked me."

I suddenly noticed the box of condoms lying near his feet, open, silver packets scattered across the floor.

Quentin's mouth crimped. "He's taking advantage of you. Right here in the kitchen where anybody might see."

Val was using me? Seriously? I stomped up to Quentin, my breasts bouncing, and jabbed a finger into his chest. "You're the one who took advantage of me. Remember that night when I'd had one too many margaritas? A real gentleman would have seen me home and said good night. But you saw yourself into my bedroom and had your fun."

For months, I'd convinced myself Quentin hadn't taken advantage of me. Today, with him staring at my body with a lustful gleam in his eyes, I no longer believed it.

I stabbed my finger into his chest so hard he flinched. "You're fired."

His eyes went wide again, with shock this time. "I'm sorry, Eve. I'll apologize to your boyfriend if you want."

Val was not my boyfriend, but that was none of Quentin's business.

"It's too late," I said. "You crossed a line, a big old red one with flashing lights on it. Breaking into my house? Attacking my guest? You and I, we're done. Get in your truck and get the hell off my property."

"Let me get my tools first."

I smacked my palm flat on his chest, making him stumble backward half a step. "I bought those tools. The only thing here that you own is your clothes and your truck. Get out of here, Quentin."

Val took a step closer, but I shook my head at him. He stayed put.

"Go," I snarled at Quentin. "I never want to see your face again. Your final paycheck will be mailed to you."

Quentin sputtered like he was trying to form words but couldn't quite do it.

I slammed both my palms onto his chest hard enough to make him stumble and trip over his own feet. "Get out!"

He spun around and bolted out of the house, slamming the door.

Val touched my arm. "Are you all right?"

"Yes."

Adrenaline spiked through my blood like an electric shock, but I would not let Quentin's invasion make me cry. I was too angry for that anyway. This energy created by my confrontation with Quentin, it burned inside me. As I focused my attention on Val, on his naked body and half-deflated erection dangling between his legs, the searing anger transformed into a different kind of energy.

An engine roared to life outside, followed by the harsh grumble and clatter of a vehicle speeding away down the gravel drive.

I blew out a breath. "We should call off what we were about to do before the interruption."

"We should," he said, but his voice had deepened into that sensual rumble again. He inched closer to me, his gaze skipping down to my breasts and lower to the hairs between my thighs before returning to my face.

My gaze dropped to his swelling dick before lifting to his face. "We really shouldn't do this."

"No, we shouldn't."

"We ought to wait until we both calm down."

He moved even closer, his cock now hard and nudging my belly. "You're right, we ought to wait until later."

The weight of lust settled low in my belly, and the need throbbed in my sex from my clit all the way down to my entrance.

I seized his face with both hands and crushed my mouth to his. Our tongues clashed, our teeth clashed, and we consumed each other like nothing in the universe, not even a nuclear explosion, could've severed our kiss.

Val pulled away only long enough to snag a condom packet from the floor, tear it open with his teeth, and roll the rubber onto his erection.

His mouth found mine again, his tongue scraping mine while his hands grasped my hips. He lifted me off the floor. Spinning around, he pinned me to the wall with his body and thrust inside me so hard and fast I gasped into his mouth. He hesitated. With our bodies joined, neither of us moved a muscle, not even our tongues that remained coiled around each other. He clasped my hands and held them to the wall above my head. Letting out a deep groan, he pumped his hips.

I moaned, the sound muffled by his mouth. God, he felt so unbelievably good. I hooked my legs around his hips, pulling him deeper inside me, moaning again from the sheer bliss of his powerful thrusts. His tongue demanded a response, and my body was beyond willing to give in to anything he wanted. I couldn't catch my breath, but I didn't care. I clutched his hands tight enough to sink my nails into his flesh, but he didn't seem to notice or care. Flesh slapped on flesh, every thrust punctuated by a wet sucking sound.

The phone rang, but my brain had shut down.

He pumped faster, rougher, and ripped his mouth away from mine to bury his face against my neck. Grunts and groans burst out of him while I fought for breath, the power of my need growing and growing, escalating into a pressure so intense my ears rang and dark spots speckled my vision.

About to come, so close, almost there.

My release blasted through me in a tidal wave of pleasure. Every spasm in my sex gripped him like a vise. The only noise I could make was a desperate whimpering as he punched into me with ruthless strength, slamming me into the wall. My neck muffled his choked cry when he blew apart inside me.

Panting, we both hung there in a suspended moment with our bodies connected in the most intimate way. His breaths blustered against my neck. Sweat drizzled down our bodies. Time seemed irrelevant, but after a few moments, we emerged from our mutual comas and untangled ourselves.

Val kissed me sweetly, tenderly, then moved away to discard the condom in the trash can.

I pushed away from the wall, wobbling a tiny bit.

He caught my upper arms with his big hands. "How do you feel? I hadn't planned on taking you like that. Not the first time."

The buzz of adrenaline had lessened, but it still had me kind of wired.

"Wow," I said, fanning myself with one hand, "that was amazing."

"I hope I didn't hurt you."

Noticing the concern on his face, I laid my palms on his chest. "Don't worry. I'm tough."

His mouth quirked. "I noticed that when you booted your handyman off the property."

"Let's go to a bed—your room or mine, I don't care which—and do that again."

"I'd love to." He drew me into his arms and kissed my forehead. "Maybe you need a glass of water first."

"Sure, that sounds good. Water and a cookie." I rolled my eyes in the direction of the cabinet above the fridge. "I hide the best ones up there."

He padded to the fridge and reached over it to open the cabinet.

Damn, he was tall enough to reach that without standing on his toes.

The phone rang.

I grabbed the handset off the wall. "Hello?"

"Evie, what's going on?" Ruth asked. "We saw Quentin stomp out of your house looking fit to kill someone, but then he drove off. That was one big cloud of dust he kicked up."

"Yeah, I fired him."

"Why?"

"It's a long story. I'll tell you later."

A long pause followed before Ruth said, "Is everything okay? Are you okay?"

"Yes, Val's taking care of me." I glanced at him, where he stood beside the fridge holding a box of cookies, a question on his face. "We'll share the story with the whole gang at lunch."

"Sure. See you then."

We said goodbye, and I returned the phone to its cradle.

Val arched one brow. "We'll share the story?"

"Not everything, obviously." I ambled up to him and took the box of cookies. Flipping the lid up, I dived my hand inside to grab a fistful of chocolate-chip yummies. I shoved a crunchy cookie into my mouth and gobbled it up. "Maybe I should crumble these all over you and eat my snack off your skin."

He chuckled. "I've had women lick whipped cream off of me, but never cookies."

"You're a cookie-crumble virgin?" I started for the hallway, aiming for his room. "Let's go. It's my first time too."

I took off at a dead run.

Val's feet slapped on the wood floor as he sprinted after me.

Chapter Fourteen

Val

After Eve had her fun crumbling cookies onto my body, we made lunch for everyone and ate with the rest of the guests in the dining hall. Eve's playful, naughty side had surprised me, but only in the best way. I supposed I shouldn't have been surprised. She might've been a workaholic who refused to go nude in public, but she did like to wear sexy outfits that showed off her beautiful body.

When Eve and I strolled into the dining hall, she was waylaid by Ruth and Sylvester who wanted to discuss what activities were on tap for the afternoon. Ollie approached me. After the usual pleasantries, he eyed my chest with a strange expression.

He leaned in a touch and asked, "Is that a chocolate chip stuck to your chest?"

I glanced down and realized it was in fact a chocolate chip, half melted and pasted to my skin. Eve had missed one.

"Ah, yes," I said, grabbing a napkin off the buffet table to wipe off the chocolate. "I had cookies earlier."

"You got cookies?" Ollie faked a pout as if the news offended him. "Eve never lets anybody near her secret cookie stash."

"How do you know she has a stash if it's secret?"

Ollie's mouth formed a sly smile. "Sometimes I help carry her groceries into her house. I saw boxes of cookies once and asked her about it. She swore me to secrecy, said she'd replace my insect repellent with sugar water if I told anyone." He waggled his eyebrows. "She must really like you if she let you see her cookie stash. It's like her own little pirate treasure. Keep expecting her to install a security system on that cabinet like something a museum might have to protect a huge diamond."

Eve didn't share her cookies with anyone, but she'd shared them with me. She'd crumbled them in her hands, sprinkled them onto my chest, and licked the crumbs and chips off my skin one by one. Her tongue had been velvety and warm, her licks gentle and—

My dick was stirring to life again.

I changed the subject quickly by asking Ollie what he did for a living. For the next five minutes, I listened to every detail about his work as a computer systems engineer. It bored the fuck out of me, but Ollie clearly enjoyed talking about his work. I liked him, and I liked all the other guests, but I despised Eve's former handyman. Good riddance, I said.

But I didn't say that to Eve.

"How long are you staying at the resort?" I asked Ollie.

"Six weeks."

"That's a long stay. Your employers must be generous with vacation time."

He bunched his shoulders, staring down at the ground with his lips pinched. "Yeah, they're real generous."

The tone of his voice implied they weren't generous at all. I might've asked him more about that, but it wasn't my business.

Ollie waved to some of the other guests. "How about a round of miniten?"

My conversation with Ollie ended there since I didn't feel like donning a thug to whack a tennis ball back and forth over a net. I wanted to get Eve alone. Preferably with cookies. Maybe chocolate syrup too.

I had to wait for my chance, but after lunch, Eve and I retreated into her house for more private time. We enjoyed each other in every room in the house until a vehicle pulled into the driveway and Eve announced it was dinnertime. She had ordered Italian food from a local restaurant. I would've preferred to have dinner with her alone in the house, so I could eat my fettuccine alfredo off her body, but she insisted on socializing with the other guests.

"I've been ignoring them," she announced while I watched her dress. "Spent most of the day having sex with you instead of tending to the needs of all my guests."

"My needs are the most pressing." I was lying on the bed in her room, where only ten minutes ago I'd been ravishing her. She stood in front of her dresser. I loved watching her get dressed, if only so I could look forward to stripping her later. "I don't think I can survive an hour without fondling your body."

She dropped onto the bed beside me and patted my cheek. "I think you'll live."

I did survive dinner, though I couldn't stop looking at Eve. Sylvester and Ruth teased me about it, but I was immune to that kind of harassment. The entire world had seen me naked, on the football field and in a sex tape, and those incidents had eradicated what little shame I'd had before that. At least Sylvester and Ruth were kind people who teased me out of affection, not paparazzi hounding me or comedians turning me into a nasty joke.

Being here with Eve and her guests, I didn't feel like a notorious scoundrel anymore. I liked the way I felt here. I'd become an almost-normal human being.

Once dinner was over, Eve invited me into her bedroom again. We were lingering in the hallway near the door to my room when she posed the question.

She hunched her shoulders and angled her head down to peek up at me through her lashes. "Would you like to come into my bedroom?"

"I'd love to, but I'm exhausted." I skimmed a hand up and down her arm. "You must be exhausted too."

"Yeah, but—" She bit down on her lower lip and stared at the wall next to me. After a few seconds, she forced a smile. "Never mind. You're right, we're both too tired. I'll see you in the morning. Good night, Val."

She all but sprinted toward her room.

"Good night, Eve," I called after her.

The door to her bedroom swung shut.

Her shyness about inviting me into her room had been adorable, but I couldn't understand why she'd felt embarrassed. Had she wanted me to sleep with her more than I'd thought? I'd assumed it was a casual request. Maybe she'd meant it as more and surprised herself with that realization.

Did I want more?

Of course not. Neither did she.

I ambled into my room but left the door open. Part of me hoped she might sneak in here in the middle of the night and crawl under the covers with me. Why was I wishing for that? We were having sex, that was all. I didn't need to feel her warm, supple body tucked against mine while I slept. I didn't need to wake up and find her head on my chest, and I absolutely did not need to dip my nose into her hair and inhale the sweet, fruity scent of her shampoo.

No, I didn't need or want any of that. I loved her body, and I loved enjoying that body, but my desire for her ended there.

For the first time in years, I had trouble sleeping. I was positive it had nothing to do with Eve.

I got up earlier than usual in the morning—not on purpose like I had yesterday, but because I couldn't sleep anymore. A hot shower sounded good until I was in the shower and started wondering if Eve would sneak in to join me.

She didn't.

Wishing she would join me in the shower had nothing to do with emotions. I wanted her like I'd never wanted any woman, and I wanted to be inside her as often as possible from today onward. Thoughts of Eve's body had me beating off in the shower, but that wouldn't tide me over for long.

By the time I walked into the kitchen, Eve was already making breakfast for everyone.

She waved toward the stool on my side of the island. "Have a seat. I'll give you first dibs on breakfast."

I perched on the stool, noting that she'd already set out plates and silverware for us. "Thought I'd beat you into the kitchen this morning."

And I might have if I hadn't needed to relieve my lust twice in the shower.

The outfit she'd chosen to wear today didn't help matters. Her tie-dyed dress held up by spaghetti straps barely covered her ass and breasts, and the gold anklet draped around her elegant ankle made me hunger to have that leg strapped around me again. The sandals she wore had the skinniest straps I'd ever seen and looked like they might snap if she took one step. The shoes didn't have me wincing and adjusting my position on the stool, though. It was the dress. Was she wearing panties under that thing? She couldn't be wearing a bra, not with that plunging neckline and those slender straps.

Eve's breasts. Naked under the dress. Her perfect tits swinging free.

My erection scraped against the underside of the island's lip.

I coughed into my fist and said, "Smells good. What are you making?"

"Sheet breakfast sandwiches."

"What is a sheet breakfast sandwich? I've never heard of that."

She smiled at me over her shoulder. "You've heard of a breakfast sandwich, right? The ones I'm making have a pancake layer on the top and bottom with sausage, eggs, and cheese in the middle. Instead of making each sandwich individually, I whip up one huge sandwich on a big baking sheet. I'm using three baking sheets today. Then I slice each big sandwich into smaller pieces."

"Do you pour syrup on it?"

"No, but I put syrup out on the buffet table for anyone who wants it." She glanced at me again, this time curling her lip. "I also have to put out hot sauce and jalapenos. Ollie and Sylvester love that stuff."

"Have you tried it? Hot sauce and jalapenos sounds good to me."

She wagged a large knife at me. "If you expect to kiss me later, better not eat any of that."

Kiss her? Yes, I wanted to do that—for hours. I loved kissing Eve.

"When can I eat one of those?" I asked. "*Estou verde de fome.*"

"You're starving, eh? Oh yeah, you look puny and weak, for sure." She turned around, holding a plate with three breakfast sandwiches on it. Setting it down in front of me, she slanted in to peck a kiss on my lips. "Can't have you malnourished, not with the things I want to do to you today."

"More cookies?" I half hoped she would do that again.

She shook her head. "I saved a bottle of caramel sauce and a tub of ice cream just for us."

"An ice cream sundae? I like those."

"Uh-uh, this one's all for me." She stretched out one delicate hand, trailing the tip of her longest finger down my chest. "You *are* the sundae."

"I like that even better." I caught her hand, lifted her outstretched finger to my mouth, and sucked on it. "But it's only fair that I should get my turn to have an Eve sundae."

She withdrew her hand, but her eyes had taken on the glossiness of desire. "Well, I guess it is only fair."

While she returned to portioning out the breakfast sandwiches, I abandoned mine and sneaked up behind her. The scent of her hair made me draw in a deep draft of it, my nose buried in her silky locks. I slipped an arm around her waist.

"Can't wait for dessert," I said. "Need you now."

"But I have to finish making breakfast. Hungry nudists are waiting, and they won't like their hot breakfast to arrive cold."

I fisted my hand in her hair, tugging her head back to expose her slender throat. Her mouth fell open. I raked my tongue up her skin from the base of her throat to the tender spot right under her jaw. "We'll heat up the food in the microwave."

She leaned into me, her hands landing on my thighs. "We can't. We shouldn't."

"Yes, we should, and we can." I glided my palm down her leg until I found the hem of her dress, then slipped my hand under it. Her skimpy underwear blocked me from touching her where I desperately wanted to, so I settled for stroking her through the fabric. "Say yes, Eve."

Her breasts heaved. Her panties grew wet.

She crooked her fingers into my thighs and whispered, "Yes."

I suckled her earlobe.

High-pitched screams erupted outside.

Eve jerked. "They're early."

"Who?"

"The Kitten Brigade." She shoved me away and whirled around, straightening her dress. "They never get here this early in the morning."

She raced out the door.

I followed at a slower pace.

There in the driveway hunkered a neon-pink motor home. Young women were still pouring out of the vehicle, every one of them wearing a simple white T-shirt dress.

Eve and I stopped ten feet from the group.

Once the last girl had exited the motor home, they all whipped off their clothes and shrieked. White dresses, the only items of clothing they wore, flew into the air and sailed down to land on the gravel of the driveway.

The gaze of every last member of their group zeroed in on me.

Whoops and shrieks exploded from them, and the throng descended.

Chapter Fifteen

Eve

Oh. Dear. God. The Kitten Brigade swarmed Val like they'd discovered a juicy T-bone steak after being on a liquid diet for a month. I got muscled out of the way as eight twenty-something women rushed at the man I'd spent most of yesterday screwing. They giggled and shrieked and barraged him with questions, all talking at once so there was no chance he could understand their questions, much less answer them.

Val stayed calm, though. He smiled and shook the girls' hands. How a naked man surrounded by nubile, nude women could remain so composed baffled the hell out of me. Most guys would've freaked out or gotten angry—or developed a raging erection. I supposed Val was used to this kind of attention. He had become a celebrity thanks to his outrageous public behavior.

When the Kittens continued to swarm Val after a couple of minutes, I shoved two fingers into my mouth and whistled. The sound pierced the babbling of the crowd, and everyone in the vicinity—the Kittens, Val, and the other guests—swung their attention to me.

"Girls," I said, "let the man breathe, okay? Having a guest suffocate under a pile of women wouldn't be good press for the resort."

The de facto leader of the Kitten Brigade, Heidi Mackenzie, sashayed over to me. She gave me a quick, firm hug and then feigned a pout. "We're sorry, Evie. But you can't expect us to ignore the hottest guy who's ever set foot on your property."

"No, but I can and do expect you to not assault him en masse."

Somehow, even while stark naked with her nipples jutting from her perky breasts, she pulled off an expression of pure innocence. Her angelic looks, with golden-blonde hair and pale-blue eyes, helped. "We didn't touch him. Not even an ass pinch. We kept our hands to ourselves even though he is a walking fudge pop begging to be licked."

Oh yeah, Val and Heidi had something in common—utter shamelessness.

Heidi leaned in to whisper in my ear, "Please tell me you've tapped that."

"You know I never kiss and tell."

"Sad but true." She backed up a step and waved her arms, summoning the Brigade. When every last one of them had abandoned Val, some adopting a fake pout like Heidi had done, she turned to address her group. "The new guy is off-limits, Kittens." The sassy girl winked at me over her shoulder. "Evie's got this one."

My mouth opened, a denial on my tongue, but I shut my trap. Nobody needed to know the details of my whatever-this-was with Val.

"And now," Heidi said, "Eve will introduce us to the new hottie."

I glanced at Val, my brows raised.

He shrugged.

And I took that as permission to tell them.

To the Kittens, I said, "This is Val Silva. He's originally from Brazil but calls LA home these days. He was a soccer star for years, even went to the Olympics, but now he's a model."

"And he belongs to Evie," Heidi said with mock gravitas.

Shelby Thomas, the shortest member of the Brigade, shook her head. "What a bummer. I was looking forward to a good cat fight. Oh well, at least I don't need to keep my hair tied up if nobody's going to use it as leverage."

The brunette ripped the scrunchy out of her, setting her long locks free, and tossed the scrunchy high into the air.

It landed on Val's shoulder.

He wrapped the strip of lavender fabric around his wrist.

Shelby giggled.

"Let me finish the introductions," I said, and pointed to each lady in turn as I told Val their names. "Heidi. Shelby. Taylor. Allison. Heather. Sydney. Jane. Leah."

Val smiled. "Nice to meet you, ladies. What a lovely bunch you are."

Some of them smiled shyly. Others grinned. A few gave him saucy looks.

Heidi rose onto her tiptoes to glance around the area behind me where the other guests had gathered. "Where's our Ollie? Isn't he here yet?"

I turned around, searching the crowd until I spotted Ollie.

At the instant I spotted him, Heidi did too. She hopped on her toes and waved her arms in the air. "Get over here, sweetie! We missed you!"

Ollie smiled sheepishly at the people around him, shrugged, and pushed through the crowd to reach Heidi and the gals.

Heidi grabbed him in a bear hug.

"Cut that out," I chided. "Do I need to recite the rules right here? I thought we could hold off on that until you get settled in."

"We know the rules," Heidi said, releasing a blushing Ollie. "But I couldn't help myself. This boy is cuteness squared."

The rest of the Kittens took their turns hugging Ollie, but in the permitted fashion. Shelby ruffled his hair. Several of them kissed his cheek. In fact, they paid more attention to him than they had to Val.

Well, they had known Ollie for years.

I walked over to Val, who now stood alone.

He draped an arm around my waist. "I seem to have lost my appeal. Can't compete with Ollie."

"Yes, he does have that adorable-nerd vibe women love."

"Would you rather be hugging and kissing Ollie?" he asked with a smirk.

"No, I prefer the notorious-exhibitionist type."

He tugged me against his side. "I'm glad to hear that."

The Kittens spotted us in our intimate pose and started cooing "ooooh." Several of them shouted various things at us—well, at me.

"Evie's got a boyfriend!"

"No, she's just licking that lollipop!"

"When's the wedding?"

"Look at those muscles! Woo-hoo, Evie!"

Ollie, still surrounded by women fighting for his attention, flashed me an impish grin. "Leave her alone, girls. If Eve wants to shack up with the new guy, it's her business."

"Shack up?" Heidi said, sidling up to Ollie. "Do tell."

"Val's staying in Eve's house."

I wagged a finger at Ollie. "Don't be a gossip. You know it's only because of the burst pipe in the guest house."

"Right, the pipe. How are those repairs coming?"

He knew damn well the repairs weren't finished. Since firing Quentin yesterday, I'd forgotten to call around and find a contractor to finish the work. If anyone would come out here. Maybe I didn't want Val to move into the guest house yet. Or ever.

Or maybe scorching sex was making me forgetful. Yeah, that was it.

Everyone stared at me and Val, their expressions running the gamut from amused to surprised.

Which might've had something to do with the fact Val had his arm around me and was hugging me to his naked body. I fought the impulse to shout, "He's not my boyfriend!" That would lead to more questions about why we were so chummy and what exactly we were doing together. In my house. Alone. Most of the day and all of the night.

I broke up the crowd by suggesting the Kittens get their tents set up. Ollie offered to help out with that, and several of the older men offered too, as did Val.

While the girls retrieved their equipment from the RV, Ollie approached me. Val and the other men had gone around the guest house to the camping area, so Ollie had me alone.

He put his arm around my shoulders. "Is Val treating you right? You're like a sister to me, and I don't want some Casanova athlete breaking your heart."

"That's very sweet, Ollie, but I'm fine. No danger of heartbreak."

"You sure?" He gave me a squeeze. "Because you two have that look."

"What look?"

"The one that usually means two people are falling in love."

"Oh please," I said. "Now you're an expert on human behavior?"

"Hardly, but I've known you for four years." He took hold of my shoulders and angled me to face him. His expression was serious. "I have never seen you act the way you do with Val. This isn't a fling, Evie. You really like him, and he really likes you."

"We met four days ago."

"You never heard of love at first sight?"

"Heard of it? Yes. Believe in it? No."

Val and I were enjoying multiple orgasms per day, not falling in love. Neither of us wanted a relationship. I wouldn't tell Ollie any of that because it was private and none of his damn business. Still, his concern for my well-being might have been the nicest thing anyone had done for me in a long time.

"Okay," he said. "If you're good, I'm good."

He jogged off to help with the tent setup.

I went into my house to finish preparing breakfast.

Ollie was wrong. No way, no how could I fall for a guy I'd met four days ago. I certainly wouldn't fall for a big-time womanizer who liked to strip in public to get media attention.

No way, no how.

Chapter Sixteen

Val

After breakfast, I observed while the other guests enjoyed a raucous game of miniten with the rules treated as suggestions and everyone laughing more than hitting the ball. Though the game was supposed to be played by two pairs, the Kitten Brigade insisted on having six players on each side strictly for fun. Eve had only four thugs on hand, so the other players took up tennis rackets. The Kittens lost to the Silver Foxes, the team name for the gray-haired guests, but no one seemed to care about the score.

Once the game ended, I followed Eve into her house. She'd announced to everyone she was going to make lunch. Considering she now had twenty-five guests to feed, she needed help. Of course, she wouldn't ask for it. The woman seemed to be allergic to admitting she needed a hand.

In her kitchen, she rounded on me. "Go back outside. You're a guest, not my sous chef."

"Don't want to be your sous chef." I looped an arm around her waist and pulled her close. "I'm your slave, remember? I do your bidding all day and all night."

"Even if I made you clean all the toilets in the guest house?"

"Yes, even then." I considered what she'd said, then asked, "Tell me you don't do all the cleaning yourself."

"I do."

"Eve, you need to hire more people to help you."

She wriggled out of my hold. "I don't have the budget for that. Maybe soon I will, now that I've paid off the bank loan, but not yet."

"I'll give you the money."

She settled a hand on the counter and drummed her fingers. "Thank you for the offer. It's very generous, but I can't accept. I'm not a damsel in distress waiting for you to rescue me."

"This is help from a friend, not charity."

Her lips ticked upward at the corners even as they puckered slightly. She shook her head. "We're screwing, Val, not knitting quilts together."

I grabbed a spatula off the island, unsure why I did it, and clenched my fist around the thing. Maybe I needed to throttle something other than Eve. Most women begged me to give them money or buy them clothes, but she would have none of it. I thumped the spatula's handle on the butcher-block surface. "Why won't you accept my help? I have more than enough money. Let me share it with you."

"Why not donate it to a good cause? Kids with cancer or abused animals really need your generosity."

Though I studied her expression, I couldn't decipher her true reasons for refusing my gift. Well, I'd known her for a matter of days, and we hadn't discussed our pasts that much. Maybe she always disliked accepting financial assistance, but the fact she'd accepted it from her parents suggested otherwise. Maybe she didn't like a monetary gift from someone she'd known for a few days.

"Please," I said, "let me do this for you. If you won't accept a gift, at least let me invest in your company."

Why was I so determined to give her money? She wanted nothing from me, and I kept pushing her to take my gift.

Eve sighed. "My God, you're stubborn. I don't want an investor who's sleeping with me. Isn't that a conflict of interest or something?"

What was the point in arguing anymore? She would never accept help of any kind from me. Maybe that was because we were sexually involved, or maybe because she didn't like my past. An infamous man made her uncomfortable. I couldn't fault her for that. Not many women, except the ones who craved fame, wanted to get involved with a man like me.

Yes, I'd made this bed for myself. Today, I had to sleep in it alone.

"Have it your way, *bebê*," I said. "I'll leave you to manage on your own."

"Thank you."

I retreated to the outdoors where the other guests were engaged in a game of charades. Nude charades might sound sexy, but in fact, it was rather awkward and silly. Tits and dicks bounced while the players tried to act out various themes, and falling down meant getting grass and dirt on their skin and in their hair. I knew from experience grass and dirt could get into many places where a person didn't want it to go. Sand was even worse, but luckily, we had no sand in the field behind the guest house.

Heidi stumbled while flailing her arms—to represent what exactly, I had no idea—and tumbled to the ground. When she got up, she had a small daisy stuck to her nipple.

Ollie snickered. "Look, she's wearing a pasty."

"The organic kind," said Willy, one of the Silver Foxes. "Very progressive, Heidi."

"Sexual harassment," I said, "is against the house rules."

Edna flapped her hand in a dismissive gesture. "Heidi knows we're joshing, and she gives as good as she gets."

"It's true," Heidi said. She plucked the wildflower off her skin and tossed it to Ollie, then blew him a kiss.

The boy blushed.

Lunch arrived a few minutes after the charades game broke up. Eve was pushing one metal cart overflowing with food while pulling another behind her. The strain of dragging them both across the dirt path between her home and the guest house crimped her whole face. She looked tired, most likely because she'd made all the food herself. Several of the men rushed to her aid. Though she tried to wave them away, Ollie took possession of the cart behind her while Willy wrested the other cart from her grasp. Sylvester hurried into Eve's house to get the third cart laden with food.

When I approached her, she managed only a half-hearted smile. "Thought you'd be first in line to wrestle for the carts."

"You wouldn't have let me, would you? I hoped you'd accept help from someone else." I glanced at the men hauling the carts toward the guest house. "I assume you aren't sleeping with any of them."

"No."

"Have you been with any of them in the past?"

One side of her mouth twisted as if she were trying not to smile. "No, I have not."

I felt strangely relieved to hear that. "Are we joining the others in the dining hall or eating in private?"

"The Kittens just got here. I'd like to eat with them so we can catch up."

Was she trying to avoid me?

I moved closer, loving the way her lips parted and her breath caught. "Heidi mentioned all of you keep in touch through email and social media. You don't need to get caught up on their lives or vice versa."

"Abandoning them on their first day here would be rude."

"Heidi ordered me to make sure you have fun. She suggested an intimate picnic at the hot spring."

"That girl needs a hobby."

"She cares about you. So—" I'd almost said *so do I.* "So let's not disappoint Heidi. Have lunch with me at the hot spring. I understand it's only a short walk away."

"That's true, but—"

"Say yes, Eve."

"Maybe tomorrow."

I lashed an arm around her waist and tugged her tight against my body, relishing the feel of her curves. "Soon enough, you'll figure out I can be much more stubborn than you. All I want is to make you feel good. Relax. Enjoy a beautiful day. You've earned it."

"This is a serious violation of nudist etiquette."

"Because I'm naked and I'm hugging you? Yes, I know." I tugged her even more snugly to my body. "In case you hadn't noticed, propriety doesn't mean much to me."

"No kidding." She gazed into my eyes, her tongue slipping out to moisten her bottom lip. "I don't have a handyman anymore, which means there's a lot of work for me to do."

"Forget about work for a while." I sealed two fingers over her lips when she started to protest. "Please, Eve, let me do this for you. It's lunch, not a handout."

She glanced at the nudists tramping into the guest house. "Okay."

We made sure the other guests had everything they needed, then grabbed some of the food and packed it into a picnic basket. From Eve's kitchen, we gathered a few more ingredients, including a bottle of wine and two glasses. Soup and sandwiches wasn't the most romantic meal, but I cared more about making sure she was well-nourished. I had a feeling if I didn't do that, she might forget to eat.

I grabbed a pair of sandals too. The trail to the hot spring was dirt, but as Eve had warned me, footwear was a necessity out in the woods. I carried the picnic basket and a blanket slung over my shoulder while she led the way, refusing to walk beside me and opposed to me holding her hand. When I tried that, she yanked hers away.

She had to be in front, naturally.

After a short walk, we arrived at the hot spring. Two wooden benches hunkered alongside the pool, and a wooden box with a latching lid held towels for any guests who might have forgotten to bring one. The box also offered bottled water. Eve thought of everything for her guests but neglected to take care of herself.

That changed today.

Steam wafted up from the blue pool, curling up into the air and dissipating. We laid out our blanket and relaxed there among the trees, listening to the birds singing while we ate and talked.

"I hope the Kittens haven't overwhelmed you," she said after consuming a large mouthful of her sandwich. "They can be a handful."

"Don't worry about me. They're sweet girls." I brushed a crumb away from the corner of her mouth with my thumb. "Besides, I grew up with two sisters. The Kittens are more exuberant than Maria and Aline, but I can handle it."

"How often do you see your family?"

"Several times a year. Sometimes I go home to visit them, and sometimes they come to America to stay with me."

"I know you live in LA, but how long have you been in the US?"

"Quite a while."

She consumed the last bite of her sandwich and wiped her fingers and mouth with a napkin. "I know it's none of my business, but I'm curious. You only have a slight accent, and you talk like an American."

Her curiosity about my life should have made me uncomfortable. After all, I wanted nothing more than a fling with her. But I discovered I liked knowing she wanted to know about me. It made me curious to learn about her.

"My mother is American," I explained. "Of Cuban descent, but both she and her parents were born and raised in Florida. She met my father when he was in Florida on spring break—he went to Harvard, like me—and they became infatuated with each other. My mother didn't go to college, but she's a very smart woman. Anyway, they kept in touch through letters and over the phone. She visited him in Massachusetts for three weeks in the summer. Six months after they met, my father proposed. She married him, and after he graduated, she moved to Brazil with him."

"It must've been hard to move to another country. Did she speak Portuguese?"

"Not at first. My father taught her." I took a sip of my wine. "She was always fluent in Spanish, but eventually, she became adept at Portuguese too. Still, she insisted I learn about America and Cuba so I would understand my heritage."

"You mentioned your father was an ambassador."

I nodded. "For three years. I told you I went to Harvard after that, but I spent summers at home. After graduation, I moved back to Brazil to join the Olympic football team. I'd played football before my family moved to Washington, and I played soccer in high school here and while at Harvard. My father wanted me to get a degree in business, so I'd be more levelheaded about financial matters, but all I cared about was football. We compromised. I got the degree, then went back to football. He was right, though. Having business training has helped me make better decisions."

"Didn't you say you moved to LA five years ago?"

"Yes, you have an excellent memory." Or was she memorizing everything I said for another reason? Did I want her to? "After the Olympics, I played for a professional club, and later for the Brazilian national football team until I retired seven years ago. My first modeling jobs were in New York, so I lived there for two years. Then, I signed a contract with an agency in Los Angeles. I've stayed there ever since."

"Wow, you're quite the international man." She took a swig of her wine. "My life can't compete."

"I've told you my story. Now tell me yours."

She swigged more wine, a bit of it dribbling down her chin. "I'm boring."

With my thumb, I wiped away the dribbling red wine. "I doubt that. You've told me very little about yourself, and already I'm enthralled."

"You're full of shit, that's what you are."

"At least tell me about your family. Do you have any brothers or sisters?"

She took another swig of wine. "Fine, if you insist. Yes, I have both. My brother lives in Portland, Maine, with his wife and their two children. He teaches high school, and she works at a community college. My sister is an accountant, and she's engaged to a great guy. She lives in Portland too. That's where we all grew up."

"How did you end up here?"

"I moved to New York, thinking I could become a professional photographer. The city didn't work out as well for me as it did for you." She gazed across the hot spring, though she seemed not to be looking at anything in particular. "I was broke. My parents had retired to Florida by then, and they wanted me to move there too. My brother and sister both wanted me to go back to Maine. I didn't want to do either, so I racked my brain for a way to make ends meet while still having time for photography."

"That must be when you had your idea for this place."

"Yeah, but it wasn't a eureka moment. It was an accident." She swung her attention back to me. "I was researching nature photography when I made a serendipitous typo. While I was typing the word nature, the search engine popped up with suggested searches, and I accidentally clicked on 'naturist.' I was going to click away from the search results, but I got curious. When I looked at the first page in the search results, I learned naturist is another word for nudist. I didn't close the browser window. I kept looking."

"A closet voyeur, eh?"

"Maybe at first," she admitted, her head bowed, looking up at me through her lashes. "But then I realized it wasn't all about sex. Some people prefer to be naked. Browsing various websites about nudism gave me an idea. It seemed like there weren't a lot of affordable retreats geared toward nudists. When my dad inherited this property, complete with a hot spring, I got my brilliant idea."

"You serve an underserved population of tourists." I traced a finger down her cheek. "You are brilliant, Eve. And hardworking. And a talented photographer, not to mention incredible in bed."

"So are you." She reached inside the picnic basket and dug out a box of cookies. "Ready for dessert?"

My cock loved the idea of Eve crumbling cookies all over me and licking them up crumb by crumb, but my curiosity pushed me to ask one more question. "How often do you see your family?"

With a soft little groan, she set down the cookie box. "We all go to our parents' house in Florida for Thanksgiving. For Christmas, we alternate between Maine and my place. This year, it's my turn."

"Are those the only times you see your family?"

"My parents like to surprise me every so often. My brother and sister have each visited a few times, and they keep pestering me to visit them." She leaned forward to settle her hand on my thigh. "May we please end the getting-to-know-you session?"

"Absolutely." I rose and offered her my hands, helping her up when she took them. "Take your clothes off, Eve, and join me in the water."

"I don't go naked in public."

"We're alone. Heidi promised to keep everyone away from the hot spring."

"Oh great. Everyone will know we're out here getting it on."

"No, I told Heidi we're having a picnic."

Eve gave me a skeptical look. "That's code for screwing each other's brains out."

I kissed her forehead. "Take a chance. With me."

"But—"

I ran for the pool and dived in.

The water was warmer than body temperature, but not too hot. Perfect for making love to a beautiful woman. By the time I surfaced at the pool's center, Eve had shed her dress and was slipping out of her panties. The sight of her nude made me hard. I'd seen her naked body before, had my hands and mouth all over her, but seeing her never failed to arouse me. It was different than with other women. I craved her more every time I had her, but with the others, I'd gradually lost interest. I couldn't imagine ever getting tired of Eve.

I swam to the shore, where a ledge offered a place to rest my arms. "Grab a condom, would you? They're in the basket."

"There aren't any—"

"Underneath everything else."

She dug around inside the basket and brought out the box of condoms. "You sneaked an entire box of them in here? Seems like overkill."

"Not with you. I can't get enough of your body."

"We don't really need these anyway." She threw me a sideways glance. "Unless you have a secret you need to tell me? About your health?"

"I'm clean, Eve. I get tested regularly."

"Okay, then. We don't need these." She tossed the box of condoms back into the basket. "I'm clean too, and I'm on the pill. Besides, I don't know if condoms work underwater. Do you?"

"No, I've never had sex in the water before."

She straightened, her brows wrinkling as she stared at me. "You have never done it in the water? But you're so adventurous."

I shrugged. "Never had the opportunity."

She approached the ledge and sat down on it with her feet dangling in the water. "You're introducing me to a lot of new things, so it's nice I can do the same for you."

"Time to get wet," I said, running a hand up her inner thigh. "Or are you wet already?"

"You know I am." She slid off the ledge into the water, dunking her head to drench her hair. "But now I'm wet all over, not just between my legs."

I pulled her into my arms and kissed her. The sensation of her silken tongue on mine, of her supple and slick body pasted to mine, made me even harder. I whisked my palms up and down her backside, from her shoulders to her ass, while she tangled her fingers in the hair at my nape and plunged her tongue deeper into my mouth. I grasped her bottom with one hand, and with the other, I covered her breast. She gasped when I flicked my thumb across her taut nipple.

When I pinched it, she clutched my hair tighter.

I gave up her lips and her tongue, dipping my head to nuzzle her throat.

"Val," she moaned, her head falling back. "Please, yes."

"Eve, you're so perfect." I slid my hand from her breast down her stomach, and lower, to push my fingers between her folds. "I love your body."

I stroked her until she wrapped her legs around me, wrapped her entire body around me.

"Skip that," she breathed into my ear. "I can't wait any longer."

Neither could I. Even touching her with my fingers, feeling how ready she was, made me throb for her. I clamped both hands on her ass and thrust into her body, groaning when her wet heat surrounded me. "You feel so good. I want you to come all over me."

"Hurry, please."

I punched into her again and again, tugging her bottom toward me to deepen every thrust. She drew her head back to look at me, her lips swollen from our kiss, her eyes half closed and her cheeks dusted with pink.

God, she was so beautiful.

With our gazes bound to each other, we gave in to the moment and to the sheer pleasure of joining our bodies. I slowed my pace, pulling out and easing back inside her, to prolong this feeling despite the desperate need to slam into her until we both exploded. Never in my life had I longed to stay inside a woman forever, to revel in the intimacy and the sensations. Her hot sheath glided along my cock, wavelets lapped around us, and her head fell back as her eyes closed. She clung to me, both arms around my neck, and locked her ankles behind my ass. Her breaths tickled my ear. Her hair tickled my cheek. I rotated my head to bury my face in that hair and fill my senses with the sweet scent of it, the scent of her.

"Faster," she murmured into my ear.

I bucked into her, gripping her bottom, yanking her into me every time I drove my cock deeper. She made a desperate noise, a cross between a gasp and a whimper, and I fucked her even faster, even harder, pounding into her while the water splashed around us and sprayed our faces.

Eve's entire body stiffened around me. She threw her head forward and sank her teeth into my shoulder when she came, her cry muffled by my flesh, her body clenched around my shaft. The pulsating waves of her climax pushed me over the edge. A hoarse shout erupted out of me as I thrust once more, the deepest and hardest thrust of all, and exploded inside her sweet body.

I'd never before come inside a woman without a condom. She'd let me. She'd wanted me to do it. A feral part of me loved the idea that I'd branded her in this way, but mostly, I loved the intense intimacy of spilling myself inside this woman with nothing separating our bodies.

We were both breathing hard and drenched. She laughed softly and tickled my nape with her fingertips. I chuckled and squeezed her ass.

"Mmm," she hummed straight into my ear, her lips vibrating against my skin. "Water sex is awesome."

I agreed, but I couldn't manage to speak yet. Being with Eve left me speechless. Maybe I should've worried about that. I didn't have the energy for worry, too relaxed to do anything except savor the warmth of her body and the afterglow of our lovemaking.

Footsteps slapped farther down the trail, coming closer.

Eve's head snapped up, and she craned her neck to peer down the trail.

Heidi emerged from the woods. When she spotted us, her eyes widened, and she stumbled to a halt.

"Oops!" she said, flinging a hand up to cover her mouth. "Sorry, guys, I didn't think—" She moved her hand away from her mouth to cover her eyes. "Didn't see a thing. I hate to interrupt, but some new guests have arrived."

"New guests?" Eve pushed me away and whirled around, sloshing water over me. "I don't have any new bookings until next week."

"Uh, they're not paying guests. It's your parents."

"What?" Eve virtually screeched the word. She slapped her palms onto the ledge and hoisted her body out of the water, scrambling to get to her feet. Water sluiced off her skin and poured from her hair, but she didn't seem to notice. "When did they get here?"

"A few minutes ago," Heidi said. She made a pained face. "They brought the whole gang."

Eve went rigid and motionless as a granite statue, her eyes wide and her mouth open. Her voice was hushed, almost a whisper. "My brother and sister? The kids? Everyone?"

"Yep."

I heaved myself up out of the water and got to my feet. Coming up beside Eve, I slipped an arm around her shoulders. "Why do you look shocked? I would've thought you'd want to see your family."

Only her eyes moved when she glanced at me. "I do, but not today. It's kind of a bad time."

She looked me up and down, her eyebrows lifting. Her appraisal stalled at my dick.

Ah yes, that. I wasn't fully aroused, but neither was I completely limp.

Eve raced toward Heidi, grasped her shoulders, and spun her to face the trail. "Don't look back. Just go. Tell my family I'll be there in a few minutes. And please, do not under any circumstances let them come out here."

"Aye-aye, captain," Heidi said with a smirk.

She lowered her hand and trotted down the trail.

Eve rushed to get dried off and get dressed.

"Relax," I said, observing her frantic movements while I slipped on my sandals and toweled off. "Your parents know this is a nudist retreat. They won't be shocked to see me."

She yanked her dress on over her head. It got stuck on her ear. She fumbled with it but seemed too frazzled to get it free.

I unhooked the strap from her ear, and the dress fell into position. "You're panicking. Is it because of me?"

She almost tripped getting her sandals on. "Ya think? I just had sex with a man I don't really know"—she flapped her arms, apparently to indicate the woods and the hot spring—"out here in the open. I took my clothes off outdoors where anyone might see me."

Eve flapped her arms again and made a face I couldn't describe. Her upper lip curled even as her mouth fell open. Her nose crinkled. She squinted her eyes and shook her head. Maybe it was shock or embarrassment, but I'd never seen an expression like that before. It was adorable. Bizarre, but adorable.

I grasped her shoulders. "Take a deep breath, Eve. This isn't as bad as you think."

"Sure, not as bad." She nodded her head with so much vigor it must've jarred her brain. "My entire family is here, everyone knows you and I are having sex, and you walk around naked twenty-four seven. My parents aren't nudists, but hey, what's to worry about?"

Her grin was sarcastic and slightly manic.

I did the only thing I could do. I gave her a quick, hard kiss and then grasped her hand in mine to lead her back to the guest house and her home. She didn't complain about the hand-holding, a testament to her frazzled state. We walked out of the woods hand in hand.

Eve froze, her eyes even wider.

An older woman with blonde hair sprinted toward us, followed by an older man with a rim of gray hair around his large bald spot. The couple halted a few feet from me and Eve, taking in the sight of us—Eve in her skimpy, tie-dyed dress and me in…well, nothing.

We'd forgotten the picnic basket, I suddenly realized.

"Mom," Eve said, struggling to catch her breath. "Dad. Hi. I wasn't expecting you."

Eve's mother squinted at me.

Or rather, at my penis.

Her lips quirked, and she puckered them like she was trying not to smile or maybe laugh. She aimed her eyes, bright blue like her daughter's, at me. "Who's your new friend, Evie?"

I kept hold of Eve's hand but offered the other one to her mother. "Val Silva."

Eve's mother shook my hand. "I'm Donna Holt. This is my husband, Larry."

Mr. Holt shook my hand vigorously. "Nice to meet you, Val. We didn't know Eve was seeing anybody."

The Holts smiled and tried very hard not to stare at my dick, though Mrs. Holt kept glancing at it, her lips twitching every time. I guessed Eve hadn't told them the resort rules.

"I'm pleased to meet you too, Mr. and Mrs. Holt," I said. "You've raised quite a woman in Eve."

The woman in question hadn't moved or closed her mouth. I wondered if she was breathing. Her chest was rising and falling, so I decided she wasn't in danger of passing out from lack of oxygen.

"Call me Donna," Mrs. Holt said. "Or maybe you should call me Mom?"

Eve roused from her catatonic state with a jolt, blinking rapidly. "Mom, honestly, I met Val this week."

"Mm-hmm." She swept her gaze over me again. "But you must really like him. You were holding hands when you came back from the hot spring, where you'd been all alone together."

"Yeah," Mr. Holt said, "and you haven't called us since last Thursday. When Mom texted you the other day, you claimed to be too busy for that. We knew something was up, and Donna bet me fifty bucks it was a boy."

No one had called me a boy in at least fifteen years.

Mr. Holt clapped me on the shoulder. "Call me Larry. Dad can wait until the wedding's arranged."

Eve spluttered for a moment before she managed to speak. "We're not engaged, for Christ's sake. I haven't called because I've been busy. A pipe burst in the guest house and then I had to fire Quentin—"

"Oh, we heard about that," Donna said. She threw an arm around her daughter's shoulders and urged her to walk. "Heidi filled us in on the soap opera, and on your new beau."

Larry gripped my shoulder hard. "Let's have a little man-to-man chat while the girls catch up. What do you say?"

What could I say? "Of course, let's chat."

Chapter Seventeen

Eve

My dad dragged Val away from the crowd that had gathered around us. I watched the two of them retreating from view behind the throng of guests and wondered what on earth my father was up to. He never interrogated my boyfriends. Not that Val was my boyfriend. What was he, then? My lover, I supposed. I did not want to tell my parents that, though I had my suspicions the other guests had spilled those beans long before Val and I traipsed out of the woods.

What should I say to my parents? *Hey, guess what, I'm screwing a virtual stranger who made a notorious sex tape and used to strip in public. You can probably catch video of both on YouTube.*

Since Val said he had the sex tape on his phone, I supposed my parents didn't need internet access to view my lover's past escapades. If they asked, he would show them. He was just that kind of shameless exhibitionist.

And I loved that side of him.

I must've lost my mind, right? Sleeping with a man I barely knew. Getting naked outdoors. Heidi had seen us in the hot spring. I hadn't been caught getting it on with a guy since my sophomore year of college when my brother Andrew had barged into my dorm room unannounced. He'd wanted to surprise me with a visit. Oh yeah, I'd been surprised all right. My brother had gotten a good look at my tits before his face turned crimson and he scampered back into the hallway. Andrew and I never told a soul about that incident.

Somehow, today had been more embarrassing. I was a grown woman, thirty years old, not a college sophomore. But this time, everyone knew what I'd been doing with a guy.

Bye-bye, privacy.

"Evie," my mom said, "why didn't you tell us you have a beau?"

I'd never been good at lying to my mom, so I told the truth—partially. "It's not like that. Val and I met four days ago. Please don't start planning the wedding."

Yeah, I omitted the fact neither I nor Val wanted a romantic entanglement, much less a commitment.

Mom slung an arm around my shoulders and gave me a good squeeze. "You might be my baby, but you're an adult. I won't judge your choices. Have I ever complained about one of your boyfriends, even the ones I didn't like?"

"No."

"I like Val."

"You met him five seconds ago."

She tipped her head side to side, then gave a decisive nod. "I can tell if a man is good or bad news in thirty seconds or less. Val is a good one."

If she knew about his past, would she feel the same way?

Why did I care? Val was fun to be with and gave me awesome orgasms. End of story.

My brother and sister ran up to us, all grins and chuckles. Andrew had that gleam in his eyes that always meant he was about to razz me big time.

"Hey, Evie," he said, giving me a quick hug. "Hope you don't mind the surprise visit. Didn't know we'd be breaking up your private party."

Krista's lips twitched like she was trying not to smirk. "Must've been some party. You're all flushed, Evie."

"Don't tease your sister," Mom said. "Can't you see she's embarrassed enough already? But Evie, really, you don't need to be embarrassed. I'm glad you've found a man who makes you happy."

"Mom," I moaned, "I told you Val is not my boyfriend."

Andrew's grin turned positively goofy. "Not your boyfriend? You run off into the woods with lots of naked guys?"

"This is a nudist resort."

"Sure, but you were out in the woods with him all alone." He pointed at my dress. "And your dress is on backwards."

What? How had I not noticed that? Val hadn't seemed to notice either.

Before I could snarl at my brother, our mom said, "Be nice, Andy. Oh, what is your father doing over there? I'd better make sure he isn't giving Val a hard time."

My brother snickered and grinned some more. "I bet Val can handle himself fine. Can't he, Eve?"

Our mom smacked his arm on her way past him. She headed for the secluded spot on the other side of the lawn where my father had cornered my lover.

Krista sidled up to me and murmured, "Good job, Evie. Val is smokin' hot."

I wasn't sure what good job I'd done and decided I didn't want to know. Krista had a filthy mind.

My sister adopted a sarcastically dramatic tone of voice when she whispered, "Ollie told us Val is staying in your house."

"Uh, yeah, his room in the guest house got flooded by a burst pipe."

Krista leaned in closer, her face millimeters from mine. "Was that an accident, or did the pipe have a little help bursting?"

"Very funny." I settled one hand on my hip. "The pipe broke before Val even got here. I had no idea what he looked like or who he was. All I knew was his name. He might've been a pudgy sixty-year-old who smelled like cigar smoke."

"But he's not. He is one guy who absolutely should be a nudist." She glanced in Val's direction and sighed wistfully. "I love my fiancé, but Jeremy wouldn't know a weight machine if it dropped onto his head."

"Muscles aren't everything," Andrew said. He clucked his tongue and spoke in a tone of mock chastisement. "Shame on you, Kris. Aren't you supposed to love your fiancé for who he is, not what he looks like?"

"Yes, but that doesn't mean I can't appreciate a beautiful man. Val is eye candy." She winked at me. "Except to Eve. I bet he's all sorts of other kinds of candy for her."

"Ech," Andrew said, feigning a dry heave. "Don't make me hurl."

With an inward groan, I resigned myself to my fate. Today was going to be a blast.

Of the atomic bomb variety.

I loved my family, but really, could they have a chosen a worse moment to pop in for a surprise visit? I guessed I ought to be grateful they hadn't all tramped down the trail to the hot spring with Heidi.

Andrew scanned his gaze over the lawn until he spotted Val and our parents. His brows squished together. "I'd swear I've seen Val somewhere before."

Oh God, don't let my brother have seen the sex tape.

Even if he hadn't, Ollie knew about Val's past and might've blabbed to Andrew.

"Man, I wish I could remember," Andrew said, frowning and shaking his head. "Is Val an actor or something?"

I kept my trap shut, sealed with invisible duct tape.

"Yeah," Krista said, "now that you mention it, he does seem familiar."

Jeremy, Krista's fiancé, jogged up to us. "Hey, Eve, great to see you." He hugged me and slipped an arm around Krista while still watching me. "Why didn't you tell us you have a famous guest?"

"Famous?" Krista said. "You know who he is? We've been trying to figure out why Val looks familiar, but Eve won't tell us."

"He's Val Silva, the soccer champ who took the Brazilian team to the Olympics and scored the goal that won them a gold medal."

Please, please, please let that be all he knows.

"An athlete?" Krista said. "Well, that explains the sizzlin' bod."

"Yeah, he was an athlete," Jeremy said. "I think he's a model now. He used to like to strip buck naked at the end of every winning game."

Aw, fuck. Why did I have such sucky luck? I'd met Jeremy several times before, but I didn't know him well. Why couldn't he be the kind of guy who played video games all day? No, of course he had to be a soccer fan.

Krista looked at me like she'd never seen me before. "Evie hooked up with an exhibitionist?"

Jeremy squinted like he was thinking hard. His expression brightened, and he lifted a finger. "I remember the rest. Val Silva was notorious for being a nudist, but he got to be really infamous after everybody saw his sex tape."

I winced. Double fuck with a side of shit and a goddamn on top. The universe was punishing me for all my past transgressions. Sleeping with Cody and Aaron. Sleeping with Quentin. Spying on Val while he gave himself a happy ending, getting naked with Val in public, doing him in the hot spring, the list went on and on. Since Val arrived, I'd become a sex-crazed moron.

No, I hadn't done anything wrong. So what if everyone knew about Val's sex tape? I had no desire to get entangled in a relationship with him. His past had no bearing on my life or anything we did together. A surprise visit from my family had knocked me off balance, that was all.

My sister gaped at me, though I got the impression it wasn't all horror. There seemed to be a bit of awe in there too. "Evie, you naughty girl. No wonder you're glowing. A man like Val could perk up any woman."

I crossed my arms over my chest and said nothing, hoping my small smile came off as enigmatic.

"Everybody thinks I'm the bad girl in the family," Krista said. "All I did was flash my tits during Mardi Gras. But Evie, you… Wow, I didn't know you had a wild streak."

She sounded impressed rather than disgusted.

I excused myself to mingle with my guests, claiming I needed to check on whether they needed anything. Really, I needed a break from the pseudo-inquisition from my smart-mouthed siblings. For the rest of the day, I juggled spending time with my family and struggling to take care of my guests at the same time. When Dad and Andrew heard about the burst pipe, they insisted on fixing things for me. Val volunteered to help them, but they needed supplies first.

Val insisted I go with him into town to get those supplies.

And yeah, he wore clothes.

Well, sort of. His shorts were so short and tight they could've passed for briefs. His short-sleeve shirt was looser-fitting. He'd opted to wear the same sandals he'd had on when we sneaked off to the hot spring. No matter what he wore, he looked good enough to lick and nibble and fondle from head to toe.

Mm, I'd done all of that this week.

I drove the truck, though Val tried to talk me into letting him take the wheel.

"You're a guest," I said. "It's bad enough you insist on helping with the repairs. I am not letting you drive. Enjoy the scenery like a good little tourist."

"Are you upset about what happened? Your family knows about us."

"Everyone knows." I glanced at him sideways. "I'm sorry about the parental inquisition. My dad has never done that before."

"Should I be offended or flattered he gave me special treatment?"

"Not sure." I steered the truck around a corner while I thought about whether to tell him what my sister and brother had figured out. What the hell. Val wouldn't care. "Andrew and Krista know about your, um, antics on the football field. Krista's fiancé, Jeremy, recognized you. And he had also seen the sex tape."

"I know. Jeremy, Andrew, and I had a good long chat. They're very protective of you."

"Yeah, Andrew is. I don't know Jeremy all that well, so I doubt he was being protective."

"He definitely was. Face it, Eve, everyone loves you."

My pulse sped up. Everyone loved me? He didn't mean to include himself in that statement, for sure. Did I wish he had?

No, of course not. We'd known each other for a matter of days.

At the hardware store, we ran into someone I'd hoped to avoid for the rest of my life.

Quentin Smith walked down the plumbing aisle toward us.

I tried to pretend I didn't notice him, focusing on the tools Val was examining. I even tried to block Val's view of the human disaster striding in our direction. I wasn't tall enough to block Val, though. Rats.

Quentin stopped an arm's length away from me. "Eve."

I pretended I'd just noticed him and pasted on a bland smile. "Quentin."

Val's eyes narrowed, and a muscle ticked in his jaw.

"Good to see you," Quentin said to me, actively ignoring the imposing man beside me. "I wanted to apologize again for the way I acted. I'm sorry. I'd like to come back to work."

Was he strung out on heroin? He couldn't seriously think I'd give him his job back.

"That's not going to happen," I said. "You firebombed that bridge."

"Any bridge can be rebuilt." He inched closer. "Please, Eve. Gimme another chance."

I didn't get the opportunity to tell Quentin to go to hell. Val beat me to it.

He moved between me and Quentin. "Eve said no. Walk away."

The dark tone of his voice implied he might resort to violence to convince Quentin to leave me alone. What happened to not being jealous? Val had sworn he wouldn't act this way.

I laid a hand on Val's arm. "It's okay. I can handle this."

His gaze flicked to me, then back to Quentin.

My former handyman glared at Val. "I'm talking to Eve, not you, Tarzan."

I squeezed between the two men, turning sideways to both of them. "Enough machismo. Val, I can take care of this myself. Quentin, I fired you and that's that. Goodbye."

Without waiting for either of them to speak again, I marched off down the aisle and swung left into the main aisle. I had no clue where I was going. Getting away from the Testosterone Anonymous meeting was my sole purpose.

Val caught up to me in the paint aisle. "Are you all right?"

"Fine. I love it when big, brawny men fight over me while completely ignoring the fact I'm standing right next to them."

"I'm sorry. I shouldn't have intervened."

A long sigh gusted out of me. "It's okay. Quentin has been a complete asshole to you."

"To you too." Val leaned against the shelves that held gallons of paint. "I won't get in your way again. Should we go back to buying supplies?"

"Yes."

The whole time we were shopping for plumbing stuff, I kept wondering why Val had been so protective of me when Quentin showed up. He'd been overprotective, actually. He despised Quentin, and my former handyman despised him. Quentin's reaction to Val made sense now that I realized Quentin had thought I belonged to him because we'd had sex once. But Val's reaction to Quentin…

He couldn't be jealous. Could he?

Nah.

On the drive home, I wondered.

Chapter Eighteen

Val

After spending the better part of a day with Eve's family, I couldn't understand why she'd been so upset when they arrived. They knew what kind of resort she owned. They knew she spent every day hanging out with naked men and women. Her brother and sister didn't mind at all, and Andrew and his wife had brought their two children who were eight and nine. The children had been here before, Andrew told me, and were comfortable being around nudists.

Eve's parents didn't mind either, so I had to wonder. Why was Eve so frazzled? Was she ashamed to have her family find out she'd been sleeping with me? I knew she cherished her privacy, so maybe that was the only reason for her behavior. Our encounter with Quentin in the hardware store hadn't helped, for sure.

I'd wanted to belt that bastard.

Just after lunch, the FedEx truck arrived. Luckily, Eve was busy entertaining her family and didn't notice the delivery I accepted from the FedEx driver. I planned to surprise her in the morning, but for now, the package I'd ordered would stay a secret.

For most of the afternoon, I worked with Larry, Andrew, Jeremy, and a couple of the other guests to repair the room in the guest house. I wondered if Eve would make me move into this room once we'd finished the work. The thought of being relegated to the guest house bothered me more than I'd expected. I had gotten used to being mere feet away from Eve's bedroom, within easy distance if I wanted to sneak into her bed—or vice versa. Skulking across the dirt path from the guest house to get into Eve's home in the dead of night did not appeal to me.

Oh, but I would do that if I had to. No chance in hell I'd give up making love to her because of geographic inconvenience. I would've traveled to Siberia barefoot in the middle of winter, swimming across the Bering Strait to get there, if it meant I could feel Eve's body around me.

I liked her. Very much. For more than her body.

The realization stopped me for a moment. I stood in the damaged room in the guest house, a hammer raised in my hand, holding a nail in position to pound it into place. Was this what people called an epiphany? I'd never had one before. I liked Eve. That shouldn't have been shocking, but I'd never wanted a woman for much more than sex. The occasional dinner, maybe. Never more. Never anything…serious. With Eve, I wanted all of it. All of her.

"You okay?" Larry asked.

His question startled me out of my thoughts. "Fine, yes. Just thinking."

About his daughter and all the nonsexual things I wanted to do with her. Ah, but I did think about sex too. I could take Eve out to dinner and then for a romantic walk along the river in town, followed by hours of sweaty, dirty sex.

"We're almost done," Larry said, oblivious of my carnal thoughts. He patted my shoulder. "You've done great, helping out with the repairs. I'm sure Eve really appreciates it. And it was a wise decision to put on coveralls."

Yes, I'd given up my preferred state of undress during the repair job. When I had thought about doing construction work in the nude, I'd suffered visions of taking a nail to the dick or the balls. Sometimes, even a nudist needed to wear clothes.

Everyone ate dinner in the guest house that evening. Eve had ordered a feast from the local Mexican restaurant in honor of her family's visit, since they loved tacos and spicy queso dip. More laughter and chattering voices filled the dining hall tonight than on any other night since I'd been here. Ollie, the Norrises, and some of the other guests already knew Eve's family.

Krista, Eve's sister, sat next to me during dinner. Eve had taken the seat on the opposite side of me, so I was sandwiched between the two lovely Holt women. I flirted with Eve and only Eve. Krista was equally beautiful, but she had a fiancé. Besides, I'd realized during our time in the hot spring I had eyes for Eve alone. No other woman, no matter how beautiful, could compare to her.

Heidi sat beside Krista. Eve's parents along with her brother and soon-to-be brother-in-law occupied the chairs across the table from us. The next closest table stood a few feet away, so we could chat with Ruth, Sylvester, Ollie, and several of the Kittens.

Eve had been right about the Kitten Brigade. They were sweet girls, but they got boisterous whenever three or more of them gathered together. Those girls made every occasion a party but never took things too far. I could see why Eve liked them so much.

Conversation stayed casual until dessert, when Krista turned to me and asked, "So, what are your intentions with my sister?"

"Intentions?" I intended to fuck her every night and as often in the daytime as possible. Her sister wouldn't want to hear that, though. "I like Eve very much, but it's a bit early to be having intentions of the kind I think you mean."

"Hmm." She eyed me like she was sizing me up. "You're hot, and you seem nice. But Evie is my sister, and I don't want her to get hurt by some has-been athlete who likes to make DIY porn."

On the other side of me, Eve was engaged in conversation with Ruth across the distance between our tables. She seemed unaware of her sister's interrogation of me. Larry and Donna Holt had gone off to mingle with the other guests, and Heidi had moved into the chair beside Andrew, regaling him and Jeremy with stories of the Kitten Brigade's antics.

Krista had me cornered.

"I have no desire to hurt Eve," I told her. "She's a special woman. I enjoy spending time with her, but I haven't known her for long."

"Yet you're sleeping with her."

"Well—" I fidgeted in my chair but resisted the impulse to look away from Krista. Her interrogation would not unsettle me, that I'd decided. "I can't discuss it with you. Anything that happens between me and Eve in private stays private."

Krista locked her arms over her chest. "Does that mean you're not secretly taping it when you screw my sister?"

"I have never secretly taped any woman. You've heard about the sex tape. I'm not ashamed of that, but the woman I was with consented to being recorded. In fact, it was her idea."

Eve's sister studied me, one finger tapping on her arm.

Her attention set my skin to itching. I fidgeted again and scratched my thigh.

"Your sister means more to me," I said, "than a costar for a sex tape. I would never knowingly hurt her."

Krista puckered her lips for half a second, then smiled. "Good. That means I don't have to get Andrew and Jeremy to tie a concrete block to your ankle and toss you headfirst into the hot spring."

The twinkle in her eyes confirmed she was joking.

I might not have been sure otherwise. Krista had seemed like a cheerful, easygoing person when I'd first met her. Here in the dining hall, she'd turned into a deadly protector of her older sister. I respected that. If I'd thought any man was using one of my sisters, I would've done the same thing.

Krista got up and walked around the table to sit in the chair beside Jeremy, which Andrew had vacated.

Eve was staring at me, unblinking.

"What's wrong?" I asked.

"I—I heard what you and Krista were talking about." She bit the inside of her lip and focused on my shoulder. "You must've been saying that stuff to make my sister happy."

Saying what stuff? With a start, I realized everything I'd said. *Your sister means more to me than a costar for a sex tape. I would never knowing hurt her. She's a special woman.* Had I sounded like a smitten man?

I'd meant every word, a fact that stunned me, but I couldn't tell Eve that. She might panic more than she already had today. But I didn't want to lie to her either.

"Yes," I said. "I, uh, didn't want your sister to think I'm using you."

"Sure, I get that." Eve relaxed, the shock dissolving into a casual smile. "Krista is my baby sister, but she likes to pretend she's my bodyguard. She likes you, though. She saves the inquisition for guys she thinks might be— Well, she doesn't do it to every guy I'm with."

Eve's parents came back to our table and spirited Eve away for a private conversation.

I wondered what she'd been about to say before she changed her mind mid-sentence.

And then I wondered why I cared.

Chapter Nineteen

Eve

After a day with my entire family and all my guests, I fell asleep the second my head hit the pillow. Val and I had both been too tired for sex, so he retreated into his room while I retreated into mine. If I hadn't been so exhausted, I would've sneaked into his room to crawl under the covers with him and go to sleep there. A couple days ago, I'd invited Val to share my bed. *Would you like to come into my bedroom?* I'd asked, the words tumbling out of my mouth before I realized what I was saying. Val had declined the offer, of course. He wanted a relationship even less than I did, but his rebuff had stung more than I expected.

The idea of sleeping with him—actually sleeping—appealed to me a lot. I tried not to think about why.

When I woke in the morning, I felt good. Wonderful in fact. I'd slept straight through the night without rousing once. Lying in my bed, I yawned and stretched my entire body. Refreshed and ready for another day of chaos, that's what I was.

"It's a stunning view from here."

Val's voice made me jump.

He leaned against the jamb of my open bedroom door, arms crossed over his chest, that gorgeously naked body on full display. His hair was mussed like he hadn't bothered to comb it yet, and his sizzling gaze gravitated to my chest. "I dreamed about those tits all night. That and other parts of your edible body."

I glanced down and realized my stretching had made the cover slide down to my waist, exposing my breasts. Not bothering to cover them, I sat up and stretched my arms above my head. "Good morning. You look edible as usual too."

"Did you dream about me?"

Oh yeah, had I ever. Sinfully hot, decadently erotic dreams about all the things I wanted to do to him and with him, not to mention the things I wanted him to do to me. I pushed the covers off the rest of my body. "All I dreamed about was you. I had half a mind to crawl into your bed last night just to sleep there."

Why on earth had I said that part about wanting to sleep with him? I hadn't meant to say it. Like the last time I'd suggested we spend the night together, the words had tumbled from my lips without permission. My mouth had a mind of its own when it came to Val and the notion of sharing a bed with him all night.

Yesterday, Val had told my sister I meant more to him than a partner for a sex tape.

A little shiver coursed through me, but not the sexy kind. Getting attached to Val was a bad, bad, bad idea. The man was a notorious exhibitionist, he made sex tapes that he kept on his phone forever after, and he loved the spotlight. I needed my privacy, would've fled from the spotlight if one had ever veered in my direction, and never took my clothes off anywhere except inside my house. We were completely wrong for each other.

Yesterday I had, for the first time ever, disrobed outdoors.

Sure, Val had been the only one there. Heidi's accidental glimpse couldn't have amounted to much. Why had I gotten naked at the hot spring? Why had I had sex outdoors? That wasn't me at all. So of course, the one time I'd done anything of the sort, I'd gotten caught in the act. At least my parents hadn't seen it.

Would it have been horrible if they had? I was an adult, after all. They knew, because my guests had gossiped about it, that I was getting it on with Val. They knew I ran a nudist resort. Would they have cared if I became a nudist? Not that I was planning to do that.

"*Qual é o problema?*" Val asked.

"Huh?"

"I asked what's wrong. You're puckering your whole face. So what is the problem?"

"Nothing, not really. I was reliving the moment when we walked out of the woods together yesterday. My family must've heard from the other guests that you and I are, um, you know."

"Fucking? Yes, I'm sure they did." He strolled up to the bed and settled his taut ass onto it in front of me. "But they would've guessed we're more than friends anyway. We were holding hands when we walked out of the woods."

Holding hands? He'd tried to do that on the way out to the hot spring, but I wouldn't let him. On the way back, I'd been too freaked out to notice anything short of Bigfoot leaping out to snarl at us. When I thought about it now, I remembered the soothing warmth of his hand in mine.

"Guess you're right," I said. "And I know I've been an idiot about all of this. I'm sorry. Please don't think I'm ashamed of having anyone know about us. I'm not."

He reached out to sweep a lock of hair away from my face, tucking it behind my ear, and grazed his fingertips down my cheek. "I tempted you to step outside your comfort zone. That wasn't easy for you, I know."

"It was easier than I'd thought it would be." That was the honest truth. I hadn't hesitated for more than a few seconds when Val suggested I strip and jump into the hot spring with him. Sex in the warm water, with him, had been one of the best experiences of my life.

Being with him was the best experience, period.

He moved closer, his hip pressed against mine, and looped an arm around my waist. "What else can I tempt you to try, *docinho*?"

Gazing into his sultry brown eyes, I forgot all about my inhibitions and silly worries about privacy. I wanted to do anything and everything with him.

I blinked rapidly as I realized he'd thrown another Portuguese word at me. "What did you say? *Docinho*? I don't know what that means."

He shifted his ass on the bed and cleared his throat. "It means sweetie."

Not long ago, I would've bristled at his use of endearments. He'd called me *bebê* and *linda*, and I hadn't minded at all. Hearing him call me sweetie in his native tongue…I liked it. A lot.

Because he meant more to me than a casual sex partner.

Holy shit. It was true. The revelation tingled over my skin, raising the hairs at my nape, but it wasn't fear triggering my response. All my anxieties over getting attached to Val and whether our lives could mesh melted away at the instant I'd realized he meant something to me, something more than the best lover I'd ever had. Sure, we still might not work as a couple. We lived in different worlds, different planes of reality. But here, now, for as long as he stayed with me, I would enjoy our fledgling connection and the silky warmth it engendered in me.

I glided my palm up his torso, from his waist to his pecs. "I think you could tempt me to do just about anything."

He tickled my bottom with one long finger. "In that case, I'll have to think about what I most want to seduce you into doing with me."

"I have an idea."

One of his dark brows lifted. "What is it?"

"Take a shower with me."

"You do realize if we take a shower together, I will ravish you."

"I'm counting on it."

We dashed into the bathroom and enjoyed a long, steamy shower. The actual steam from the hot water filled the stall, but we also created our own steam. I locked my legs around his hips while he backed us up to the wall, directly under the shower head, and drove into me again and again until we both hit that peak together.

Then we did it again.

Our morning sex might not have been the most creative ever, but it got our day off to a blissful start. By the time I'd gotten dressed and walked into the kitchen, Val was busy preparing breakfast—for an army.

"What's all that?" I asked as I perched on a stool at the island.

"Breakfast for the guests and your family."

"Making breakfast is my job, not yours. Guests don't do manual labor."

He paused in stirring scrambled eggs in my largest frying pan and glanced over his shoulder at me. "I thought I was more than a guest by now."

Had I hurt his feelings? I hadn't mean to, but it sure seemed like he was wounded by the fact I'd called him a guest.

I rubbed my forehead. "All I meant was that you are paying to stay here. You shouldn't be making breakfast for everybody. I get paid to do that."

"You need employees, Eve. Since you won't hire any, I'll fill in until you change your mind."

"Until you go home, you mean."

He was staring down at the eggs again, stirring them with a wooden spoon while they gradually congealed into fluffy masses of sunny-yellow goodness. His shoulders bunched the tiniest bit.

Why did I get the feeling I'd hurt his feelings again? I couldn't figure it out. Yes, I'd realized I liked being with him for more than sex. He'd told my sister something similar. But he hadn't expressed any interest in staying beyond the two weeks he had originally booked. I didn't know if he meant anything by the statements he'd made to Krista yesterday, or if holding hands meant anything to him either. He was a self-professed player who'd assured me he didn't want a relationship.

Since when did I sit around contemplating the status of my relationship, or lack thereof, with a man? Something about this thing between me and Val, whatever it might be, had turned me into a frazzled mess.

Until this morning. Today, I felt much calmer and more like myself.

I pushed off the stool and sidestepped the island to stand beside Val. "All I meant was that you had planned to stay two weeks. Are you changing those plans? Do you want to stay longer?"

He froze, his gaze nailed to the eggs. "Would you want me to stay longer?"

"Yes."

Only his eyes moved, his gaze homing in on mine. He didn't blink.

"Are you going to make me beg?" I asked. "I'll probably do that if you don't say something in the next three seconds."

He dropped the wooden spoon into the frying pan of full of eggs, whirled toward me, and hauled me snug against his body with his big hands spread over my buttocks. "Yes, Evie, I want to stay longer. Much longer."

"Like another week?"

"As long as you'll have me."

My pulse sped up, and I couldn't help grinning.

He grinned too.

I patted his ass. "Why don't you get out the breakfast sausages while I whip up some biscuits."

"Already did that. The biscuits and sausages are staying warm in the oven." He turned around to pick up the frying pan by its wooden handle. "I'll put the eggs in there too, while we eat the breakfast I made for you."

"How did you whip up a meal so fast? It didn't take me that long to get dressed."

Those luscious lips of his curved into a sexy smirk. "I got up before you. The biscuits were cooking while we were in the shower."

I hadn't smelled them cooking, but then, I'd been a little distracted by hot shower sex.

"You didn't have to do that," I said. "But thank you, Val. I really appreciate it."

"Sit. *Café da manhã* will be served in a moment."

"The what now?"

He smiled and laughed. "*Café da manhã* is what Brazilians call breakfast. It literally means morning coffee. This is a special variation known as Café Colonial."

I waited on a stool across the island from him while he gathered the delicacies he'd already whipped up for a separate meal, this one exclusively for the two of us. My stomach growled. Loudly.

He grinned at me over his shoulder. "Hungry?"

"Sorry for the rude noises my body made. I'm starving, and the food smells soooo good."

"You can start with this." He reached into the oven and brought out a small basket overflowing with golden muffins, or maybe they were biscuits. He set the basket down in front of me. "*Pão de queijo*, or cheese bread. It's a Brazilian specialty made with Minas cheese from the southeastern part of Brazil."

"Is that near where you're from?"

"Further to the northeast." He retrieved two glasses from the refrigerator and set them down on the island. "I've noticed you don't drink coffee, so I made chocolate milk. I've never been a coffee drinker myself."

"Thank you."

"You're welcome, but I'm not done yet." He spun around, grabbed a bowl out of the fridge, and spun around again to plop it down in front of me. "Papaya and açaí."

I barely had time to notice the dark-purple berries nestled among the orange papaya slices before Val produced another basket of some type of bread from the oven and placed it in front of me.

"*Pão francês*. Literally, French roll." He gathered jars of jam and jelly from the fridge and placed them beside the rolls. "I've already buttered them."

The hunks of butter melting on the rolls had already clued me in to that fact.

"Looks yummy," I said, rubbing my palms. "May I dig in yet?"

"One last thing." He grabbed a plate off the counter which had been covered with a dish towel and put it in on the island. "*Cuca de banana*. That means banana cake. It has German origins and is something like streusel."

"German? I thought you were making me a Brazilian breakfast."

"I am. Brazil has a deep German connection." He eyed the items he'd laid out before me. "I don't normally eat this much for breakfast but being with you has given me a powerful appetite."

"Me too." I picked up a piece of cheese bread and plucked a sliver off it, chewing the bite before I spoke again. "Delicious. You're quite the cook."

"I had wanted to make more, but I didn't have time. Couldn't resist making love to you in the shower." He smirked. "Twice."

Making love. Until this morning, he'd called it fucking or ravishing me. Should I ascribe meaning to his change of phrasing? Probably not. Lots of people called it "making love" even when no love was involved.

I ate some of everything—most of everything, actually—because Val's cooking was incredible. I loved all the traditional dishes he'd made me, and I loved learning more about his homeland through those foods.

"Where did you get all the ingredients?" I asked. "The grocery store in town doesn't have Amazonian fruit or Brazilian cheese."

"I had them rushed here by overnight delivery."

"All the way from Brazil? That must've been expensive."

"You're worth it, and I can afford it."

I gnawed on my lip for a moment before deciding to just ask him. "Do you go all out for every woman you sleep with?"

"No." He picked at a hunk of cheese bread, peeking up at me with his head down. "Only for you."

His statement set my tummy to fluttering and gave me a strange glowy feeling behind my ribs. To avoid thinking about why, I redirected the conversation to general topics unlikely to lead to accidental intimacy.

After we'd finished our breakfast, Val tried to wash the dishes. I shooed him away. Since he'd made breakfast, for us and for the guests, I insisted on taking care of the cleanup.

Val insisted on drying the dishes. The man was incapable of not lending a hand.

While he was drying the last thing I'd washed, the frying pan, he peered out the window above the sink. His brows scrunched together, crinkling the spot above his nose.

"Are the Kittens prancing around naked out there?" I asked.

"No, it's not them."

"What's so fascinating, then?"

He tore his focus away from the window and set down the frying pan. "It's nothing."

Did he really think that would staunch my curiosity? I rose onto my tiptoes and peered out the window. My jaw dropped. Seriously. It dropped, possibly down to my belly button.

Out there on the lawn, my family was prancing around in the nude playing miniten with the Kittens and Ollie. My niece and nephew had kept their clothes on, but my parents and my brother and sister, along with their significant others, had stripped. They all seemed to be having a great time and seemed oblivious of their own nakedness, like they'd always been nudists.

I dropped back onto my soles on the cold, hard floor.

"Well," Val said, "it looks like your family has no problem with nudism."

Chapter Twenty

Val

Out here on the lawn, I watched Eve while she watched her family enjoying a friendly game of miniten while in the nude. How could I look at anything but her? The dress she wore, with its thin straps and above-the-knee hem, barely covered her curvy body. The way the fabric swished around her thighs whenever she moved had me fantasizing about whether she wore anything under it.

When she'd first seen her family through the kitchen window, her expression had gone from relaxed to abject shock in a millisecond. I'd never seen anyone look as stunned as she had been at that moment. She saw nudists every day and didn't bat an eye, but seeing her family jumping into the lifestyle left her speechless.

Literally. Eve had not spoken a word since she'd gotten her first glimpse of her family au naturel.

When she had wandered outside, I followed. We loitered at the edge of the lawn where a group of smiling, laughing people engaged in a game of batting a tennis ball back and forth over the net with the wooden thugs that covered their hands. I'd never played miniten, but observing a game made me want to try it.

"Let's join them," I said to Eve.

She jerked and veered her wide-eyed gaze to me. "What?"

"Relax," I said, laying a hand on her shoulder. "I meant let's join the game. You can keep your clothes on."

She did relax, a touch, and her eyes were no longer bulging. "I don't play miniten."

"Neither do I. But how hard can it be? Senior citizens are doing it."

"Miniten isn't usually so vigorous, which is why nudists like it. This group is really going for it, though."

On the playing field, Sylvester leaped up to smack the ball with his thug. His own balls flapped along with his dick. The tennis ball sailed over the net. Krista tried to hit it but missed, succeeding only in making her tits flap.

Eve twisted her mouth into a look of half embarrassment, half amusement. "I've never understood how nudist women can stand having their boobs flailing around like that. It hurts, you know? Unless you're flat-chested, it can be rather painful."

"Have you tried playing sports in the nude?"

"No, but I do occasionally go without underwear."

"I know, and I love when you do that." I slipped an arm around her shoulders. "Makes it easier for me to get you naked. Or to fuck you while you're dressed."

"You haven't done that yet."

She was right, I realized. I'd done pretty much everything else with her, but I hadn't pushed up her skirt and taken her that way.

I bent my head to whisper in her ear, "Are you wearing a bra and panties?"

Her lips kinked into a sexy, mysterious little smile as she angled her head to look at me. "Neither."

She trotted toward the miniten field, shooting me a grin over her shoulder. "Come on, Val. Let's play."

I ran after her.

We joined the Holt family's team, but that left the Kittens and Ollie with two less players than we had. Krista and Jeremy offered to defect to the other team to even things out. Despite her lack of undergarments, Eve played with as much enthusiasm as the Kittens. She jumped up to hit the ball, raced back and forth, and even spun around once to hit her final shot. It seemed like she'd executed that move strictly to show off.

The Holts won the game.

Well, the Holts and me.

"You're an honorary member of the family," Donna told me when I joked that I was the odd man out on this team. "Besides, you might be an official member soon enough."

Her mother's words made Eve stop blinking, though her eyes didn't widen like earlier. Her gaze swerved to me.

Official family member? That could mean only one thing. Donna Holt thought I might marry her daughter. The idea surprised me as much as it seemed to surprise Eve. The implication that her family might want me as an in-law floored me. I'd never met a woman's family before, but I'd always assumed if and when I did, I wouldn't receive a warm welcome. What parents would want their daughter to be involved with a notorious show-off?

My lifestyle and my choices had never bothered me before Eve. Now, I wished I hadn't done those reckless and rather narcissistic things to get attention and find a new career. I wished I'd been the kind of man with whom a woman like Eve might want a future.

I wasn't. I couldn't change that.

After another game of miniten, I led Eve away from the group. She slipped her hand into mine, threading our fingers. I loved the feel of her warm little hand wrapped around mine. I loved the soft smile on her lips too, and the matching softness in her eyes. We meandered around the guest house to the backside where no one ever seemed to go. The Kittens had set up their tents in the makeshift campground, a grassy area screened from our view by trees.

Eve glanced at the rolled-up yoga mat lying on the ground. "Somebody left their mat here. I'd better take it into the guest house and—"

"I put it there, *amorzinho*. For our private use."

"Our use? I thought you brought me back here to get it on, not do yoga."

"Both." I picked up the mat and unrolled it, laying it out on the grass. "I'm going to fuck you while we do yoga together."

Her eyes flashed wide for a heartbeat, but then a sexy smile curved her lips. "Nude erotic yoga? I've never tried that."

"Let's start with a warm-up...kiss."

I pulled her into my arms and kissed her, gently at first, relishing the taste of her while my cock stiffened and her nipples hardened against my chest with only the thin fabric of her dress separating us. I devoured her mouth like I was drunk on the flavor of her. And I was. I couldn't get enough of her lips, her slippery tongue, her breathless moans that I swallowed.

"Get rid of your dress," I murmured against her mouth.

She stepped back a few inches, just enough to let her whip the dress off over her head. It fluttered down to the ground beside the yoga mat.

I set my hands on her hips and backed her up until she stood on the mat. "Ready for a workout?"

Glancing around, she bit down on her lower lip. "What if someone sees us?"

"Everyone is on the lawn, on the other side of this building." I skated my hands down to cup her ass. "Let go, Eve. Let me have you here, now, please."

She hesitated for only a second. "Let's do it."

I moved behind her, my cock brushing her ass, and skimmed my hands up her sides. When I reached her arms, I used my hands to encourage her to lift them and join her palms above her head. "Do exactly what I say. I'm the teacher, you're the student seeking bliss."

"Val the yogi? Sounds like bliss to me." She craned her neck around to shoot me a saucy smirk. "Not sure this will be standard yoga, but I'm all in for whatever you've got in mind."

"Good." I gave her bottom a light slap. "Follow my instructions."

"Yes, sir."

I laid my palms over her joined hands and guided them down, past her face, to her chest. "Place your palms on your breasts with the nipples sticking out between your fingers."

She followed my command, smirking the whole time, the expression carving out dimples in her cheeks.

I placed my hands over hers and flicked my thumbs across her rosy nipples.

She sucked in a breath.

"Now spread your legs to hip width," I said, scraping my thumbnails back and forth over the rigid peaks of her breasts. "Are you wet?"

"Oh God, yes."

I glided my hands down to her belly and tugged her tight against my body so she could feel the hard line of my erection against her back. Her body felt so good, so warm and soft and tempting, that I couldn't resist rolling my hips into her, grinding my cock against her, while I slid my fingers between her folds. A deep groan vibrated my chest. "You're so fucking wet."

The sensation of her slick heat on my fingers amped up my lust, that slender thread of control fraying. I'd wanted to take my time, but this woman drove me out of my mind. She would do anything

I asked of her, anything, and never question it. Eve might've been straitlaced on the outside, but she had a deep, hot wild streak like no other woman I'd known.

"Downward dog," I said, my voice rough and low, strained by my need for her and only her. "Do it now."

She bent from the waist, planted her hands on the mat, and walked them forward until she'd stretched her body into an upside-down V.

A perfect downward-dog pose. Her luscious ass was in the air, her legs spread enough for me to do what I needed to do. To her. With her. Because of her.

I grasped her hips. "You are the sexiest woman alive, *amorzinho*. No other woman has ever made me come as hard as I do with you."

"Same for me. Sex with you is the best ever."

"Don't move." Before she could say anything, I pulled my hips back and thrust into her. "Hold the pose, and don't come until I tell you to."

A laugh sputtered out of her. "Not sure I have any control over that, especially with you."

I pinched her bottom, making her gasp. "Give it your best shot."

"Yes, sir."

Gripping her hips, I pumped into her in a steady rhythm, slow and easy, giving her time to adjust to the new position before I unleashed my lust on her. Holding back like this was maddening. I wanted to shove us both over the edge right now. More of her, I needed more of her, needed to go deeper, harder, faster, until her body clenched me and I erupted inside her. Somehow, I maintained the measured pace despite the intoxicating feel of her slick sheath around me. The pressure in my cock, the pressure to let go and come inside her sweet body, had me gritting my teeth.

She twisted her head around to look at me, desire tightening her features. "Forget yoga. I need to feel you come inside me right now. Please."

The huskiness of her plea snapped the slender thread of my willpower.

"Hold on," I growled as I lifted her legs and shuffled forward until she hung upside down with her hands flat on the ground and her legs bent. I slid my hands up to her ankles, one at a time. "Okay?"

"Yes. Do it."

I thrust into her, sinking deeper than ever inside her lush body, and paused there for a moment, letting myself fall into the pleasure of taking her. Then I plowed into her fast and hard, her cream making a sucking sound and my balls slapping on her skin, every movement rough and hungry. If my eyes had been open, they would've rolled back in my head from the indescribable pleasure of her body around me, so wet and warm and supple. When she came, I let out a strangled cry at the sensation of her sheath tightening around my cock and her body milking me. I threw my head back and punched into her even harder, twice more, spilling everything I had inside her depths.

"God, Evie." I lowered her feet to the mat, carefully, and hooked an arm around her waist to draw her up into a standing position. With her body plastered to mine, I wrapped both arms around her and rested my chin on her shoulder. "That was incredible. You are incredible, *amorzinho*."

"That was earth-shattering, I'd say." She wriggled around to face me, enfolding me in her arms, her cheek against my neck and her breaths tickling my skin. "What was that you called me? *Amorzinho?*"

"It means love or sweetheart." I kissed the top of her head. "You are sweet, and perfect, but you're also brave and wild and passionate. I love being the only one who sees this side of you."

Her fingers plunged into my hair while she whispered into my ear. "I love it too. And I love the way you keep calling me affectionate things in Portuguese."

"Can't help it. I feel affectionate toward you."

"Me too."

This time when I'd spent myself inside her, I had experienced more than a sexual release. Something inside me had let go too.

I held her for a long moment, caressing her silken hair.

She pulled her head back to look at me and smiled that sensual little smile. "Let's do more erotic yoga."

"Love to."

What we'd just done had been more than sex. We both knew it.

The sound of a car door slamming made us both freeze.

"What was that?" Eve asked. "There aren't supposed to be guests arriving or leaving today."

"I'll check. Wait here."

I trotted to the corner of the guest house and peered past it to the driveway.

Quentin Smith's truck was backing up, turning around at a dangerous speed. Gravel sprayed up when the vehicle rocketed down the driveway toward the road.

What the hell had Quentin been doing here?

Eve came up behind me, laying a hand on my shoulder. "What is it?"

"Your former handyman just left. Took off like he was running from an erupting volcano."

"He probably stopped by to pick up his last check."

I turned to face her. "I thought you mailed that to him."

"Planned to, but he called and said he'd pick it up. I told him not to." She pursed her lips. "He doesn't listen very well."

No kidding. The man heard only what he wanted to hear. He'd probably hoped to find Eve alone and try to wheedle his way back into her life.

"I left his check in an envelope taped to the door of the house," she said, linking her hands behind my nape. "He's gone. Let's get back to dirty yoga."

I grinned. "Lots more poses to try."

"Command me, oh wise and scorching-hot yogi master."

We both laughed.

After less than a week with Eve, I felt closer to her than I had with anyone else in my entire life. I might've dismissed it as nothing more than the thrill of tempting a straitlaced woman into doing things she'd sworn she would never do. Deep down, I realized what we'd done today had been more than a conquest. It had been more, period.

I had no idea what that meant.

Chapter Twenty-One

Eve

Val stayed, even after the Kittens left. The day before the girls took off in their RV, Val and I walked in on Ollie and Heidi kissing in the downstairs hallway of the guest house. Both of them blushed and stammered excuses they didn't need to make. Afterward, Val and I agreed that Ollie and Heidi made a cute couple and seemed perfect for each other. Later, Heidi confided in me that she had liked Ollie for a long time but thought he didn't like her. They were going to try a long-distance romance.

It was so sweet. They were so sweet. I loved seeing two of my favorite people find happiness together.

After the Kittens left, things quieted down. Some guests left, new ones arrived. The guest house stayed at full occupancy, thanks to the guys finishing the repairs to the water-damaged room. When they'd completed the job, Val sought me out to inform me it was done. He found me in the kitchen making lunch.

"The room is ready," he said, lingering by the door to the outside. "All the repairs are done, and no one will ever guess a pipe had burst in there."

"Great." I put a pan of muffins into the oven and shut the door, brushing my hands off on my apron. "It's a relief to have that fixed. Thank you for helping out."

He shrugged one shoulder. "We were all happy to pitch in."

The way he was loitering by the door made me wonder if he was anxious about something. When he began to shift his weight from foot to foot, I knew he was.

"What's wrong?" I asked, walking up to him.

"The room is ready." His mouth pinched at the corners the same way his eyes did. "The room meant for me."

"Originally meant for you."

"Yes." He scratched the back of his neck. "Should I…ah…move there?"

"What? No, of course not." I got anxious then, rubbing my arms. "Unless you'd be more comfortable there."

"I wouldn't." He pulled me into his body, dipping his head to nuzzle my nose. "I'm the most comfortable when I'm with you."

"Well then…" I looped my arms around his neck and tickled his nape. "Maybe you should sleep in my room from now on. It's silly for you to go back to your room after we have sex."

"Are you sure?"

"Positive. Are you okay with that?"

His lips eased into a grin. "Yes, Evie, I'd love to sleep with you every night."

"Good."

My heart did a little cartwheel every time he called me Evie.

Time zipped by. My family left after twelve days. Both my mom and my sister told me how much they loved Val and that we made a great couple. Even my dad and my brother liked Val. They saw through his infamous past and got to know the real man underneath, the good man who refused to let me handle chores on my own and who insisted on making me breakfast every morning.

He'd even started bringing me breakfast in bed.

During the day, in between prepping meals and otherwise taking care of the guests, we would head to the hot spring, take walks, go into town to buy supplies, or anything we felt like doing. We talked a lot too. I learned more about his childhood in Brazil and what it was like moving to America, first as a teenager and later as an adult. I told him all about my family, my childhood, everything and anything he wanted to know. Every time I did photo sessions for the guests, Val wanted me to take more portraits of him—in and out of clothes. He kept trying to convince me to pose while he took pictures of me. I kept saying no, mainly because he wanted naked pictures of me. Besides, though I was a photographer, I didn't like pictures of myself.

One afternoon, Val and the guests went on a nature hike. I bowed out since I had boring business stuff to do in my office, like the task of filing my quarterly taxes. Maybe I should've found it strange that I no longer thought of Val as a guest, but I'd stopped trying to rationalize everything. I enjoyed his company, and I hoped he'd stay for a good long while.

After I finished my taxes, I headed out across the lawn toward the main trail.

Feminine shrieks emanated from deeper in the woods.

I stopped at the trailhead and tilted my head to listen. Why were women screaming? Val had probably made an off-color joke or done something flamboyant like grabbing a Frisbee and leaping up to toss it high in the air and then catch it. He liked to show off his athletic prowess.

Footfalls pounded. Twigs cracked.

A large figure barreled toward me.

I ducked sideways right when Val rocketed out of the woods. He kept rocketing straight past me and onto the lawn. Gasping for breath, he stumbled to a halt and doubled over with his hands on his thighs.

"What's wrong?" I asked when I rushed over to him.

He held up a hand, one finger raised.

I waited while he caught his breath.

Guests meandered up the trail toward the lawn. Ollie, Ruth, and Sylvester approached me and Val while our newest guests, the young ladies who must've been the ones screaming, trotted off to the guest house. Their smiles and giggles suggested they hadn't been terrified when they shrieked.

"What happened?" I asked Ollie.

"Val should've listened. You and everybody else told him to use the bug spray. He said he didn't see bugs, so why did he need to spray chemicals all over himself?" Ollie shook his head at Val. "Humility, man. You've gotta have a little humility when you're a naturist out in the woods."

Sylvester snickered. "Ought to listen to your girlfriend too."

I realized with a start Sylvester meant me. Was I Val's girlfriend? Was he my boyfriend? I guessed those labels did apply to us. After all, we were essentially living together.

"The rest of us used the bug spray," Ollie said to me. "We only got a few bites."

"What was all the screaming?" I asked.

"Val started shouting and swatting at the air, then he took off down the trail like a rabid bull on a rampage."

The bull in question straightened and faced me.

And that's when I noticed the red marks all over his body.

I winced. "Oh honey, you ran into no-see-ums, didn't you?"

He nodded, looking miserable.

"Why didn't you use the insect repellent? I warned you about the no-see-ums."

"Didn't see any insects."

"That's why they're called *no*-see-ums."

He scratched at a swarm of bites on his chest. "Didn't hear them either."

I bracketed his face with my hands. "Poor Val. You're all bitten up. Don't worry, I'll take good care of you."

Ollie raised his hand. "I got a few bites. Do I get the Evie special treatment too?"

"Sorry, it's for ex-footballer guests only."

I shepherded Val back to the house and made him lie down on my bed on his back. It seemed like the no-see-ums had mainly bitten him on his front side. I snagged a bottle of calamine lotion, a box of cotton swabs, a pill bottle, and a glass of water from the bathroom. Thus armed, I straddled him on the bed.

"Take this," I said, holding out a pink pill and the glass of water.

He eyed the pill with suspicion. "What is it?"

"Don't trust me enough to take it no questions asked, hm? It's an antihistamine." I glanced at his bites. "Maybe you need two pills."

"One will do." He nabbed the pill and the glass, popped the pill into his mouth, and swigged the water. As he set the glass on the bedside table, he said, "Thank you for taking pity on me."

"It's not pity. I've been swarmed by no-see-ums. It's awful." I set to work daubing the lotion onto every single bite with the cotton swabs. "Besides, you're as pitiful and miserable as a lost puppy in the rain."

"Pitiful? The itching might drive me insane, but I am not a lost puppy."

"Relax. I wasn't insulting you. Your misery is cute."

"I'm glad my condition amuses you."

"Shush. I'm working here." I bent to kiss him. "Once I finish tending to your wounds, I'll distract you from your itching."

"How?"

"I was thinking a striptease might do the trick."

Despite his discomfort, he pulled off a naughty smile. "Yes, please."

"Followed by sex."

He grinned. "You're a genius, *meu amor*."

"I don't think they give out a Nobel Prize for sex."

"They should create one for you."

"Don't hold your breath for that one." I raised my brows. "What did you call me this time?"

He went stone-still, his eyes unblinking. After a few seconds, when I was about to check for a pulse, he relaxed and smiled. "Never mind."

I let him get away with that only because of his pitiful condition. And because I wasn't sure I wanted to hear the answer. We had developed some kind of bond between us, but we hadn't talked about it. I had no idea if all his endearments were nothing but smooth talk he used with all the ladies.

No, I didn't believe that.

And I was pretty sure whatever he'd said included the word love.

By the time I finished covering him with calamine lotion from head to toe, Val was gazing at me with sleepy eyes.

"Ready for a nap?" I asked.

"Yes. The antihistamine helps, but it's making me too groggy to enjoy a striptease."

"We'll do that later."

He patted the mattress beside him. "Lie down with me. Please."

I dutifully crawled onto the bed and stretched out alongside his body.

Raising one arm, he invited me to cuddle up to him.

How could I resist? He'd become as pink as a baby pig thanks to the calamine lotion, but I'd risk getting the stuff all over myself for the chance to cuddle with him. Tucked under his arm, I nestled my head into the hollow of his shoulder.

Five seconds later, he was snoring.

We never did get around to the striptease.

One afternoon about a week later, following a series of portrait sessions with guests, Val repeated a request he'd made several times before.

I had just taken the memory card out of my camera and was plugging it into my laptop to download the images.

He came up beside me—nude of course—and said, "Pose for me, Eve. Please. Keep your clothes on if you like, though I love your naked body. You have nothing to be ashamed of."

"Not ashamed."

"Why won't you explain to me why you won't pose for pictures?" He leaned against the wall, beside where my computer table butted up against it. "I keep asking, and you keep sidestepping."

"I know, I'm sorry." I scrubbed hands over my face, groaning. "Explaining the reasons why I don't want to pose might offend you, and the last thing I want to do is make you uncomfortable or unhappy."

When I glanced up at him, he was staring at me with a blank expression.

"See?" I said, dropping my forehead into my raised hand. "I've already hurt your feelings by saying I'm afraid I'll hurt your feelings."

"I'm not offended." He knelt beside my chair, peeling my hand away from my forehead. "I was surprised, that's all. But I love that you care about me, and I care about you the same way. You can tell me anything, Evie. Whether I like what you say or not, I will never lash out at you because of it."

"Yeah, I know that. I'm not good at sharing my feelings, though."

"Neither am I. We're learning together, aren't we?"

"Guess we are." I relaxed back into my chair. "I don't like pictures of myself. It's not that I'm ashamed of my body. You know I have zero problems with wearing short-shorts and tank tops and other skimpy stuff. I'm not comfortable in front of the camera, that's all."

"There's something else. I can tell."

I squirmed in my chair. "If I were to pose for you, what would you do with the pictures?"

"Nothing. They're yours."

"But you like to flaunt your nudity. I don't."

He studied me for a moment, his lips tightening. His lips curled into a little smile, and he shook his head. "I think I understand. I only publicize my own nudity. I would never share photos of you, in or out of clothes, without your explicit permission."

"Not worried you'll post naked pictures of me online. Your assistant leaked your sex tape. What if somebody leaks my photos this time?"

"I won't let that happen." He took my hands in his. "I care about you, and I will never let anyone hurt you. After my former assistant leaked the video, I not only fired him but also implemented new security measures. My phone can only be accessed with an iris scan, and my home computer requires a password." He grunted, one side of his mouth twisting into a sardonic expression. "My password used to be the word password followed by the number of my football jersey. Now, it's something no one will ever guess. Besides, like I keep telling you, I'm not demanding you pose nude. I would love to have a photo of you, that's all. You're beautiful, on the inside and the outside."

His words set off a lovely warmth in my chest that blossomed outward. He cared about me. He loved the way I looked no matter what I wore or didn't wear. In the three weeks that we'd known each other, he'd done nothing except protect my privacy and help me in any way I'd let him. Even that day at the hot spring when we'd made love in the water, he hadn't pressured me to undress. I'd done it because I wanted to do it.

I slanted in to touch my lips to his. "Okay. I'll pose for you."

"Thank you, Eve." He kissed my cheek. "You won't regret this."

"Can't regret anything we've done together." Rolling my chair back, I stood and picked up my camera, then offered it to him. "All yours."

He accepted the camera and rose, scrutinizing the various buttons and switches on it. "I've never used a high-end digital camera like this one."

"Don't worry, it's easy. I'll show you the ropes."

For the next ten minutes, I demonstrated the basics for him, and he mastered all of it right away. I tested the lighting by having him lie down on the crimson cushion. When I held the light meter near his hips, he smirked.

"Is it critical," he said, "to make sure my cock is properly lit?"

"Oh, absolutely." I withdrew the light meter. "Can't have your gorgeous dick hidden in shadows."

He lunged up to grab me around the waist and haul me down onto the cushion on top of him. "It's your turn in front of the camera."

"It'll be hard for you to photograph me while I'm lying on top of you."

"You're right, though I hate to give up fondling you." To prove he meant that, he cupped my bottom with both hands. "But I suppose I must."

He rolled us over and hopped to his feet.

I tossed him the light meter.

Catching it, he headed for the table where I'd set down the camera.

While he had his back turned, I got ready for my photo session.

Val, camera in hand, turned to face me. He stared at me for a moment, but then his mouth stretched into a grin. "Evie, you saucy little vixen. After everything you said—"

"What you said changed my mind." I stretched my arms above my head, petting the crimson cushion, and bent one knee. The velvet felt divine against my naked skin. "How's this pose?"

"Perfect." He raised the camera and began snapping pictures. "You are the most beautiful woman in the world. Your body deserves to be captured on digital film for posterity. In fact, I might call the Louvre to offer them the modern masterpiece that is Eve Holt."

He paused in his picture-taking to wink at me.

"Very funny," I said, rolling onto my stomach, propped up on my elbows. "I know you won't really do that. But if you should plaster my nakedness all over the Internet, I'll show everyone the picture I took yesterday."

"What picture is that?"

"You tripping over a twig, about to fall flat on your face. Your mouth was wide open, and I think your tongue was sticking out."

"Do you honestly think I'd be embarrassed?" He dropped to his knees three feet from the cushion where I lay. "You know me better than that."

"I do. And I love your complete lack of shame."

He set down the camera and crawled toward me, stopping at the cushion's edge. "I don't expect you to be shameless like me, and I'm not sure I'd want you to be. I want you exactly the way you are."

"That's the nicest thing any man has ever said to me." I plunged a hand into his hair, pulling him closer. "I want you just the way you are too, sex tapes and all."

"Just so you know, I deleted the sex tape from my phone two days after we met."

"Why would you do that?"

"For you, Eve. I don't need a memento of my liaison with another woman."

"Glad to hear it."

I drew his head closer until our lips met.

He fell onto the cushion, half on top of me, braced on his elbows. The kiss deepened swiftly, hot and sensual and imbued with more emotion than any of our previous kisses. I latched my arms around him, spreading my legs. I was all but begging him to take me, and I felt no shame at all about it.

"My camera takes video too," I mumbled against his lips.

Val pulled his head back. "No, Eve, I don't want to tape us. What happens between you and me is strictly private. I don't want to share our intimate moments with the world, and I don't need a replay to remind me of how much I love being with you."

"I love being with you too."

We made love right there on the crimson cushion, like we had started to do the first time he had posed for me. After that, he insisted I let him take more pictures of me—and he insisted I wear clothes. He told me he wanted a picture to put in his wallet and one to have as his wallpaper on his phone. I took pictures of him with clothes on too, for the same reasons. By the end of the day, we had both changed our phones to display the photos we'd taken of each other.

That night, while I slept with Val's body spooning mine, questions niggled at me. Was I in love with him? Was he in love with me? The most important question kept me awake until after midnight.

Could we, two opposite types of people from two different worlds, really work out in the long run?

Chapter Twenty-Two

Val

The day that marked one month since I'd arrived at Eve's place fell on a Saturday. I had plans to celebrate the date with a date—a real one this time. Dinner in the nude while seated at the kitchen island didn't count. Dinner under the stars on a picnic blanket on the lawn, also in the nude, didn't count either. I wanted a genuine, fully clothed date with her.

I wanted to romance the hell out of Eve Holt.

Since I'd never in my life tried to impress a woman this way, I resorted to calling my sister Maria. After the usual greeting and pleasantries, I got to the point. "I want to ask Eve out on a date, the kind that takes place in a restaurant and involves nice clothes. How do I do that?"

Maria laughed. "*Como*? I must have misheard. You couldn't have said Val Silva finally wants to ask a woman on a date."

I growled under my breath. "That's what I said."

She laughed harder. " *Ó pá*! It only took you thirty-seven years."

My whole family spoke Portuguese, of course, but both of my sisters spoke English as fluently as I did. We often conversed in that language since I'd gotten accustomed to it over the years. Our mother liked English too because it was her native tongue. Sometimes we reverted to Portuguese, particularly if Maria or Aline wanted to scold me or mock me.

"I'm asking for your help," I said. "Will you stop laughing at me and tell me what to do?"

"My big brother needs my help. Give me a moment to enjoy this."

Another, louder growl rumbled out of me. "Forget it. I'll call Aline."

"*Porque?* Aline knows nothing about dating. She married the first boy who asked her to a dance." Maria paused, no doubt for dramatic effect. "Here's what you need to do. Are you listening? Write this down so you don't forget."

"Get on with it."

"Speak these precise words. Eve, will you please go on a date with me?"

My sister burst into laughter again.

"Thank you, Maria. I'm glad my anxiety entertains you."

Her laughter faded away. "You really are anxious about this, aren't you? This woman must mean a lot to you."

"She does."

"Go with your heart and be yourself. She must like you the way you are, eh?"

"I think so." Though Eve had her doubts about my past behavior, I believed she accepted me the way I was. She'd told me as much, but still… "What if being myself offends her?"

"Then she's not the woman for you."

She was the woman for me. I'd known it for a while. Whether I could be the kind of man she needed remained to be seen. I'd try as hard as I could to become that kind of man.

Maria and I talked a bit longer, mostly about our family and what everyone had been doing since the last time we'd spoken. After we said goodbye, I wandered through the house until I found Eve in the living room, sitting in an armchair. She had her legs crossed with her feet on a footstool, and her laptop was balanced on one thigh. Shorts and a tank top concealed only the most private parts of her body. The parts she saved for me alone.

The light of the sinking sun bathed her in a golden, pinkish glow.

When I walked into the room, she smiled. "Hey, gorgeous. Were you on the phone? I heard you talking."

"I called my sister Maria."

Eve angled her head to the side like she was analyzing me. "What's wrong? You look nervous, which isn't like you at all."

She was right. I felt nervous, and that was a rare experience for me.

I perched on the edge of her footstool with her bare feet nudging my ass. "I need to ask you a question."

Clapping her laptop shut, she set it on the table beside her chair. "Shoot."

My pulse throbbed faster, thumping in my ears. I scratched my head, fidgeted, and avoided looking her in the eye. Maria would've found this highly amusing. I wanted to grab the nearest blunt object and hit myself in the head with the thing. *Snap out of it*, I commanded myself.

For the first time ever, I had clammy palms because of a woman.

I cleared my throat. "Eve, I was thinking about what we should do for dinner tonight."

"This is Chinese night, remember? I placed an order already."

"For the guests." I fidgeted again. "For us, I wanted to, uh, make some kind of, um, special arrangements."

"Special?" Her eyebrows cinched together over her nose. "Like what?"

Be yourself, Maria had advised.

Eve liked me the way I was. Right?

She poked me with her big toe. "What's the matter? Did Ollie beat you at soccer? Sorry, I meant to say football."

"I didn't play a game with Ollie today." I took a deep breath, straightened, and met her glittering blue gaze. "*Como vai, gatinha?*"

"Huh?"

"It's Portuguese."

"What does it mean?"

"The phrase is a Brazilian pickup line." I angled in and laid a hand on her bare thigh. "How's it going, baby? That's what it means."

She laughed. "That's your great pickup line? How did you ever become a ladies' man with material like that?"

"It's all in the delivery. *Gatinha* literally means kitten."

Her laughter bubbled out again, light and musical. "Kitten? You should try that line on Heidi and her gal pals."

Making her laugh had relaxed us both, so I forged ahead. "Will you go out on a date with me, Eve? In our clothes, at a restaurant, the right way."

Her cheeks dimpled with a lovely little smile. "Yes, Val, I will go out to dinner with you."

"Wear something nice. I want this to be a formal date."

Those dimples got deeper. "I don't have much in the way of fancy clothes, but I'll do my best."

"Anything you wear will be perfect." I skimmed my gaze up and down her delicious body. "But you do look best in nothing at all."

"Same goes for you."

We ambled through the house hand in hand, splitting off in the hallway so I could go into my room and she could go into hers. Though I slept with her every night, I'd kept my things in the other room to avoid cluttering up her space. Ten minutes later, I was ready. When I knocked on Eve's door, she told me to "go away, please" because "a woman needs more than ten minutes to get beautiful." I considered reminding her she was always beautiful, with or without prep time, but I had the feeling she was as nervous about our date as I was.

I waited in the kitchen, perched on a stool, my foot tapping a fast rhythm on the floor. My gaze stayed glued to the clock on the microwave.

Fifteen minutes later, Eve swept into the room.

And my heart stuttered.

I couldn't move or speak. Her dress, a rich shade of sapphire blue, draped over her curves like it had been made for her body and only her body. The off-the-shoulder design showcased her beautiful shoulders, and the neckline plunged low enough to show off the slopes of her breasts. The flowing skirt dropped almost to her ankles, but one side featured a slit that exposed most of her thigh. Her elegant dress sandals each had a single strap over her toes and another that encircled her ankle. Their blue color matched her dress.

Her hair cascaded over her shoulders in lush waves, and her makeup accentuated her beauty rather than overpowering it.

She was stunning.

Those bright-blue eyes found me and flew wide for a second, then her lips curved into a satisfied smile. "I prefer you naked, but that suit is really doing it for me."

I glanced down at my gray suit. "I've had this for years. It's not even designer."

"Who cares?" She sashayed up to me, her hips swaying, and spread her palms over my chest. "It's damn hot. That's all that matters."

"Glad you like it."

"I'd rip this suit off you right now, but I'm looking forward to our date."

"So am I." Peeling her hands off my chest, I clasped one and guided her toward the door. "Let's go. It's time to romance you, Eve."

Her dimples returned. "I like the sound of that."

Chapter Twenty-Three

Eve

When was the last time I'd had a real date? Years, for sure. I couldn't remember exactly. Once I'd started my business, it had consumed the majority of my time. The word vacation had no meaning for me anymore. Time off consisted of kicking back in front of the TV to binge-watch all the buzzworthy shows I'd missed because I was working seven days a week.

Val took me to the nicest restaurant in town, a steak house. Despite its designation, the place offered a superb atmosphere and superb food as well as live music and a dance floor. Val pulled my chair out for me and pushed it back in once I'd sat down, the way I'd seen men do in movies but had never experienced before in real life.

Oh, that suit. I loved it. As in "I want to tear your clothes off with my teeth, Val." The gray color suited him, and the fit highlighted every one of those muscles I adored. Why had I agreed to a clothing-on date? I wanted him naked this instant.

The restaurant probably didn't allow nudism. Damn.

Val ordered a huge T-bone while I ordered the filet mignon. My choice seemed to surprise him, given the way his brows shot up. Once the waitress had taken our orders and left, he rested his elbows on the table and studied me.

"What is it?" I asked. "Do I have something stuck in my teeth?"

"No. But you are the only woman I've ever met who would eat a steak dinner in my presence. Or eat much of anything."

"If that surprises you, be prepared for a real shocker when you see me eat it."

"Yes, I know how you eat with gusto. I love that about you."

"Can't help it. I love food." I unfolded my napkin and placed it on my lap. "I don't eat steak often, so it's a treat for me. That means I will devour it."

"I have firsthand experience with the way you devour something you're craving."

"Even filet mignon can't compare to the flavor of you."

He reached across the table to grasp my hand. "You are a one-of-a-kind woman, Eve. Meeting you is the best thing that's ever happened to me."

My cheeks grew warm. "You sure know how to compliment a girl."

"It's the truth. You've changed my life."

Though I tried to speak, whatever words I'd meant to say got stuck in my throat. My cheeks flamed, but it was the fluttery sensation in my chest that rendered me speechless.

His thumb caressed the back of my hand, and his tender gaze was focused exclusively on me.

"You've changed my life too," I said when I finally regained the ability to speak.

And it was true. Before Val, I would never have taken time to relax in the middle of the day, much less taken my clothes off outdoors. His shamelessness encouraged me to stop worrying about what people thought of me. The only opinion that really mattered to me these days was his.

The waitress arrived with our drinks, interrupting our moment.

Val withdrew his hand and sat back in his chair.

I wanted to crawl onto his lap and cuddle up there.

We talked about everyday things while we ate our meal. Val smiled every time I shoved a chunk of steak into my mouth and moaned with satisfaction. For dessert, we ordered the darkest, most sinful chocolate cake I'd ever tasted. When I moaned at the deliciousness of it, Val's smile turned hot and hungry.

I'd expected he would whisk me home immediately after dinner, but he surprised me again.

He stood and offered me his hand. "A dance, Eve?"

A few couples occupied the dance floor, swaying to the romantic melody played by a piano and a string quartet.

I placed my hand in Val's.

He led me onto the floor, raised our joined hands, and placed his other palm on my back.

And we danced.

With our bodies barely touching, his hands provided the most solid link between us. No, that wasn't right. Something else, something far less tangible, provided the strongest link. I rested my cheek on his chest and let him sweep me around the dance floor. The music seemed like a waltz, and we moved in time with the rhythm, round and round, my dress swishing around our legs and his hand on my back anchoring me to him. He smelled so good, like woods and spice and man.

I lifted my head to gaze up at him.

He kissed my forehead.

My pulse accelerated. A delicious tingle swept over my skin, chased by a warmth that originated in my chest and bloomed outward to suffuse my entire body, my entire being.

Once the song ended, we headed back to our table to pay the bill. I offered to pay half, but Val shook his head.

"No, Evie," he said. "A gentleman always pays for dinner."

"What if I invited you? I should pay then."

"Maybe, but you didn't invite me. I asked you out."

We made it to the car before we lost control. I started it, climbing onto his lap in the driver's seat and kissing him like a sex-starved nympho. His hands whisked up under my dress, and he pulled his head back to arch his brows at me.

I shrugged. I hadn't worn any underwear.

He made love to me right there in the parking lot. We took it slow, every stroke of his cock lush and intoxicating. I gripped his shoulders, and when I came, it hit me so hard I jerked into the steering wheel.

The horn blared.

Val punched into me one last time, choking back a shout.

I wrapped my arms around him, breathing too heavily to speak, with his semi-firm shaft still inside me. He kissed my throat and worked his way up to my jaw, and finally, to my mouth. I couldn't respond at all, too stunned by the pleasure he always gave me and by the fact I'd had sex in a car for the first time ever. Sex in the parking lot of the most popular restaurant in town. Where anyone might've seen us. Maybe that should've embarrassed me, but I realized it didn't. Nothing much embarrassed me anymore, not since Val.

We drove home and rushed into my bedroom, our clothes gone by the time we got there, and made love again with the same leisurely pace, like we both needed to memorize every sensation. I'd never felt more connected to anyone, or more at ease and fulfilled. Afterward, he pulled the covers over us and hugged me to his side. We fell asleep that way, contented and spent.

Our first date had been bliss

Chapter Twenty-Four

Val

Ilay on a lawn chaise soaking up the sunshine, my eyes closed behind my Ray-Bans. The noises of the guests playing badminton reminded me of my first day here. Back then, the guests had been playing miniten, but the sounds were similar. Eve had greeted me at the gate on that day, and I'd been smitten from the first second I'd seen her. She was more than beautiful. She was smart, accomplished, determined, and beloved by all her guests. Even the new ones took to Eve as soon as they met her. She worked hard to ensure the guests had everything they needed, and she made a concerted effort to socialize with them too.

Three days had gone by since our first date, but I'd been here for over a month. I no longer thought of myself as a guest. Neither did Eve. She kept talking about "the guests" but not including me in that designation. I wanted to take her on another date, but I had no idea how to top our evening at the steak house. Dinner, dancing, and sex in the parking lot. That was hard to outdo.

"Shit!"

The hissed curse from nearby made me open my eyes and glance toward Ollie, who lay on another chaise a few yards away. He had been reading a paperback. Now, he held the book over his groin, his cheeks red, and darted his gaze around as if making sure no one was looking.

"What's wrong?" I asked, praying it wasn't no-see-ums again. I'd needed seven days to get over that episode—seven days of

Eve tending to me, but still, I had no desire to repeat the experience.

Ollie eyed me sideways. "I, uh, have a little problem."

He shifted in his chair, squinting his entire face and taking great care to keep the paperback positioned over his groin.

"It's embarrassing," Ollie muttered out of one corner of his mouth.

Ahhh, I finally understood. Every nudist male had the same problem once in a while, though not often. I grabbed my towel off the grass and tossed it to Ollie. "Here. This ought to help."

He caught the towel but didn't use it. Squinting his face even more, he said, "This won't help. The problem is too...big."

I flattened my lips to suppress a laugh. "You're a nudist, Ollie. These things aren't shocking to the rest of us, so it shouldn't bother you. Roll onto your side for a bit or go walk it off."

"Don't think that will help. This isn't the usual kind of problem."

Since I could see the tip of his dick sticking out from under the paperback, I decided he wasn't exaggerating. "What precipitated the problem?"

He tipped his head in the direction of the badminton game.

I glanced there and spotted our newest guests having a good time whacking the ball around with some of the older guests. Kelly and her husband Todd, newlyweds on their honeymoon, had arrived yesterday. Kelly was very sexy, though she couldn't compare to Eve. Still, every time Kelly jumped to hit the ball, her breasts bounced. Every time she scored a point, she did a little victory dance with her knees bent, pumping her fists in the air in time with the thrusts of her hips. The young woman didn't mean it in a sexual way. She was having fun. But her dancing exposed the area between her thighs.

Well, I did see Ollie's dilemma. What man wanted a beautiful woman to see him in that unfortunate state, especially with her husband watching? Ollie couldn't help it, and I sympathized with his plight.

Not that I had ever been embarrassed about such a thing.

Ollie's gaze flicked toward Eve's house. His eyes bulged right before he squeezed them shut. "Oh fuck. Kill me now."

I glanced back.

Eve was moseying toward us wearing her favorite short-shorts and tank top with a pair of flip-flops. She smiled and waved at Ollie before aiming her brightest smile at me. Eve blew me a kiss.

Ollie moaned pitifully and sank down in his chair.

"Put the towel over yourself," I told him, "then lay the book on top of that."

He straightened somewhat and followed my advice.

Eve reached us as Ollie got himself covered. She ruffled my hair. "Scoot over."

I scooted, and she squeezed in beside me.

"This is a serious etiquette breach," I said, pretending to be offended. "Physical contact? Shame on you, Evie."

"This is our resort, and we can do whatever the hell we want." She wriggled to get in a better position. "Besides, I am showing incredible restraint by not copping a feel."

"I stand corrected. You are behaving admirably."

Kelly scored another point and did her inadvertently erotic dance.

Ollie moaned, shaking his head and squeezing his eyes shut again. He ran a hand over his mouth, sat up, and announced, "I'm going for a walk."

"We'll go with you," Eve said.

Ollie's eyes bulged again.

She tried to get up, but I slung an arm around her waist to hold her in place.

Eve glanced at me. "What are you doing?"

"I…" How to explain this without embarrassing Ollie further? I patted her hip. "I'm too comfortable here. Let's stay put and talk about what our next date should be."

She relaxed and cuddled up against me again. "Sure, let's do that."

Ollie looked so relieved I almost thought he might collapse. Eve didn't notice because she had aimed her adoring gaze at me.

Rolling onto his side away from us, Ollie dropped his book and got up while holding the towel in front of him. He hustled off toward the nature trail.

By the time he'd disappeared into the woods, Eve's expression had turned expectant. "What will our next date be? When will it be? I'm liking the romantic treatment."

"Hasn't fucking been romantic?"

"Sure, but it was nice to go out to dinner. And I loved seeing you in a suit."

"But you tore it off me the second we got home."

"I loved doing that too."

"You were stunning in that dress." I stealthily palmed her breast with the arm I had draped over her shoulders, making sure no one else would see it. "But I loved taking it off of your body."

She drew figure eights on my chest with her finger. "You know, I still haven't given you that striptease I promised you after the no-see-um attack."

My cock woke up at her suggestion, and I was on the verge of developing a stiffer problem than Ollie had. "Let's go in the house and do that right now."

A scream reverberated through the clearing around the lawn and the buildings.

Eve jumped out of the chaise at the instant another scream echoed from the nature trail.

I leaped up too. We both stared in the direction of the nature trail, the apparent origin of the outbursts. The screams hadn't been pitched high enough to be a woman. It must've been a man.

"What the hell?" Eve said, squinting to peer down the trail.

Ollie barreled out of the woods, without his towel, flapping his arms in the air and screaming again. "Run! It's after me! Shiiiiiiiit!"

The guests playing badminton froze, their gazes swiveling to Ollie.

He got halfway to Eve and me before we saw the thing that was after him.

A porcupine hustled out of the woods, quills raised, making a beeline for Ollie.

"Shiiiiiiit!" he hollered again.

Eve rushed toward one of the guests, grabbed the gray-haired woman's badminton racket, and bolted toward the onrushing porcupine.

Well, if you could call what the creature was doing "onrushing." Though he moved fast for such a large, bulky creature, he was in no danger of catching up to Ollie.

I hurried after Eve, but she didn't need my help.

Eve stopped, planted her feet wide, and swung the racket in the direction of the porcupine. She snarled and shouted and stomped one foot, all while brandishing the racket in sharp, whooshing swings.

The porcupine turned around and hustled back down the nature trail.

Ollie fell to his knees, breathing hard and red-faced. He collapsed onto his side on the ground and rolled onto his back spread-eagled. "I think I'm dead. That bright light must be heaven."

Eve approached him, thumping the racket on her palm. "That's the sun, Ollie. You're not dead, though you sure made an unholy ruckus. What happened?"

He shut his eyes. "I was walking down the trail, kind of distracted and not paying attention to where I was going." He opened one eye to peek at me and winced. "I was looking down, and I sort of stumbled into the porky. He wasn't happy about it."

"Why on earth were you staring at the ground?" Eve said. "You know better than that. Keeping an eye on your surroundings is critical in the woods."

"I was—" He flushed even redder, almost crimson, and couldn't quite look at Eve. "I had a problem and needed some alone time."

"But why—"

"Give him a break," I said to Eve. "He's embarrassed enough as it is."

She glanced at me as I came up beside her. "You know what his secret problem was, don't you?"

"Yes, but I'm not going to tell you. It's one of those secrets between men."

Ollie nodded solemnly. "Thanks, man."

Eve's mouth twisted into a half frown. "Manly secrets? What does that mean?"

"It's the bro code," Ollie said. "Don't mess with it, okay?"

Her attention flickered between me and Ollie for a moment before she gave up and shrugged. "Whatever. I guess the secrets of man are not for woman to comprehend."

Ollie pushed up into a sitting position. "Think I'll go take a nap. Getting chased by a crazy porcupine took a lot out of me." He exhaled, his shoulders sagging. "I'm having one crap day."

Eve watched him while he got to his feet. "Did something else happen? I mean, besides the porcupine and your secret manly problem."

He ran a hand over his cheek. "I got an email from Heidi. She's back with her ex."

"Poor Ollie." Eve wrapped her arms around him. "I'm so sorry."

Ollie grimaced.

I decided he was concerned about a recurrence of his manly problem, so I dragged Eve away from him. "Let's go do that private thing we talked about earlier."

She grinned. "Yes, let's."

While Ollie shuffled off toward the guest house, Eve and I headed into our house. Yes, I'd started to think of it as "our" house, which didn't bother me the way it might have a few weeks ago. We were living together after all.

And I liked it.

Chapter Twenty-Five

Eve

My clothes lay here, there, and everywhere in the bedroom. I'd tossed them away without a thought for where they might land, more concerned with getting Val hot and bothered with my striptease. Not that it took much to get Val in the upright position for takeoff. Sometimes all I needed to do was wink at him. His easygoing nature did not extend to our intimate times. He could be tender, sure, but he could also become the most scorching, inventive, and energetic lover.

That explained why I was currently lying half on top of him, my cheek on his chest, lazing in the afterglow of sweaty, mind-blowing sex.

I pushed up on one elbow to admire the tattoos on his arm and chest. The dragon that snaked down his biceps had intrigued me since the day we met, but I'd never quite gotten around to asking about it. I traced the tattoo's lines with my fingertip.

"Does this dragon have some meaning?" I asked.

"The design is inspired by Amaru, the winged serpent of Tiwanaku, but it's a stylized version." He took hold of my finger, dragging it along the tattoo while he explained. "It has the body of an anaconda and the head of a bird. Amaru represents the power of nature, and to the Incas, it became a protective deity. No one knows what the people of Tiwanaku thought of Amaru, since their civilization died out many thousands of years ago. Tiwanaku is in the mountains of Bolivia."

"Wow, you're a history buff. I learn something new about you every day." I tickled his skin with the finger he still held. "Your love of ancient mythology is wicked sexy."

"I also know about legends of Brazil. Would it turn you on to hear about those?"

"Absolutely." I wriggled my finger free of his grasp. "Does touching your tattoo give me magical powers?"

"You don't need magic to entrance me."

I bent to lave my tongue over the lines of his tattoo, beginning with the tail and gliding my way up to the wings and the head.

He sucked in a breath.

I swirled my tongue around the dragon's head.

Val dived a hand into my hair, cradling my head, halting my exploration. "Don't awaken the beast unless you want to be devoured."

"As much as I'd love that, I should check on the guests." I hopped off the bed and started collecting my clothes. "I need to cheer up Ollie. He's really bummed about Heidi."

"What are you going to do? He has a broken heart, but it will heal."

"I should do something." While I pulled on my panties, I mulled the problem. By the time I got my bra on, no ideas had come to me. I paused, hands on my hips. "How does a woman console a man she's not sleeping with? I mean, I know how to make you feel better, but a blow job doesn't seem appropriate for Ollie."

"While I'm sure he would love that, I'd rather you didn't."

Tugging on my shorts, I pretended to be confused. "Really? And I thought you were such a bohemian."

He sat up and shimmied to the foot of the bed, reaching out to grasp the waistband of my shorts and pull me toward him. "I'm an exhibitionist, remember? Never claimed to be a bohemian. I'd share my sunscreen with Ollie, but I won't share you with anyone."

"I won't share you either."

"Good." He placed his open mouth over my belly button and swirled his tongue inside it. "Sharing is overrated."

"Have you ever done a threesome?"

"Twice. I prefer to have one woman all to myself."

"I do love your one-track mind."

Those lips traveled higher while his hands slid down my thighs. "How can I think of anything else when I'm with you?"

A breathy moan whispered out of me, but I gathered what little willpower I had left after spending more than a month with him and backed away. I wagged a finger at him. "No more sex. Not until after dinner. Well, maybe mid-afternoon. Oh, just let me talk to Ollie and then you and I can get back to getting it on."

Val laughed. "That's my insatiable girl."

"Me?" I shook my head at him. "You are the one who drags me into the woods for quickies, and drags me behind buildings for quickies, and—"

"I confess to the crime of being addicted to you, Evie." He held out his hands, wrists together. "Lock me up in your dungeon. I hope it's a life sentence."

Those two words stopped me. Life sentence. He'd been joking of course, but the term implied he wanted to stay with me for good. Or maybe he expected me to go to LA with him.

Did I want to go with him? What would I give up to have him in my life for good?

To avoid thinking about that, I finished getting dressed, kissed Val on the cheek, and hustled out of the house to find Ollie. He was nowhere in the guest house or on the lawn. I ran into Ruth and Sylvester, who were relaxing in chaises.

"Have you seen Ollie?" I asked them.

"Yeah," Sly said. "He went down the nature trail again, this time wearing clothes and holding on to a badminton racket."

"That dear, dear boy," Ruth said. "How could Heidi break his heart? She's such a sweet child. This doesn't seem like her at all."

"We don't have to hate Heidi because she dumped Ollie," I said. "Sometimes things don't work out between two people. I'm sure Heidi didn't mean to hurt him."

Part of me wanted to be angry with Heidi, the protective part of me that thought of Ollie as a little brother. Mostly, I wanted them both to be happy. Too bad that hadn't happened for them as a couple.

"Don't forget," Sly said. "Ruth and I are leaving tomorrow."

"Yeah, I know. I'll miss you guys."

Ruth leaned forward to clasp my hand. "We'll miss you too, Evie, but we'll be back for the fall color."

Sylvester chortled. "Maybe we should build our own little bungalow in the woods and live here. Sure would save us the trouble of driving or flying here."

His wife tsked. "You'd miss the alligators and the early-bird specials."

Yeah, they lived in Florida. Alligators were one reason I would never move there.

I chatted a little more with Ruth and Sylvester before I headed down the nature trail in search of Ollie. I found him at the hot spring. He was sitting on one of the benches, his gaze aimed straight ahead though his focus seemed to have retreated into a distance only he could see. His hair was wet, but his clothes were dry. Rather than looking melancholy, he seemed relaxed and content.

I sat down beside him and patted his leg. "Hey, Ollie."

"Hey, Eve." He turned his face toward me and smiled a little. "If you're worried I might drown myself in the hot spring, you can relax. I'm okay."

"Are you sure? Getting dumped sucks."

"Yeah, it does." He braced his elbows on his thighs. "I should've known better. Heidi and her boyfriend were always breaking up and getting back together. Being the rebound guy is never a good idea."

"No, I guess not. I still feel bad for you."

"Don't. I'm fine, really." He waved one finger toward the water. "Took a dip in the hot spring, did a lot of thinking, and realized I'm not as bummed as I thought. Sure, I like Heidi. We don't know each other that well, so what I was feeling was only a crush."

I bent forward too and rested my cheek on his arm. "I'm still sorry. You deserve to find a woman who appreciates you."

"Heidi dumping me wasn't what really bothered me." He frowned at the ground. "I got laid off."

"What?" I sprang upright and scrutinized him for a moment until the shock of his statement waned. "That's awful. When did it happen?"

"A week before I came here. That's why I wanted to extend my stay from two weeks to six weeks." He ran a hand over his mouth and sighed. "Thought I'd feel better if I got away from home. It didn't work. Knowing I have to go back there and look for another job... Man, that sucks way worse than Heidi dumping me."

"Wish I could help you out somehow." I got an idea and leaped to my feet. I grabbed Ollie's hand and tugged. "Come on."

He eyed me with suspicion. "What are you up to, Evie?"

"Let's canvas the guests for ideas on how to get you re-employed."

"Oh no, come on." He made a pained face, his voice evincing the faintest whine. "I don't want pity from the other nudists."

"Don't you mean naturists?"

His lips tightened into a smile he was trying to suppress. "Yeah. I still don't see how the other naturists can help."

"Won't know unless we ask."

For the next half hour, Ollie and I talked to everyone—except Val, who had sequestered himself in the spare bedroom claiming to have "important phone calls" to make. Everybody had an idea for Ollie, though none seemed quite right for him. He wrote down everything they said, accepted business cards from those who offered him one, and thanked each and every person who gave advice.

By the time I returned to the house, Val was in the kitchen. He perched on a stool at the island.

"I've been waiting for you," he said when I walked into the house.

Despite being naked, he managed to look serious. Not suicidal serious, but rather, contemplative serious.

"What's up?" I asked as I parked my butt on the stool beside his. We faced each other, our knees inches apart.

"I have a proposition for you."

"Don't you think it's a bit soon for a proposal?"

He rolled his eyes. "Not that kind of proposition. What I'm offering is a business proposal."

"Okay," I said cautiously. Whatever he was up to, I hoped it didn't involve a massive grant from the private foundation he'd spent the last few hours setting up for this purpose.

Val slanted toward me, his gaze intent on mine. "I want to be your business partner."

"Business?" I searched his face for some sign it was a joke, but he still looked serious. "Partner? Do you mean, like, an official partner? I have an LLC, you know."

"Yes, I know. I want to buy into it and become a full-fledged partner."

My mind seemed to have screeched to a halt. I couldn't form thoughts, much less words. When I managed to speak, I babbled and even laughed nervously while I did it. "My company is a single-member LLC. I'd have to, uh, redo it somehow. I mean, a partnership LLC is different and— Are you sure about this? I've made some strides with the business, but you might lose your shirt."

He smiled. "I lost my shirt years ago. Best decision I ever made."

"You know what I mean." I wrung my hands and bit the inside of my lip. "Risking my own money is one thing. Risking yours… If I bankrupted you, I'd feel awful."

"I wouldn't enjoy bankruptcy either, but I want to do this." He slanted in more, his gaze aimed straight into mine. "For you, I'll take any risk."

A rock hardened in my throat, its edges sharp and rough. Take a risk with Val? I'd done that already, several times over, and it had been the best thing I'd ever done. But personal risks were a whole other thing from professional ones. I might bankrupt us both, and we'd wind up living in a tent in the state forest.

I hadn't worried about losing everything until he'd announced he wanted to be my business partner.

"Trust me," he said, his tone as earnest as the look on his face. "I know the risks, and I want to take them with you."

"What about your modeling career? Your life in LA?"

"I've had enough of that. Earlier, I called my agent and gave her the news. I'm retiring from modeling. After that, I called a real estate agent and put my house up for sale."

My mouth dropped open. "Why would you uproot your whole life?"

"Come on, it can't be that hard to understand." He cupped my face in both his hands. "I'm doing this for you. I want my life to be here with you, running this resort together."

"But why?"

"You still don't understand, do you?" His lips formed the sweetest smile I'd ever seen. "I love you, Evie. You are *meu amor*, my love. That's what I called you the day of my unfortunate encounter with invisible insects."

"I love you too, Val." The words poured out before I considered what I was saying. His declaration had hit me like the mythical arrow fired by Cupid, sinking deep into my heart. I loved him. The idea might've scared me a month ago, but today, loving him felt like the most right thing I'd ever done. "I really do love you. An awful lot."

"Me too." He smirked. "I love you an awful lot, not myself."

"You're one hundred percent sure you want to run this place with me, as official business partners."

"I do."

"Well then." I peeled his hands away from my face and clasped them to my chest. "Yes, Val, I accept your proposition. I will be your business partner."

"I'll call my lawyer so he can get started on the paperwork."

"Sounds good."

He leaped to his feet, swept me into his arms, and carried me off to our bedroom. For the next hour, we celebrated the best way we knew how—with plenty of grunting and moaning, a few screams, and lots of enthusiasm.

Chapter Twenty-Six

Val

The next day, with our new partnership in the works, I drove into town to visit the hardware and grocery stores—as a business partner, not as Eve's lover. This was my first official outing to buy supplies for the resort. Eve had wanted to come with me, but I'd convinced her to stay home and take care of our guests.

Our guests. I liked that.

I wandered into the hardware store feeling better than I had in years, since before I'd made a public spectacle of myself for the attention and become the accidental star of a sex tape scandal. My old life no longer appealed to me. The thought of going back to LA to finalize the sale of my house and collect my belongings made my jaw tighten. None of that mattered anymore, because I had the right life now. My life with Eve, working with her and living with her, was all I needed.

Ten minutes after I walked into the store, I was talking with an employee who seemed very knowledgeable about paint. Eve had looked at the store's paint selection online and had given me strict instructions to buy only the colors white and seafoam green. If I came back with gray or bright blue she would, she'd promised, sick a horde of no-see-ums on me.

Jeff, the paint expert, was explaining the types of paint to me. I nodded and pretended I understood the differences, knowing I would buy whichever kind Jeff suggested.

Out the corner of my eye, I noticed a figure moving down the aisle toward us. I glanced in that direction and gritted my teeth.

Quentin Smith stopped in the middle of the aisle, looking surprised like he hadn't noticed me before. A muscle ticked in his jaw.

With a herculean effort of willpower, I relaxed my jaw and turned my gaze away from him, back to Jeff. The young salesman seemed unaware of the tension between me and Quentin and had not paused in his description of the types of paint.

"Like I said," Jeff told me, "the paint and primer in one is the easiest to use and has the best coverage. If you want stain protection—"

I swore I could feel Quentin's gaze burning into me. I glanced at him, moving only my eyes.

He had his fists clenched now, along with his jaw.

Fuck him. I would not give the bastard the satisfaction of goading me into a confrontation. I had Eve. He didn't. End of story.

Naturally, the bastard refused to walk away. He marched up to me and growled, "Shouldn't you be going back to where you came from? The worms in the swamp must miss you."

His insult sounded like something straight out of a schoolyard. I almost laughed but quashed it because that would inflame him more. Eve wouldn't want me to beat the shit out of her former handyman. As good as punching him would feel, it wouldn't solve the problem.

Quentin was obsessed with Eve.

I gave him my back and asked Jeff to explain the stain-protection options again.

A hand slapped down on my shoulder. "I was talking to you, nature boy."

"Please excuse me," I said to Jeff. "I need to deal with a personal matter."

Jeff glanced from me to Quentin and back again three times. "Uh, sure. I'll be at the paint counter when you're ready to order."

The young man hustled away.

I turned to face Quentin, maintaining a calm demeanor even while I imagined the various ways I might pummel him. "What do you want, Mr. Smith?"

His eyes narrowed to slits, and he squeezed the words out between his clenched teeth. "I want you to stay the hell away from Eve."

Quentin's attempt to intimidate me failed. I folded my arms over my chest, casually, like I didn't give a damn what he said or did. Well, as long as he was badmouthing me, I didn't care. If he said one rotten thing about Eve…

"I'm not leaving," I said. "Eve and I are partners, in every way."

"Fucking her doesn't make you partners."

"My relationship with Eve is none of your business."

His mouth flattened into a slash, and veins stood out on his neck. "She'll see through you eventually. Eve isn't one of you nudie freaks. She's a real lady."

I glared at him. "Yes, Eve is a lady. But a real gentleman would never seduce a woman who'd had too much to drink. What does that make you?"

Quentin jerked backward as if I'd kicked him in the nuts. "She wasn't drunk. A little tipsy was all."

"Any amount of impairment should have been enough to stop you." I jabbed a finger into his chest. "You are the one who's a worm."

He stared at me, his face blank, for a few seconds.

I hoped he might give up and go away, but of course, he didn't.

Quentin snarled, "You son of a bitch. I won't let you ruin Eve."

He pulled his fist back and swung it at me.

I caught his fist in one hand and slugged him in the gut with the other.

Spluttering, Quentin doubled over and staggered backward.

"Never show your face to me or Eve again," I said.

He glowered up at me, still bent over hugging his midsection. "This isn't over."

"Yes, it is."

I stalked down the aisle and out of sight of Quentin. For fifteen minutes, I wandered the aisles collecting the rest of the supplies before I headed back to the paint department. Along the way, I passed the checkout aisles. Quentin was making his purchases there, engaged in conversation with the cashier, a perky young woman who seemed to think Quentin was hilarious. Her giggles faded as I hurried past the checkout lines. She eyed me like I was a cobra about to pounce and sink my teeth into her throat.

Who knew what lies Quentin had told the girl.

Once I'd paid for all the supplies, I drove home to Eve. The tension that had lingered ever since Quentin first approached me dissolved the instant I got out of the truck.

Eve raced out of the house and threw her arms around me. She crushed her lips to mine. With her feet dangling off the ground, she broke the kiss and grinned at me. "I'm so glad you're home."

"I am too. But you're acting like I was gone for months, not a few hours."

"Can I help it if I missed you?" She pecked my lips again. "Besides, I'm excited about having you as my business partner."

"That's obvious." I hugged her tighter to me, loving the feel of her warm, supple body. "I need to get out of these clothes."

"Yes, you do." She slid down my body until her feet touched down. "Let's get naked."

She stripped off her tank top and tossed it onto the truck's hood.

I gaped at her, sure I must've been hallucinating. Eve Holt stripping in public? Well, it wasn't exactly public. This was our nudist resort, but still, I'd never imagined Eve would join the natives.

She removed her shorts next, followed by her bra and panties. Her sandals stayed on since we were standing on the gravel driveway. She scanned me up and down. "Why are you still dressed?"

"Your striptease entranced me." I whipped off my clothes, ditching them on the truck's hood with her garments. I held out my hand. "Shall we check in on our guests?"

"Absolutely."

She settled her smaller hand in mine, and together we headed for the lawn where our guests were lounging on picnic blankets. Ollie was playing the guitar and singing a pop song I recognized but couldn't quite name.

"Ollie sings?" I said to Eve as we reached the lawn's periphery.

"Yeah," Eve said, smiling. "He's great, isn't he?"

"He is."

The whole gang suddenly noticed us. Every gaze swung in our direction, and a flurry of surprised sounds and expressions ensued.

Eve didn't blush or turn away. She faced the group head-on, smiling and waving to them, and called out "hello" to each and every guest. She used their first names, even for the ones who'd arrived today. The woman had an amazing memory.

Ollie set down his guitar and hurried up to us with Ruth and Sylvester close behind. The older couple were leaving this afternoon, but they'd stayed long enough to witness Eve's first foray into nudism.

"Evie!" Ruth said as she dragged Eve into a quick bear hug. When she released Eve, Ruth patted her arms. "You finally did it. Doesn't it feel wonderful to get rid of those itchy clothes?"

"Getting rid of my bra sure feels good," Eve said, then flashed me a sly smile. "Though there are certain benefits to wearing clothes."

I loved watching her strip. That was the unspoken benefit.

After everyone had their chance to congratulate Eve on taking the plunge, she and I returned to the house to make lunch for the guests. Unfortunately, that meant we needed to wear clothes during the food prep and while carrying it to the guest house. Once we'd done that, though, we shed our clothes and joined the other nudists for lunch.

For the entire afternoon, Eve stayed nude.

Though nudism wasn't about sex, I had trouble holding back my hunger for her when I spent hours admiring her naked body. By three o'clock, I couldn't stand it anymore. I asked Eve to take a walk down the nature trail with me, but she guessed my intentions as soon as we set foot on the trail.

"Will it be the hot spring again?" she asked. "Or do you have other plans for where we'll have sex this time?"

I patted the blanket I'd slung over my shoulder. "Thought we'd try it on the ground."

"Let's go to the meadow where all the wildflowers are in bloom."

"Perfect."

We made love there in the meadow, surrounded by colorful flowers with the sun warming our bodies and the birds serenading us. It was beautiful. She was beautiful. I loved her body, but I loved her heart and her mind even more.

That night, we made love again and fell asleep with our bodies entangled.

In the morning, I rose before Eve and performed my usual task of making a special breakfast for her. When she moseyed into the kitchen, naked, and stretched her arms above her head, I nearly vaulted over the island to ravish her. I'd developed an enormous amount of willpower since meeting Eve. If I gave in to my desire every time it seized me, we would've done nothing but have sex since the day I'd arrived here.

"Mmm," she hummed as she reached the island. "Smells wonderful in here. What did you make me today?"

"Your favorite. Café Colonial."

"Oooh." She rubbed her hands together. "Breads and cheese and sweet stuff. Yummy."

Eve took a seat on one of the stools, where I'd already laid out the place settings.

I served her a few minutes later and sat down beside her.

"You are an amazing cook," she said while chewing a mouthful of cheese bread. "I'm one lucky girl to have landed a guy like you."

"No, I'm the lucky one." I wiped crumbs from the corner of her mouth with my thumb. "You took a chance on me in spite of my past."

"The best decision I ever made." She glanced around as if she'd forgotten something.

"If you're worried about the guests," I said, "it's taken care of. I made the food, while clothed, and Ollie helped me take it all to the guest house."

She froze mid-chew. "What time is it?"

"Eight o'clock."

Her eyes went wide. "Why did you let me sleep so late?"

"Because you needed the rest. You have a partner now, which means you don't need to work so hard."

Her lips curved into a sweet smile. "I love you, Val."

I kissed her cheek. "I love you too."

A fist banged on the door, rattling it, and a familiar voice shouted, "Eve! Open the door. It's an emergency."

The tone of Ollie's voice confirmed his statement.

Eve and I both ran to the door. She yanked it open.

Ollie was breathing hard like he'd been running. He was wearing clothes too.

"What on earth is wrong?" Eve asked, laying a hand on his arm.

"Just got a call from Sam Walsh at the hardware store."

Sam owned the hardware store, but I couldn't imagine what kind of emergency would compel him to call Ollie.

"He tried to call you, Eve," Ollie explained, "but you didn't answer your cell and he didn't have the landline number."

Eve shook her head. "I don't understand. What's the big emergency?"

"There's a passel of reporters heading this way." Ollie glanced toward the driveway. "Some of them already made it to the outer gate. I ran there to check. Since the gate doesn't have a lock, I'm guessing they'll be through it soon enough."

"Wha— I—" Eve looked to me, her mouth open, then looked at Ollie again. "Why would reporters be swarming this place?"

Ollie held up a cell phone. Its screen displayed a social media post that read, "The bad boy of international football is at it again. Val Silva is living in a sex commune where all the guests pose for erotic photos and engage in orgies."

The post included a photo of me and Eve.

Naked. Behind the guest house. Fucking.

Chapter Twenty-Seven

Eve

My vision blurred and drifted back into focus as my mind struggled to comprehend what I was seeing. Me and Val. That day we'd had sex behind the guest house. How could anyone have photographed us? How could anyone have known what we would be doing that day? They couldn't have known, but if a tabloid reporter had followed Val here, that person could've been spying on us since the day he arrived.

Why not? The naked truth about Val Silva, bad boy ex-athlete turned model, would make for a splashy headline.

And there it was. The headline. The splash. The lies.

Ollie stuffed the phone back into his jeans pocket. "What should we do? If those paparazzi or whatever they are want to get in, they can climb over the outer gate. The inner gate isn't shut, but even if we close it, they can climb over that too. Should we call the police?"

I couldn't speak. My thoughts whirled, and I couldn't grab on to any of them.

"This is private property," Val said. "They have no right to invade the privacy of our guests. Yes, we will call the police."

"Sheriff's department," I mumbled.

Val slipped an arm around me, tugging me into his side. "It will be all right, Eve. Once they realize there's nothing to see here, they'll lose interest and leave."

A sour taste crept into my mouth. I needed to talk to Val about all of this, but not in front of Ollie. So I told Ollie, "Call the sheriff's department and then inform the guests of what's happening. I'll come to the guest house in a few minutes, as soon as I get dressed."

And figure out what the hell to say.

Ollie nodded and trotted back to the guest house.

I pushed the door shut with my foot and wriggled out of Val's embrace.

He shook his head slowly, his mouth open, and spread his hands. "Eve…I'm so sorry."

"How did paparazzi find out about my resort? How did they know you're here?"

"Only my family knows I came here, and they would never tell anyone." He reached for me, but I scuttled away from him. "Eve, please, let me help."

"Help how? A horde of gossipmongers are invading my home, my business. How can anyone feel comfortable staying here again? Privacy is paramount for a nudist resort."

"I know. I'll do anything I can to make this right." Head bowed, he rubbed his forehead. "I don't understand how anyone found out I'm here. Someone has known for weeks, based on the photo of us."

"You mean the one of us screwing." I backed up to the island and hugged myself, suddenly cold from head to toe. "What if my family sees that? What if these scumbag paparazzi track them down and harass them? Whoever took that picture of us might've photographed everyone who's been here lately."

Val scrubbed a hand over his mouth. "This is my fault, I know. Please believe me, Eve, I never meant for my life to crash into yours. I left all of that behind, or I thought I did."

"Obviously not. Maybe your new assistant blabbed to the tabloids."

"He didn't know where I'd gone." Val shuffled closer but didn't try to touch me. "Once this initial shock passes, we'll both be able to think more clearly and figure out how this happened. We're partners. Nothing will change that."

"Everything has changed. My business will be toast. My guests will never trust me again."

"Don't assume the worst. Nudists can be very understanding."

He almost smiled when he said that but couldn't quite accomplish the expression.

I had no fucking idea what I felt, what I should feel, what I should do. The numbness of shock had penetrated me to the core. He was right. I needed time to recover from the sucker-punch jolt of learning my privacy and the privacy of my guests had been shattered.

Was it Val's fault? I had no clue. Not yet.

He wouldn't do this, a voice in my head whispered. *He loves you.*

Yes, I believed that. Right now, it was the only truth I was certain of. But if his past had precipitated this disaster, I needed to reconsider whether a relationship with him was the best thing for me, no matter how much I loved him.

I straightened and cleared my throat. "I have to get dressed and talk to my guests. Everything else will have to wait until the dust clears."

"By 'everything,' you mean us."

"Honestly, Val, I don't know. This is all too much right now. I have to focus on protecting my guests."

Before he could say anything in response, I hurried down the hall to my bedroom, slamming the door behind me. Tears pricked at my eyes, but I had no time to cry. Later, maybe I'd collapse onto my bed and sob for a while. At this moment, I needed to minimize the damage as much as possible.

How was I supposed to do that?

I pulled on jeans and a baggy T-shirt along with socks and sneakers. I almost forgot underwear but remembered before I walked out of the bedroom. The last thing I needed was a photo of me, braless and panties-less, splashed across the Internet. Sure, it wouldn't be as bad as the porn photo already out there, but I refused to add fuel to the gossip fire.

On my way out of the house, I grabbed my phone. Val seemed to have retreated into the spare room, considering the door was shut and he was nowhere in sight. I had no time to hash things out with him. My livelihood was in critical condition, on the verge of death.

Val was my partner. Not officially, not yet, but yeah. My partner. Should I include him in my decisions? I paused on the threshold of the outside door. Sunshine spilled through the opening into the kitchen, dispelling the shadows. The darkness inside me crept closer and closer.

I rushed out and yanked the door shut.

Ten minutes later, I stood in the dining hall in front of all the guests. They occupied chairs at the tables, and all of them wore clothes thanks to Ollie convincing them it was the smart thing to do under the circumstances. Everyone watched me and waited to hear what I would say. Fabulous. I had to come up with a reassuring and inspiring speech that would convince everyone I hadn't fucked up royally. No problem.

Rolling my shoulders back, I lifted my chin and began. "Thank you all for being so patient. I know you're wondering what's going on. Ollie told you a little about it, but I need to explain exactly what's happened and what we—" I hesitated for a split second, realizing I'd used the word we, implying I had a partner. "What I am doing to ensure your privacy and security. Nothing matters more to me than providing a safe and comfortable environment for all of my guests."

I paused, scanning the crowd to gauge their reactions. No one glared at me, so I figured I was okay for the moment.

"The sheriff's department has been informed," I said, "and they are sending deputies. The state police are also sending two troopers. That's all they can spare, but I doubt we'll need more. The people trying to get into the resort are tabloid reporters who want a juicy story. We are not going to give it to them."

"Why are they here?" someone asked.

The voice originated from the rear of the dining hall, and I couldn't see the speaker's face through the crowd.

I didn't want to tell them Val had been the bait that lured the paparazzi here. I still didn't know how they'd found out he was here. Until I could tell them that, I would not mention Val's connection to the craziness about to descend on us.

"Because of me," a voice behind me said. Val's words echoed through the dining hall. "This is happening because of me."

My heartbeat sped up as I swiveled my head to glance at him. He wore clothes, dark-blue jeans and a conservative tan shirt. He looked edible as always, but I couldn't muster any lust. His expression made sure of that. Sorrow was the best description of what I saw in his eyes.

"You all know about my past," he said from just inside the doorway. Though he spoke to everyone, his gaze remained locked on mine. "I've never tried to hide it, and in spite of my past behavior, you have welcomed me into your family. I'm very grateful for that. I wish I could turn back time and make it so what's happening today never happened, but I can't. All I can do is make sure no one else is harmed by it."

I clutched my hands over my belly, my body rotating toward him like it had a mind of its own. The look on his face, it pierced straight into my heart. My throat went thick. My mouth went dry. I had a sinking feeling I knew what he would say next.

"That's why I'm leaving," he said. "To protect you."

He was talking to me.

I swallowed hard, but my throat got thicker, tighter, constricted by a terrible emotion I couldn't quite name. He was leaving me. For my own good. Just a few minutes ago, I'd wondered whether I should continue our relationship. He'd made the decision for me.

All the guests jumped up and swarmed us, babbling things I couldn't understand. My focus had telescoped down to me and Val. Nothing else got through the haze of a new, colder shock and the pain that swept in behind it.

Guests asked me questions that I tried to answer as fully and honestly as I could. Noise outside made some of them run to the windows. I could see vehicles pulling up between my home and the guest house, people tumbling out of them even as others ran up the driveway and through the open gate. There hadn't been much point in closing the gate. It had no lock, and besides, the paparazzi could've climbed over it.

By the time I'd fielded all the questions and the group had settled down, Val was gone.

I hurried outside, arriving as the sheriff's deputies drove up in one vehicle and the state troopers in another. Talking to them took more time. I kept glancing back at the house, wondering if Val was in there or if he'd already left. The paparazzi tried to surround me, but the law enforcement officers forced them back and escorted me toward the house. I noticed Val's truck parked behind the house as usual, so he hadn't left yet.

The paparazzi rushed for the door of the house.

I hopped onto my tiptoes, craning my neck to see what they had seen.

Val had stepped out of the house carrying his suitcase. He held up a hand to quiet the crowd. Once they settled down, cameras raised and mics positioned, he said, "I'm leaving."

Several voices shouted complaints.

Val held up his hand again. He grinned and said, "Follow me back to LA, and I promise you'll get a better show than anything you'll see here."

He winked and trotted toward his truck.

That grin and wink had been totally fake. Sure, his act had been a stellar performance. Nobody else would've noticed the slight clues to his true emotional state. He was luring the paparazzi away from this place, away from me.

I wanted to run after him, kiss him, tell him he didn't have to do this.

My feet wouldn't budge. It wouldn't have made a difference if I could've moved. Val wanted to be the hero who saved me and my business from shame and ruination. Maybe it was for the best. What we had might not have lasted.

Bullshit, a voice in my head snarled.

I ran toward his truck, ran as fast as I could, shoving paparazzi out of the way, elbowing the ones who hissed nasty curses at me. By the time I'd plowed my way through the crowd, Val's truck was gone. I couldn't even see it rolling down the driveway. He'd taken off, kicking up a cloud of dust in his wake.

The vultures descended on me. They fired off question after question, their voices overlapping.

I ducked my head and charged through them until I stumbled up to the door of my house. They tried to follow me inside, but I slammed the door in their faces.

The cacophony of shutters activating filled the air.

Stern voices shouted things I couldn't make out, but I realized it was the state police and sheriff's deputies attempting to wrangle the herd.

Keeping my head down, I ran through the house shutting any open windows and yanking all the curtains closed. I locked the windows and the outside door. I called Ollie and instructed him to keep the other guests inside the guest house until the cops drove the paparazzi away. After we said goodbye, I collapsed onto my bed and slung an arm over my eyes.

Val was gone.

Chapter Twenty-Eight

Eve

A little while later—I'd lost count of the minutes or hours—a crisp knock lured me out of my bedroom and to the door to the outside. When I peeked out the window beside it, I saw one of the deputies. I also noticed the herd had thinned. Only a handful of paparazzi loitered out there.

I pulled the door open.

"Ma'am," the deputy said, nodding. "We got the reporters to leave. Most of them, anyway. Once we threatened to lock them up overnight, they seemed to lose interest in harassing you."

"Yeah, it was really Val they wanted."

"That was Val Silva, wasn't it? The soccer player whose team won the Olympics?"

I was more grateful than words could express that he hadn't mentioned the sex tape or Val's flagrant nudity whenever his team won games. Maybe this deputy didn't know about that, or maybe he was being tactful. Either way, I could've kissed him for it.

"Thank you," I said. "I really appreciate you guys stepping in to clear out the vultures."

"No problem, ma'am. The state guys are heading out, but my partner and I will hang around for a bit to make sure the rest leave."

"Would you guys like a bite to eat or something to drink?"

"A drink would be great."

I listed all the beverages I had on hand. He chose pop, and I gave him four cans so the other law enforcement men could have some too.

They all smiled and waved to me.

I couldn't move away from the doorway. Though only a few paparazzi remained, the idea of stepping outside and into the fray again left me paralyzed. I shut the door and retreated into my bedroom, curling up on top of the covers with my knees pulled up to my chest.

Would Val come back? Did he want to?

More time passed while I lay there, not sleepy, but mentally exhausted. Thoughts ricocheted through my mind like ping-pong balls. Should I have tried harder to stop Val from leaving? He would call me. Wouldn't he? Once he got home, he'd let me know everything was okay.

A knock roused me from my lethargy, and I headed for the front door.

Ollie was there when I opened the door. "Are you okay, Eve? I've been calling, tried your cell and the landline, but you didn't pick up."

I had a vague memory of hearing phones ringing, but I'd left my cell by the island and there was a hallway between me and the kitchen. The noises had seemed far away.

Yeah, I'd also been in a semi-catatonic state on my bed.

"Sorry," I mumbled. "Needed a break after all the craziness."

He touched my arm. "You okay, Evie? We all heard what Val said and saw him leaving. When's he coming back?"

I hunched my shoulders. "Don't know if he is coming back."

"Of course he is. Val's crazy about you."

A half-hearted shrug was all I could muster in response.

"You're wiped out," Ollie said. "Get some rest. I'll take care of lunch and dinner. If you don't mind me invading your kitchen."

I shrugged again.

"Be back in a few minutes," he said. "Gotta put some clothes on to make the food. You always tell us we can eat naked, but you have to make and serve the food with clothes on."

"Uh-huh."

He gave my arm a squeeze and trotted back to the guest house.

I slept all afternoon. Though I'd missed lunch, I didn't feel hungry at all. Ollie insisted I eat, even sat there watching me to make sure I did eat something. The food tasted like cardboard. Ollie's cooking wasn't the problem. Nothing would've tasted right to me. Nothing felt right either. My home had been invaded, my privacy torn to shreds, and my reputation blackened. Would anyone come to my resort ever again? I'd probably lose my business and be forever known as the slut who screwed Val Silva behind the guest house. Maybe I was overreacting, but I couldn't stop the crazy thoughts from whirling inside my head.

None of that mattered half as much as the fact he'd walked out on me.

After I dutifully swallowed food I couldn't taste, Ollie hugged me and left. I grabbed my cell phone and called Val. His voicemail picked up. I left a stammering message, sounding like an idiot. Two hours later, I left another message. At midnight, I tried again.

When I finally went to bed, I didn't get much sleep. Crying kept me awake.

The next day, I picked myself up and got back to it. Though my eyes were gritty and puffy and had dark circles under them, I refused to wallow any longer. I showered, got dressed, and started working on breakfast for the guests. Ollie showed up and insisted on helping. It seemed strange to see him in clothes, but he turned out to be an excellent helper. He also insisted on taking care of the other guests, handling any problems or requests they had.

When I caught him cleaning the toilets in the guest-house rooms, I told him, "You are a guest, Ollie. You shouldn't be doing janitorial work."

He kept scrubbing the toilet while he told me, "I don't mind. It's nice to do something constructive instead of being stuck in a cubicle. Besides, this place is like a second home to me. You're like a sister, and the other guests are my crazy aunts and uncles." He paused in his scrubbing and looked up at me. "I love you, Evie. Anything you need, I'm here to help."

I didn't know what to say to that other than the truth. "I love you too, Ollie."

We went on like that for a week. Ollie served as janitor, handyman, sous chef, receptionist, and guest coordinator. He had no official job here, but he worked as hard as any full-time employee. He wore clothes most of the time since the health code required him to wear clothes while cooking and serving food and, well, it would've been icky for him to go nude while cleaning toilets. In his duties as my receptionist and guest coordinator, he preferred to go au naturel.

Every day, at least five times a day, I tried to call Val. I gave up on leaving voicemails since he ignored them. I texted and emailed, but he ignored that too. After ten days, I gave up. Val was never coming back. My chest ached and tears blurred my vision every time I thought about him. Part of me wanted to hunt him down and kick his ass for running out on me. The rest of me, the larger and far less brave part, preferred to hide.

Another week dragged by with no contact from Val, not even a piddly email offering a half-assed explanation. The biggest excitement I had that week was of the unpleasant variety. I had decided to repaint the dining hall and went to the hardware store for the necessary supplies. Ollie had offered to handle the supply run, but I needed to get away from the guests for a while.

I was holding a gallon-size can of paint, reading the fine print on it, when I spotted a figure approaching in my peripheral vision. Glancing up, I nearly dropped the paint can.

Quentin nodded and offered me a tight smile. "Eve."

My brain couldn't generate any response to his appearance. Since I didn't care to stammer like an idiot, I opted for the silent treatment accompanied by what I hoped came off as a hard stare.

He hunched his shoulders and jammed his hands in his pants pockets. "I, uh, ought to explain."

I clutched the paint can to my belly. "Not interested in any explanations from you."

"You'll want to know this." He scrunched up his face and refused to look at me. "I'm the reason the paparazzi found out about you and Val."

The room did a pirouette around me. I hugged the paint can tighter, unable to speak until the spinning stopped. Even then, I opened my mouth but couldn't muster words. Quentin had called the paparazzi? How had he even known who to call?

He bowed his head, his shoulders hiking up even higher. "I'd been kinda jealous of Val. Started talking to the pretty new cashier Sam hired. More than once, I talked about Val and how he's a nudist, how he did all kinds of crazy shit that anybody can see online."

"You were blabbing about my private life to the checkout girl."

"Well…" He coughed and peeked up at me before averting his gaze again. "It was kinda like therapy for me. I got all my frustrations out and, after the third time, I realized I'm not jealous anymore."

"Hooray for you." I shoved the paint can onto the shelf where I'd found it and rounded on Quentin. "You feel better, so you decided to call in the hell hounds?"

"No, I—" He raised his face to me. "The cashier girl did. Just now, I was talking to her. She was upset the paparazzi didn't hang around for longer since she was looking forward to our little town getting on the evening news. That's why she told them about Val. She went to the website of one of those tabloids and submitted a tip. I think she got paid for it too."

We hadn't made the evening news. Not even our sex photo had gone that wide.

"Did you take that photo of me and Val?" I asked.

He covered his eyes with his hand, wincing. "Yeah. I went back to the resort to grab my last paycheck and a few tools I'd left behind. That's when I saw you two. I showed the cashier the picture on my phone. She wanted me to text it to her, so I…did."

You bastard, I wanted to scream. Shock paralyzed me, though, and I could manage only to stare at him. "Those tools belong to me. I bought them."

"After I saw what I saw, I left without taking any tools."

I glared at Quentin. "Let me get this straight. First, you beat up Val. Then, after I fire your ass, you start blabbing to the hardware store cashier. Next, you take a dirty picture of me and Val. Finally, you give that photo to the fucking cashier so she can sell it and all the gossip you told her to the first scummy tabloid she can find online. My life got blown up, and it's all because of you."

"Yeah, it's my fault. I'm sorry, Eve. I'm so sorry."

"I never want to see your face again. Not in the hardware store, not in the grocery store, not even when I drive past your truck on the street." I jabbed a finger into the air near his face. "Do you understand?"

"Don't worry, you'll never see me again. I got a job in Salt Lake City."

Maybe I should've felt relieved hearing that. All I really felt was sad. I'd lost a friend because he betrayed me and proved he'd never been a friend at all. I'd lost my privacy and my sense of security thanks to the invasion of the tabloid vultures.

I'd lost Val.

Maybe I couldn't change any of that stuff, but I could sure as hell change one thing. I pushed past Quentin and marched straight to Sam's office at the back of the store. The door hung open as usual, so I walked inside and dropped onto the empty chair beside his desk.

Once I'd explained the situation, I didn't get a chance to demand he fire the cashier.

"She's gone," Sam said. "I'll inform her right away."

Getting the cashier fired didn't make me feel better. Well, not a lot better. At least one person who'd screwed with my life had paid for it. When I got home, Ollie suggested I talk to a lawyer, but suing Quentin or the stupid girl who'd tattled to the paparazzi wouldn't help anything. I'd spend money I didn't have in an attempt to get restitution from a girl who earned minimum wage. Quentin wasn't rolling in dough either.

So, I took the high road and let it go.

A good wallow sounded awesome, but I had no time for that. The attack of the rampaging paparazzi had triggered an unexpected side effect. The resort was now fully booked for the next six months.

When the calls had started to pour in, I'd contacted my regular guests to find out when they might want to return, to make sure they got a spot reserved.

Ruth had told me, "We're coming right away, sweetie. You need all the support you can get."

"I'm fine, really. Ollie's sticking around to help out."

"We're coming, Eve. No arguments."

A few days later, Ruth and Sylvester arrived in a chartered bus.

When I saw the huge vehicle, I gaped at it and at the gaggle of people disembarking. I knew all of them. There was Ruth, Sylvester, my parents, my brother and sister and their significant others, my niece and nephew, and the entire Kitten Brigade. Well, almost all of them. Heidi wasn't among them. Shelby told me Heidi had gotten engaged and was too busy to come, but she'd sent a care package. It contained fancy things that might be found at a spa, things like goat's milk soap and bath beads. I loved Heidi in spite of the way she'd dumped Ollie. He still cared about her, I knew, but he'd recovered from their breakup better than I was recovering from mine.

Every member of my family hugged me. Even Krista's fiancé, Jeremy, hugged me.

Surrounded by my family and Ruth and Sylvester, I studied the vehicle they'd arrived in. "Why did you guys charter a bus? I would've picked you up at the airport. My old bus isn't luxurious, but it would've fit all of you."

"We didn't charter the bus," Mom said. "Val bought it for you."

"Yeah," Sylvester said, "he seems to think he's your business partner."

"What?" I started gaping again, my gaze flicking from Mom to Sly and back again. "But he went home. I haven't heard from him in two weeks."

"Don't know anything about that," Sly said, "but I heard him saying, clear as day, he bought this bus for your business."

"He said 'our business,' honey," Ruth corrected. "He meant the resort because he and Eve run it together."

"But—" I couldn't finish the thought because it had already fled my brain. Val bought me a bus. He called it "our" business. And yet he hadn't responded to a single damn voicemail, email, or text since the day he'd left.

"Give her the papers," Ruth said to her husband.

Sylvester pulled a sheaf of papers, folded in half, out of his back pocket and offered it to me. "Val said to give you these."

I took the sheaf and unfolded it. An envelope fell out and fluttered to the ground.

Krista snatched it up and handed it to me.

"You go inside," Mom said, "and look through that stuff alone. We'll join you in a little while, after we get unpacked and settled in."

"I don't have enough rooms for all of you," I said. "I was expecting Ruth and Sylvester, not a small army."

"An army of people who love you," Krista said. "It was a surprise. We knew if we told you all of us were coming, you'd tell us not to."

I couldn't argue with that. I probably would have told them to stay away.

But I loved them so much for being here.

"We brought tents," Jeremy said. "And the bus is pretty sweet too, comfortable enough to sleep in."

My surprise guests headed for the guest house, and I returned to my house to read the papers Val had sent. Seated at the island, I set the sealed envelope on the wood surface. I wasn't ashamed to admit I was afraid to open that envelope, afraid of what I'd find inside it. The papers consisted of legal documents that altered the structure of my LLC to allow for a partner and that also iterated the terms of our partnership. Val had signed the documents. They required only my signature to become real. Little sticky flags marked the places where I needed to sign.

I stared at the envelope for a couple minutes after I read the legal documents. Then, finally, I summoned the nerve to rip it open. The envelope contained a single sheet of paper, a letter written in Val's hand. I read slowly, making sure I didn't miss a single syllable. A tingle chased over my skin, a kind of excitement I hadn't experienced before or since Val had been in residence here. I read the note three times, despite the fact the damn thing consisted of only eleven words.

"Wait for me," he said. "Thirty days and I'll be coming for you."

Coming for me? What, like I was a dog he'd sent to a kennel? He couldn't not call me for two weeks and then expect me to be thrilled he might come back for me in another month. He could've called or texted or emailed. Instead, he left me hanging.

And he expected me to sign the papers.

The sound of bare feet slapping on the wood floors pulled me out of my contemplation. I glanced over my shoulder to see Ollie racing out of the living room.

"You've gotta see this," he said, breathless.

He hugged my laptop to his chest.

I waved a dismissive hand. "I trust you to handle whatever it is."

Ollie had become my de facto assistant manager. He handled everything from paying bills to cleaning toilets, so I didn't understand what could be so important that I needed to see it.

"Not this," he said as he plopped onto the stool beside me and flipped up the laptop's lid. He pointed at the screen. "Look. Somebody sent you money."

I bent forward and squinted at the screen. It showed the company PayPal account, and there was indeed a new transfer. It had come from Valentim Silva.

"Val sent you ten thousand dollars," Ollie said.

The amount sounded familiar, and I grabbed the legal papers to flip through them again. Yep, there it was. Val's initial investment in the company, required to become a partner, was ten thousand dollars.

Why would he send the money before I signed the papers? Was he trying to force me to accept him as my business partner? I couldn't believe he would do that. Maybe I didn't know everything about Val, but I knew him well enough to realize his investment in the company was his way of showing he still wanted to be a part of my life.

So answer your damn phone, Val.

"Thank you for showing me this," I told Ollie as I leaped off the stool and grabbed the papers. "I have some private calls to make."

"No problem."

I turned to leave the room but hesitated. I looked at him over my shoulder. "Could you handle everything if I, um, took a vacation?"

"Sure, but maybe you should hire a real assistant manager for that."

"No time." I clutched the papers to my chest. "I'm leaving as soon as I can make the arrangements."

Assuming my first phone call went the way I hoped it would. I needed answers, and I was sick of waiting to receive them. Time to go get them myself.

My family wouldn't mind me leaving them right after they'd arrived. Once I explained why I was doing this, they'd understand.

"Where are you going?" Ollie asked.

"California."

Chapter Twenty-Nine

Val

Waves swelled and broke on the shoreline outside the picture windows, seeming dark and foreboding under the gloomy sky. Slouched in an armchair, I stared at the breakers and sipped my glass of bourbon. I'd always loved the view from my living room. Ever since I'd left Eve, nothing was beautiful anymore. I hated my house, I hated the ocean, and I hated the fucking paparazzi. Most of all, I hated myself for hurting Eve.

I would get back to her. If she'd have me.

A large breaker crashed onto the shore, spraying the beach.

Whatever I had to do to make this up to Eve, I would do it. Somehow, I had to make her understand why I'd abandoned her. Maybe I shouldn't have sent her the legal documents without at least calling first to explain. A phone call wouldn't be enough. I needed to look into her eyes when I told her.

I hoped I'd be kissing her seconds after that, but it might've been wishful thinking.

God, I missed her.

Why the hell did you leave her, then?

The doorbell chimed.

I groaned and swigged the last of my bourbon. Seeing anyone appealed to me about as much as wrestling with a porcupine. Poor Ollie had almost done that. A smile tugged at my lips but couldn't quite take hold. I missed Ollie too, and Ruth and Sylvester, even the Kitten Brigade. They'd become like family to me. Eve had become so much more.

The doorbell chimed again, three times in quick succession.

Christ, whoever it was had a hard-on for talking to me.

I slapped my glass down on the table and shoved myself out of the chair. The wood floor chilled my bare feet, but I didn't care. When I reached the front door, I swung it wide open. A wave of shock broke over me, but it swiftly transformed into a warm and welcome relief.

Until she spoke.

"*Você partiu meu coração.*"

A pain tightened the back of my throat, roughening my voice. "I know I broke your heart. I'm sorry, Evie, I'm so sorry."

"Yeah, I know you are."

What could I say? What could I do? I'd abandoned her. Now she was here, standing on my doorstep, and I was paralyzed.

"You know," she said, "we haven't seen each other in more than two weeks. I think it would be appropriate for you to kiss me."

That was all the invitation I needed.

I threw my arms around Eve and dragged her into me. She tried to speak, but I silenced her with my lips. She melted against me, moaning, opening her mouth and welcoming my tongue. She tasted even better than I remembered, sweet and sexy—if "sexy" were a flavor. With Eve, it definitely was. The taste of her and the feel of her body intoxicated me more than any alcohol.

Finally, I relinquished her lips. I held on to her body, though. No force on earth could make me let go.

"Well," she said breathlessly, "that answers one question."

I arched a brow. "What question is that?"

"Did you miss me."

"Of course I missed you. *Penso em você o tempo todo.*" I brushed stray hairs away from her face. "That means I think about you all the time. Missed you so much I want to drag you down to the floor and fuck you with the door wide open."

She laughed. "Same old Val."

The words she'd spoken a moment ago replayed in my mind. "Where did you learn Portuguese? You pronounced that phrase perfectly."

"I talked to your sister Maria. She suggested I ought to tell you in Portuguese how much you'd hurt me by taking off like that." Eve hunched her shoulders. "I figured what the hell. My voicemails and texts in English weren't getting through to you."

Yes, I'd done that. I'd taken off, then I had ignored her attempts to contact me. How could I explain the reasons for my behavior? I'd convinced myself I was protecting her.

We both fell silent for a moment, our gazes bound to each other, neither of us knowing quite what to say.

At last, I broke the silence. "You know I'm glad you're here, but why are you here?"

"Did you really think a crappy eleven-word note was enough?" She tapped a finger on my chest. "You ought to know better. Wait and I'll come for you? Please."

"Hmm." I grasped her bottom with both hands. "I suppose you're right. The Eve I know would never sit still for that."

"Damn right." She pulled out of my grasp. "What the hell were you thinking? Running away without even saying goodbye? I get a deafening silence for weeks, then legal papers and a half-assed note. I deserve better than that, Val."

"Yes, you do." I noticed my neighbors across the street staring at us and clearly whispering to each other about the scandalous sight at the home of the infamous footballer. "Come inside, Eve. Public nudity is still illegal in California."

A slight smile tightened her lips as she scanned me up and down. "I had thought you were exaggerating when you said you always go naked at home. But here you are, answering the door in your birthday suit."

I stepped back, and she walked inside. As I shut the door, I asked, "How angry are you?"

She ambled down the hallway toward the living room, visible at the hall's end. Glancing back at me, she gave me a sarcastically sweet smile. "Angry? Why would I be angry? Just because I fantasized about castrating you, that doesn't mean I'm mad."

I followed her into the living room, wondering how I was going to make this right. My plan had sounded reasonable and even noble at the time. Looking back, I realized how stupid I'd been.

Eve sat down at one end of the sofa.

After a brief hesitation, I settled onto the opposite end.

She watched me, her mood unreadable.

It was a challenge for me to explain, but I forged ahead. "I'm sorry, Eve. I did what I thought was necessary to protect you from the paparazzi, but I realize now it was a stupid idea. I'd intended to lure them away from your home for long enough that they would get bored and move on to the next pop star who goes into rehab. Did it at least work? Have the paparazzi left you alone?"

"Yeah, they're gone."

"This was all my fault."

She snorted. "No, it was all Quentin's fault. He blabbed to the cashier at the hardware store, and he took that photo of us. The cashier sold it all to a tabloid."

"Christ, I can't believe it. After all of that, and considering what I've done since I left you, I'll understand if you never want to see me again."

Her steady gaze remained fixated on me. "What have you done?"

"You must've seen the photos and videos."

"What photos? What videos?"

"On the internet."

She flapped a hand, dismissing the suggestion. "Oh, I don't look at stuff like that online. I don't even use social media."

How had I not known that about her? I'd learned a lot about Eve Holt over the past six weeks, but I still had much more to learn.

Eve angled sideways, leaning back into the sofa's corner. "What kind of trouble have you been getting into without me?"

I scratched my cheek. "Well, I needed to distract the paparazzi, to keep them away from you. That required…a splash."

"And by 'splash' I'm guessing you mean 'tsunami.' Right?"

"Yes." I crossed my ankle over the other knee, fidgeted, and tucked my foot under my knee. "I danced naked on the beach in broad daylight while singing Brazilian pop songs. And I did that every day for a week."

Her expression blanked. For a few seconds, she neither spoke nor moved.

Until she burst out laughing.

By the time she stopped laughing, her eyes were watering. She grabbed a tissue from the box on the coffee table and wiped her eyes. "Honestly, Val, I was expecting something more scandalous than that. What, no sex tape this time?"

"Of course not. I'm in love with you, Eve. I would never sleep with anyone else."

The humor washed out of her expression. She blew her nose and crumpled the used tissue. "I know you wouldn't do that. I was joking."

"I'm glad to hear that, but you must be upset with me for making a spectacle of myself."

"Why would I be upset?" She held up the tissue, glancing around like she was searching for something. "Where's the trash can?"

"Under the table behind you."

She twisted around, spotted the trash, and tossed her tissue into it. Straightening, she squared her shoulders and looked at me. "If you really love someone, you accept them the way they are."

"But the things I've done—"

"Are part of what makes you...you." She scooted a little closer. "I wouldn't change who you are, and I don't want you to do it because you think that's what I want. All I want is you."

"We haven't known each other that long."

She tilted her head to the side, studying me. "I know enough. We might be different, but we have a lot in common too. I may not ever strip naked in a packed sports stadium, but I love that you are the kind of man who might do that. I know you would never do anything to humiliate me or hurt me. I trust you, Val."

"But I flaunted my nudity in front of the paparazzi."

"I get that you expected me to castigate you for that, but I'm not the least bit embarrassed by anything you've done."

Entranced by her eyes, so clear and bright and focused on me, I couldn't think of anything intelligent to say. "Why not?"

"Why am I not ashamed of you?" She shook her head, her lips curling up at the corners. "Because I love you. How many more times do I need to say that before you believe me? I love you, and that means I accept all of you—your past, your present, and anything flamboyant you might do in the future." She scooted closer still, halfway across the sofa now. "I don't even care that your neighbors, some of whom are celebrities, saw me talking to a hot, naked Brazilian sex maniac."

I chuckled. "Sex maniac?"

"Maybe sex god is more appropriate."

"Yes, I prefer that one." I inched nearer to her. "Does this mean you'll have me?"

"I've already had you. Many times, in many positions, indoors and out."

"Eve, you know what I meant."

"Yes." She slid closer. "Of course I'll have you. I signed the legal papers on the plane. Why did you send the money before I'd signed?"

"To show you I'm serious. About being your business partner, and about our relationship."

"In that case..." She swung a leg up and over to straddle my lap. "We'd better seal the deal."

"That's it? I was expecting to jump more hurdles before you would forgive me."

She linked her hands at my nape. "I forgave you on the plane too."

I touched my lips to hers. "Thank you, *meu amor.*"

"You're welcome." She raised her brows. "Dancing naked? That was the best you could come up with?"

"My only other idea was to lie on the beach masturbating."

She threw her head and laughed.

I pulled her shirt up. When she raised her arms, I tugged it over her head.

As the shirt landed on the coffee table, she grinned. "You like stripping me, don't you?"

"No, I don't like it. I love it." To prove my point, I unhooked her bra and stripped it off her body. "Clothing does have its purposes."

I flipped us so she lay stretched across the sofa with me on top of her.

She unfastened the button on her jeans and eased the zipper down. "Let's see how fast you can get the rest of my clothes off."

"A challenge? All right." I hooked my fingers inside her waistband and yanked off her jeans and panties in one sweep. They got stuck on her shoes, so I yanked those off too along with the socks. All of it fell to the floor within ten seconds. "Fast enough for you?"

"Very impressive." She bent one knee, tipping it to the side, exposing her slick, pink flesh. "I do have one more question."

"Now? I'm about to fuck you."

"Then answer quick." She clasped her hands above her head. "Are you moving to Oregon?"

"Yes. You already knew that." Though her body tempted me to forget everything else, I sat back and said, "I have an offer on my house, so I need to settle that and some other financial matters before I can move. That's why I said I'd come for you in thirty days."

"There's no need to wait. Your lawyer, your real estate agent, and your financial manager can handle that stuff."

"How do you know?"

"Because I talked to your lawyer. His name and phone number were on the documents you sent." She nudged me with her big toe. "How do you think I found your house? You never told me the address. The legal papers had your lawyer's address, not yours."

"I should've known I can't hide from you."

"Did you want to hide?"

"No, not anymore. Not from you." I lowered my body onto hers, and my cock brushed against her wetness. "Thought I'd have to work harder to get you ready for me."

"Honey, all it takes is your naked body. One glimpse of that, and I'm beyond ready."

"You must be very frustrated since I'm naked most of the time, often in front of other people."

"I would never describe the way you make me feel as frustrated." She locked her ankles behind my ass. "With you, I feel alive and free."

"So do I, Evie. Because of you."

Chapter Thirty

Eve
Ten months later

I tore my gaze away from the glowing screen of my laptop and surveyed the beach around me. A few mare's tail clouds wisped across the blue sky. Nude men, women, and children cavorted on the sand and in the water while delicate swells lapped at the shore. It was May, but here in southern Brazil, below the equator, that meant autumn. Porto Alegre boasted a subtropical climate that made it hot in the summer and temperate in the winter. Being in the southern hemisphere felt strange, but today it was in the seventies. I could get to like it here.

My gaze drifted away from the frolicking strangers and settled on the very familiar figure lying nude on a large beach towel beside me. Val wore sunglasses and nothing else, his bronzed body stretched out and on full display. This was a clothing-optional beach, after all. I was the only person wearing a swimsuit, though my bikini barely qualified as clothing.

I admired Val for a few more seconds, then returned my attention to the computer on my lap. I sat cross-legged, the laptop balanced on my thighs. On the screen, my half-written email awaited me. I typed the rest of my response to the newest guest at Au Naturel Naturist Resort LLC. She would arrive tomorrow. "Sorry I won't be there to greet you," I typed, "but my assistant manager will take great care of you. I'll be back from vacation next week. So glad you've chosen

Au Naturel for your holiday." After clicking the send button, I shut down my laptop and slipped it into its protective case.

Ollie had become my official assistant manager as well as the secretary and treasurer for the LLC Val and I owned together. Thanks to Val's resources, we could afford to expand and update the resort. The interior of the guest house had undergone major renovations, we had a real tennis court, and over the summer we planned to build guest bungalows and other stuff to make Au Naturel a top-notch nudist resort while keeping it affordable and family friendly.

I yawned, stretched, and said, "It's time."

Val lifted his sunglasses enough to peek at me. "Time for what?"

"This." I rose and stripped off my bikini. "I'm making my nude debut in Brazil."

He smiled in that sexy way that made me shiver with heat, not cold. "I wondered how long it would take you. Eve Holt going nude at her own resort is one thing but doing it on a public beach in another country is something else."

Yes, I'd finally embraced naturism. Since we'd recently hired people to cook and serve the food at our resort, Val and I were free to go without clothes whenever we liked. I still wore clothes when I greeted new guests—and I made Ollie and Val do the same, though they groused about it—because it seemed like the most professional way to go. A lot of our guests were new to nudism and needed to ease into it.

Val did on occasion walk down the driveway while naked to get the mail. He enjoyed the hike, and I was pretty sure he enjoyed the risk of someone seeing him. His exhibitionist streak might have gotten narrower, but it would never disappear. I didn't want it to either. I loved him exactly the way he was.

Here on the only nude beach in the vicinity of Val's parents' house, I twirled to give him the full view of my nakedness.

Val smirked. "Bringing you to a nude beach might have been a mistake. The sight of your naked body always makes me hard."

"Let me take one dip in the water before we go back to your parents' house."

"Make it quick." He licked his lips, and his voice turned huskier. "Or I'll be forced to drag you behind the nearest tree and make you scream."

I sprinted for the water and leaped into it. Water sprayed up around me. I ducked under the surface to get thoroughly drenched and bobbed up again. My breasts emerged from the water, bouncing. Brushing my hair back, I glanced toward Val.

He was sitting up, holding my laptop case over his lap.

I had a feeling he was experiencing the same kind of problem Ollie had suffered from once upon a time. I took pity on Val and got out of the water to pull my towel around my body.

He stood but kept the laptop case in front of his groin. "I suppose we should be going. My family is waiting for us."

I slipped on my bikini. "Ready to go."

"But are you ready to meet my sisters?"

We'd been here for a week, and I had yet to meet Maria and Aline, though I'd spoken to Maria on the phone back when Val had been avoiding me. Based on that conversation and the stories Val had told me about his sisters, I had a feeling I'd like them.

He glanced up and down the shore, seeming anxious. "Let's go farther down the beach to see if we can find a secluded spot."

"Thought we needed to go."

"A few minutes more. Please." He set down my laptop case and offered me his hand. "Come with me, Eve."

I shrugged and took his hand, dropping my towel on the sand so it covered the laptop.

He guided me down the beach past the smattering of people who lounged on towels or splashed in the water. We came to a stand of palm trees, and he led me into its midst. Shielded from view, we seemed to have satisfied his desire for seclusion.

Eying the palm fronds above our heads, he nodded as if he were satisfied with the location, but he still looked anxious.

"Is everything okay?" I asked.

He dropped to one knee, still holding my hand. My left hand. "I love you, Eve. All I want is to spend the rest of my life with you, running our business and, I hope, raising our children together." He hesitated, swallowing visibly. "Will you marry me?"

"Yes, Val, I would love to marry you."

He blew out a breath, the anxiety flooding out of him.

"Did you actually think I might say no?" I asked.

"I am a notorious exhibitionist, and I abandoned you for two weeks."

"We talked about all of this. I love you the way you are." I knelt in front of him, looping my arms around his heck. "As for the ditching-me thing, I'm way over it."

"Glad to hear it." He nuzzled my nose. "No one will believe I'm getting married."

"The bad boy bachelor settling down. Yeah, that might make news all around the world." I held up my left hand, wiggling the third finger. "Aren't you forgetting something?"

His grin disintegrated. "Fuck. I forgot the ring."

Val scooped me up and carried me all the way back to our towels, where he set me down on my feet. He unzipped a small pocket on my laptop case, a pocket I never used, and dug around inside it. With an "ah-ha," he brought out a small velvet box.

When he started to kneel, I said, "No need to do that again."

He did it anyway. "I'm doing this the right way."

"Nude on a beach? Not sure that's the traditional method for proposing."

"For nudists it is." He plucked the ring out of the box and held it toward my left hand. "Your finger, please."

I stretched out all my fingers.

He slipped the ring onto the correct one, kissed my palm, and rose. "Now it's official."

"Time to meet your sisters and make the big announcement, eh?"

"Yes, it is."

We drove back to his parents' house, which perched on the side of a hill and overlooked the coastline, though it had no beach access. Val's parents had neighbors who owned a private beach, but nudism was not allowed there. Val had put his clothes on before we left the beach since he couldn't go nude at his parents' place. They had no problems with his lifestyle, but their house featured many large picture windows that their neighbors could see. Not all of them were okay with nudism, and he understood that.

His sisters were already there when we got to his parents' place. Both Maria and Aline hugged me and oohed over the gorgeous diamond ring Val had given me. Thankfully, he hadn't bought a ring with a diamond so large it might blind astronauts in space if the sun hit it right. He'd chosen a tasteful yet beautiful ring.

Over dinner, I got to chat with Val's sisters. Maria laughed with gusto and loved to tease her brother affectionately. Aline was more subdued than her sister but also loved to tease Val. Both his sisters and his parents were thrilled he was getting married, and they didn't mind at all that he planned to live in America for good. They knew he and I would visit Brazil as often as possible. They also vowed to visit us often.

When we said goodbye to Maria, she pulled me into another hug and whispered in my ear, "I've never seen Val so happy before. Thank you, Eve. Now have some babies, would you?"

She kissed my cheek, winked, and left.

Babies? Val and I hadn't talked about that yet.

Once Val's parents had gone to bed, he and I lounged on the sofa. With his arm around me, I nestled into him and sighed with pure contentment.

He kissed the top of my head. "Exhausted?"

"Yes, but in a happy way. I love your sisters."

"They love you too." He hugged me a little tighter. "Maria and Aline both asked me when we'll start having babies."

"Yeah, Maria mentioned that to me too." I bent my head back to look at him. "Do you want kids? We never talked about that."

"I would love to have children with you, Evie. But if you don't want that, I understand."

"Oh Val, you really are the most unbelievably sweet and considerate man." I spread a palm over his cheek. "I would love to have kids with you."

"Should we wait a while to start a family? We do have all the changes at the resort to deal with."

"Do you want to wait?"

"No. Do you?"

I wriggled around until I was on my knees with his arm still around me. I kissed him softly. "Let's start right now. I'm still on the pill, but we could practice."

"Right here on my parents' couch?"

"No, I guess not." I tapped my chin, considering the options. "Let's do something naughty."

"What do have in mind? You know I'm up for anything."

"Let's sneak onto your neighbors' beach and have sex in the moonlight."

He pulled me onto his lap, wrapped both arms around me, and got to his feet while maintaining his hold on me. "Let's do it."

And we did just that. On the beach, in the moonlight, we made love for an hour. The naughtiness factor made it a little more exciting, but it was Val who made our time on that beach a night to remember.

When I'd first met Val, I had thought he was the wrong man for me. On the surface, we seemed like complete opposites. In the months I'd known him, I had realized how much we had in common and that our differences made our relationship stronger and more exciting. When my instinct was to play it safe, he encouraged me to take risks. When his instinct was to go a little too far,

I reined him in, but only enough to keep us both from getting arrested. I loved his wild side, his caring side, his intelligence, his humor, his body. I loved him, period.

Naked or clothed.

Epilogue

Ollie
Six Days Later

I scratched my chest through my shirt, not used to wearing clothes. Eve had instituted a new policy that decreed not only did employees have to wear clothes when greeting new guests, but we also had to wear a uniform. The fabric was itchy. She swore she'd order better ones soon, but for today, I had to act friendly while my whole body begged to be scratched.

A taxi rolled up the driveway, gravel crunching under its tires. The driver parked but did not get out to help the woman in the backseat get her things out of the trunk.

Everybody in town knew Au Naturel was a naturist resort full of naked people. Most locals didn't mind, but some thought it was a freak show. I recognized the taxi driver. Phil Johnson didn't mind sneaking a peek at the female guests whenever he drove someone out here, but he refused to set foot on the property. His shoes stayed firmly in the taxi.

As usual, he peered out the windshield hoping to catch a glimpse.

Since the other guests had gone inside for lunch, the perv was disappointed.

I hurried forward to pull the back door open.

The woman inside had her head down, focused on fiddling with her purse. Auburn hair fell over her shoulders and curtained her face.

Offering her my hand, I said, "Welcome to Au Naturel."

She slipped her hand into mine and climbed out of the taxi. Her head lifted, and she smiled a little. "Thank you. I'm Mara Severins."

I already knew that, but I couldn't manage to say anything in response. She was beautiful. Her almond-shaped eyes, an amazing shade of jade green, sparkled in the sunshine. Her skin was a golden tan, like it was her natural complexion and not made in a tanning bed or the result of a sunbathing addiction. The form-fitting dress she wore showcased her slender body and especially her breasts. They weren't large, but they weren't small either. Just the right size, I decided.

Her pouty lips tightened, and her brows drew together. "Is something wrong? Is this the wrong day? Sometimes I do that, I get the dates messed up and show up at the wrong time."

"I— whuh—" Yeah, those were the first syllables I spoke to the prettiest girl I'd ever seen. Shit. What was wrong with me? I still held her hand in mine, and her skin was so soft.

She squinted at my chest, then swung her gaze up to mine. "It's nice to meet you, Oliver."

How did she know my name? I glanced at my chest. Duh. The name tag pinned to my shirt told her.

Time to suck it up and act like a mature adult.

I rolled my shoulders back and released her hand. "Yes, I'm Oliver Jackson, the assistant manager. You can call me Ollie if you want. Let me get your bags for you."

"Thank you, Oliver."

"Open the trunk," I said to Phil. The lid popped up right when I reached the trunk. Inside it lay four large suitcases and one smaller case. Who brought this much clothes to a naturist resort? Maybe she had a shoe fetish and brought her entire collection. I hefted the suitcases out of the trunk and set them down alongside the driveway. Shutting the door, I called to Phil, "Thanks, man. See you next time."

Phil backed up and turned around, waving as he headed off down the driveway.

I waved back. Picking up two of the large suitcases, I stifled a grunt. Damn, these things weighed a ton each. I'd have to come back for the rest.

"Follow me," I said and started lugging the bags toward the guest house.

Mara Severins toddled after me, her high heels making it harder for her to walk across the gravel drive and the dirt path to the guest house.

I slowed down to let her catch up. "Might be easier if you take off your shoes."

"Right." She smiled shyly and removed her shoes, carrying one in each hand. "I'm not used to the outdoors since I live in Philadelphia, but that's why I came here. To commune with nature or whatever."

"You can definitely do that here."

When we reached the guest house door, she held it open for me.

"Sorry, that's supposed to be my job," I said, lugging the suitcases across the threshold.

"My fault. I overpacked. Always do."

The door shut behind us.

She pulled in a deep breath, her eyelids sliding half shut, and blew out the breath she'd held. "Mmm, I smell food. Haven't eaten since I left Philly early this morning."

"The other guests are having lunch. Why don't you join them while I take your things upstairs? They're nice people, and they love meeting new guests."

"You don't mind? I mean, I'm leaving you to carry my bags. I know they're heavy."

"It's my job." I nodded toward the door a dozen feet down the hall. "Dining hall's in there. Go on, have fun."

She smiled, and her cheeks dimpled. "Thank you, Oliver."

I readjusted the load I was carrying, unable to stop myself from admiring her backside while she trotted toward the dining hall door. She had a great ass.

Mara swerved into the dining hall.

And screamed.

I dropped the suitcases and bolted to the doorway.

Mara had stopped a few inches inside. Her shoes lay on the floor where she must've dropped them. Her mouth gaped, and her eyes bulged.

The other guests stared at her but seemed more confused than scared.

She stammered wordlessly before she managed to squeak out, "W-what is this place?"

I came up alongside her, touching her arm. "What's wrong? Are you having an epileptic seizure or something? I can take you to the hospital if—"

"No, I'm not having a seizure." Her voice sounded breathy. She squeezed her eyes shut and turned toward me. "Why is everyone naked?"

"Oh. Yeah, that. I know at some naturist resorts the guests dress for meals, but here we have a less formal way of doing things." I studied her face, which she had scrunched up tight. "Are you sure you're okay?"

"Fine. Yes." The syllables were clipped. She pried her lids apart to look at me. "Why would birdwatchers eat in the nude?"

"Birdwatchers? Some of our guests enjoy doing that, but what's clothing got to do with it?"

"Everyone is naked."

"Uh, yeah, that's kind of the point." I laughed, trying to sound casual though I'd started to feel uncomfortable. "This is a naturist resort."

She threw her hands up, huffing. "Like that explains it?"

"Well, sure it does."

Mara stalked out into the hallway where she couldn't see into the dining hall.

I followed her. "I'm confused. Why are you so upset that all the naturists are naked?"

"Because—" She flapped her arms and huffed again. "Public nudity is illegal."

"This isn't public. It's a private resort." I held up my hands, trying for a conciliatory tone. "Listen, you can dress for meals. Nobody will care."

Jeez, I'd never met an uptight naturist before. She was beautiful, but I'd started to think she might have a few screws loose.

"Oh, how generous," she said in a haughty tone. She scrunched up her face harder than before, her lip curling. "I'm allowed to wear clothes if I want. Shouldn't you be more concerned about disturbing all the other guests who don't want to eat surrounded by naked people?"

"Um, those are all the other guests in there."

"Everyone eats in the nude?" She grasped her head in her hands, her eyes wild, seeming on the verge of a nervous breakdown. "What kind of place is this?"

"It's a naturist resort." I touched her arm. "Relax. This is a clothing-optional resort, not a clothes-free one. You can take your time getting acclimated before you ditch the clothes. You haven't done this much, have you?"

"Done what?"

"Gone nude."

She lowered her hands, her gaze narrowing. "What do you mean it's a clothing-optional resort? I thought this was a naturist retreat."

"It is." A realization dawned on me, and I raised my brows. "What exactly do you think a naturist resort is?"

"A place where people go to enjoy nature and see the wildlife."

Seriously? I stifled a groan. "Miss Severins, you're at a nudist resort."

Her eyes bulged again as her face went pale. Her knees began to wobble.

And she fainted.

I caught her. "Miss Severins?"

Her lids fluttered open. "Nudist?"

"Yeah, that's right. Some of us prefer naturist, though."

She closed her eyes and moaned.

I helped her to her feet. "How did you not know? It says right on our website, and on every travel site where we're listed."

"Never saw any website. I hired a travel agent to book my vacation. She said this was a place where birdwatchers and other nature lovers come to enjoy the outdoors."

"Sorry. I don't know where she got that idea." I glanced at her suitcases. "You want to go home right away?"

"I can't." She threw head back and moaned again. "I bought non-refundable, round-trip airline tickets. Are there any motels in town?"

"Sure, but they're all booked up. The Renaissance fair is this week."

Mara slumped against the wall.

"I'll take your bags up to your room," I said. "And if you still don't feel comfortable eating in the dining hall, I can bring food to your room."

She managed a weak smile. "You're a good man, Oliver. How did you ever wind up working at a nudist retreat?"

I tried not to wince. She must've assumed I always wore clothes since I was wearing them now. The rude awakening could wait until later, after she'd calmed down and gotten used to the idea everyone else around here was naked.

"Never know," I said as I hefted her suitcases off the floor. "You might decide to give naturism a try."

She straightened and smoothed her dress. "I doubt that."

Mara Severins lifted her chin and marched off down the hallway barefoot.

I snagged her shoes from the dining hall and hurried after her. An uptight city girl at a naturist resort? Oh yeah, this would be tons of fun.

Not.

Ollie and Mara will return in _Natural Impulse_.

Did you love

Natural

Passion?

Visit

AnnaDurand.com

to subscribe to her newsletter
for updates on forthcoming books in this series
&
to receive free gifts for signing up!

Anna Durand is a bestselling, multi-award-winning author of contemporary and paranormal romance. Her books have earned bestseller status on every major retailer and wonderful reviews from readers around the world. But that's the boring spiel. Here are the really cool things you want to know about Anna!

Born on Lackland Air Force Base in Texas, Anna grew up moving here, there, and everywhere thanks to her dad's job as an instructor pilot. She's lived in Texas (twice), Mississippi, California (twice), Michigan (twice), and Alaska—and now Ohio.

As for her writing, Anna has always made up stories in her head, but she didn't write them down until her teen years. Those first awful books went into the trash can a few years later, though she learned a lot from those stories. Eventually, she would pen her first romance novel, the paranormal romance *Willpower*, and she's never looked back since.

Want even more details about Anna? Get access to her extended bio when you subscribe to her newsletter and download the free bonus ebook, *Hot Scots Confidential*. You'll also get hot deleted scenes, character interviews, fun facts, and more! Plus you'll receive the short story *Tempted by a Kiss* and mutliple bonus chapters in both ebook and audiobook formats.

Visit AnnaDurand.com to sign up.